W9-API-590

WILDFIRE

Nick Oldham

This first world edition published 2020
in Great Britain and the USA by
SEVERN HOUSE PUBLISHERS LTD of
Eardley House, 4 Uxbridge Street, London W8 7SY.
Trade paperback edition first published
in Great Britain and the USA 2020 by
SEVERN HOUSE PUBLISHERS LTD.

British Library Cataloguing in Publication Data
A CIP catalogue record for this title is available from the British Library.

ISBN-13: 978-0-7278-8959-1 (cased)
ISBN-13: 978-1-78029-682-1 (trade paper)
ISBN-13: 978-1-4483-0386-1 (e-book)

All Severn House titles are printed on acid-free paper.

Severn House Publishers support the Forest Stewardship Council™ [FSC™],
the leading international forest certification organisation.
All our titles that are printed on FSC certified paper carry the FSC logo.

FSC www.fsc.org MIX Paper from responsible sources FSC® C013056

Typeset by Palimpsest Book Production Ltd.,
Falkirk, Stirlingshire, Scotland.
Printed and bound in Great Britain by
TJ International, Padstow, Cornwall.

For Belinda

THE PAST
2009

For the time being at least, Detective Chief Inspector Henry Christie had seen enough of death.

It was a Sunday evening in October when he pulled up in his own car outside a council house in Bacup, Lancashire, which was a hive of police activity: two patrol cars, a plain CID car, a crime scene van and a dog patrol. The front door of the house was open; light flooded out, silhouetting the two uniformed constables standing at the front step, giggling at something.

Henry had been the senior on-call night detective for the whole of the county since the previous Monday, meaning he still had his 'day job' to do, yet also had to live by his mobile phone out of office hours, not have any alcohol and be prepared to turn out at a moment's notice, or at least offer any advice sought, usually to manage a murder or other serious crime such as armed robbery or kidnap.

He had already attended the scenes of three murders that week.

This would be the fourth – quite a lot for a fairly quiet county such as Lancashire – but at least they had all been manageable 'one-on-ones', as they were known colloquially. Simple jobs as such, although Henry knew from experience as a detective that no murder was simple for anyone involved or touched by it. However, in terms of the police dealing with them, none of the three had required the turnout of a fully staffed murder squad or the establishment of a MIR – Major Incident Room – just a focused, well-managed clean-up job for each one.

That did not make it an easy week, though.

Each of the murders had been the culmination or breaking point of severe domestic abuse.

Two of the victims had been vulnerable, downtrodden women in terrible relationships they could see no way out of for a variety of reasons: kids, money, fear, intimidation or a combination of all of these factors.

One young woman – only nineteen years old – had been pummelled to death by her boyfriend's fists as they had walked home from a drunken night out in the pub. He'd accused her of flirting with one of his mates, giving him the 'come on'. She had vehemently denied this, and in a jealous but misguided rage the boyfriend had launched into her. Ninety seconds later he was standing breathlessly over her unmoving body.

That was Monday night's murder, the first of the week.

Tuesday night brought the murder of a sixty-year-old woman whose head had been stomped on by her irate husband because she wanted to go away on a girls' weekend to Benidorm with her sister and a few mates. He hadn't liked the idea.

Thursday night's victim had been strangled because she had actually made steps to leave her abusive, controlling husband.

All three men, reflecting from the chill of their police cells, had discovered just how easy it could be to murder someone.

The call to the fourth murder, the one Henry had just arrived at, had been taken halfway through a late Sunday roast dinner with his wife, Kate, and had a slightly different twist to it.

Henry had wolfed the remainder of his meal and grabbed his coat even with his mouth full, aware of Kate's sad eyes.

'Sorry,' he said.

'It's fine,' she lied.

'I could do without it,' he said. 'I've seen enough dead people this week.'

'And all women.'

'Not this one, though.'

He drove from his home in Blackpool all the way across the breadth of Lancashire to the 'deep east', as he called it, and found the address in Bacup easily. Many years before, he had been a uniformed patrol constable in the Rossendale Valley in which Bacup was situated and he still knew the area well. The geography of the place was imprinted on his brain from just those brief years working those streets as little more than a lad.

The journey took just short of an hour.

He wasn't in a particular rush so he enjoyed travelling through well-remembered towns and streets at the end of the motorway

– Haslingden, Rawtenstall, Waterfoot and finally Bacup, parking up outside the address.

He looked up at the house, knowing what he would soon be seeing, having had it described in detail already, yet still feeling the trepidation he always felt on entering a murder scene. The butterflies never left, nor did he want them to; when they did, it would be time to call it a day and settle for a shiny-arsed job at police headquarters. Trepidation gave an edge.

'Whatever,' he murmured to himself and got out of the car. He went to the boot and fished out a new forensic suit. He clambered into the suit, pulled on a pair of elasticated overboots and latex gloves, then turned towards the house, out of which emerged the detective sergeant who had called him earlier.

Jo Howard was dressed in a baggy forensic suit too, with the hood up and a surgical mask covering her nose and mouth.

Henry watched her stop, pull down the mask, pull off the hood and take a few deep breaths of fresh air. He saw her shoulders rise and fall as she inhaled, exhaled, clearing her lungs.

Then she saw him approaching and visibly pulled herself together – Henry could tell she was having 'a moment'; he'd had many in his career. It was allowed.

'Boss,' she said.

'Hi, Jo,' Henry greeted her. She was in her mid-thirties, had been a detective sergeant for two years and a DC for three years prior to that, and before that a uniformed constable. Henry had been on her promotion board interview panel. She was good, clever, well respected, and had an excellent record as a thief taker and a compassionate cop – two qualities that rarely blended. Giving her the nod for promotion had been one of his easy decisions. 'What've we got?'

Although she'd briefed him over the phone and he'd made notes, a face-to-face update was always better.

Which confirmed why this murder was different from the previous ones that week.

The background circumstances were similar. Abuse. Humiliation. Misplaced jealousy.

That volatile mix.

The difference in this case was it was the wife who had cracked and, in a cold-blooded, calculating manner, stood behind her husband as he lolled drunkenly in an armchair, snoozing after an extended lunchtime drinking session with his mates, and had struck him on the crown of his head with a sixteen-ounce Stanley FatMax Steel Claw one-piece hammer.

'It could have been the first blow that actually killed him,' Jo said. 'I've a feeling we might never know for sure.'

'Why do you say that?'

Jo raised her eyebrows. 'Because she hit him forty times.'

Henry digested this. 'Forty times?'

'That's what she told me. Who am I to argue?' She tilted her head. 'Come on, boss.'

Henry followed Jo into the house on the designated route that anyone with a legitimate reason to enter the crime scene would have to use.

'She locked herself in a bedroom after she killed him,' Jo explained over her shoulder to Henry. 'The section lads left her in until I landed, just a couple of minutes behind them. I talked her out and that's when she told me she'd hit him forty times.'

'Right. And you arrested her, cautioned her properly?'

'Yep. Got a couple of PCs to convey her to the nick at Greenbank. I had a DC waiting for her arrival, who supervised everything – forensic, DNA, fingerprints.'

'OK.'

Jo entered the living room, Henry one pace behind her.

He folded his arms at the threshold, letting his eyes take in the scene.

A living room: three-piece suite, coffee table, big-screen TV.

The husband was sitting up in one of the chairs.

Henry had to agree it probably wouldn't be possible to ascertain if the first blow to the head had been the one that killed Billy Devlin. Or the fifth. Or the twenty-seventh.

Henry was looking at a man who had been murdered in a frenzied attack. His skull had been mashed to a pulp of red, blood, brain, bone. Blood was splattered across the room, over the furniture, up the walls.

Henry's eyes roved, took in everything – including the discarded murder weapon which had been dropped on the carpet behind the chair, still in situ until he gave permission for it to be moved, bagged and tagged, which would not be until the crime scene investigators and forensic people had recorded everything, taken their samples, done their job, and until a Home Office pathologist had been to the scene to make an initial assessment.

Henry never allowed himself to comment out loud on a murder scene, other than from a professional viewpoint, but inwardly he said to himself, 'Wow.'

'Yeah, forty seemed about right.'

Henry was sitting across from the wife – her name was Lauren Devlin – in an interview room at the custody suite in Blackburn Police Station, now situated on the outskirts of the town, close to the Whitebirk roundabout, which gave quick access to the Lancashire motorway network. Jo Howard sat next to him and she was essentially carrying out the interview as Henry had now delegated the case to her. He was pretty much 'second jockey', just along for the ride.

Lauren Devlin, having been arrested at the scene and on suspicion of the murder of her husband, had been meticulously put through the identification and forensic mill – fingerprints, photograph, DNA swabs, seizure of clothing, blood samples, fingernail samples – and given the chance to make a phone call and elect to be represented by a solicitor. She made a weepy call to her mother and chose the duty solicitor who was now sitting alongside her in the interview room, having had a private consultation previously.

She had been allowed to have a shower – after a full forensic swab, body search and a check-over by the police surgeon – and then given a paper suit and slippers.

The body of her husband was lying in the public mortuary at Royal Blackburn Hospital. He was in a chiller cabinet and the post-mortem was scheduled for ten o'clock the next morning. Henry would be attending; although he had delegated the investigation to Jo Howard, he believed that going to PMs was an essential requirement for an SIO.

Henry said, 'Why forty? Seems a very precise figure.'

He watched Lauren Devlin blink and think about this. Her hair was scraped back tightly from her face and tied in a ponytail. She had piercing green eyes but with heavy bags under them, pale skin, tight, thin lips, and initially Henry thought she had an abject air of defeat about her.

She breathed in through her nose, her nostrils dilated. A tear formed in the corner of her left eye, tipped out and scuttled down her face like a transparent bug.

'Why forty?' he asked again, wondering if Lauren had been thinking of Lizzie Borden, who had supposedly given her father forty whacks with an axe. He was curious, but his voice was gentle, unthreatening.

'I sat down last night,' she said at length, then paused.

The almost inaudible whirr of the tape deck could be heard in the silence as the cassettes turned, recording for posterity, as did the camera positioned up in the corner of the room.

'I had a pen,' she went on, 'and a pad and I started to write it all down. Y'know, a bit like prisoners do on walls to count the days – four marks down and a dash across, so there were five marks, yeah? Then another five, until I had eight blocks of five. You get my meaning?'

'Forty marks on a piece of paper,' Jo said.

'Yeah, that's right – because I remembered every single time, *every* single time.' Her voice was flat and emotionless.

'What did they represent?' Henry asked. He thought he already knew the answer.

Lauren Devlin raised her eyes to his. 'The number of times he raped me over the last four years since we've been married.'

Henry felt everything in his body and soul tighten up as though being squeezed by a fist.

Jo said, 'He raped you forty times?'

Lauren nodded. 'Tried to strangle me twice, proper. They got their own little ticks.'

Henry swallowed.

'Beat me up regularly from a slapping to a kicking.' She tilted her head and gazed at the fluorescent tube on the ceiling. 'I've had black eyes, a broken cheek bone, two broken ribs . . . you name it. Bruised to fuck!'

'And you never called the police?' Henry asked.

Her eyes came back to his. 'You need to check your records – all that "advice given" shit.'

'It's no comfort, Lauren, but I will.'

'So, yeah,' she reiterated, 'forty seemed about right. One, two . . .' she began. In her eyes, Henry could see her reliving the moments. 'I'd wanted to keep up a steady pace – bash, bash, bash. You know, I had that Bee Gees song banging through my head, the one they tell you to do CPR to.'

'"Stayin' Alive"?' Henry said.

She nodded. 'Bit of an irony that, eh? So, anyway, that was in my head.' She demonstrated by bringing an imaginary hammer down. 'Thing was, though, I couldn't keep a steady beat. In the end, I was just smashing it down on to his head, screaming each number as I hit the bastard. I do remember getting to forty, but after that it all got a bit blurred, and next thing I knew I was upstairs in the bedroom.' She shrugged. 'Could've been fifty, easily.' She took a nervy sip from the mug of hot, sweet tea that had been provided for her. 'I could feel his blood splashing my face. It were hot.'

The detectives let her speak for as long as she was willing to go on. She talked for two hours and by the end of the interview she was exhausted, as were the two detectives and the solicitor. She was taken away to a cell by a gaoler and as soon as she lay down on the hard bench and pulled a rough blanket up to her chin, she was asleep.

When the solicitor had departed, Henry and the DS walked to the CID office to discuss strategy for the enquiry – what had to be done, how, when – but as they chatted through things, Henry saw that Jo appeared to be struggling to keep her mind on track.

'You all right?'

'Yeah, yeah . . . just thinking about Lauren and her life,' she said with a curl on her lips. 'Poor sod.'

'Grim – but she could have left him.'

'We both know that's not always possible, boss. If it was, things wouldn't end up in such a horrible mess. Sounds like we weren't much use to her either.'

Henry saw her chin begin to wobble a little.

She turned away from him, wiping her face.

'You sure you're all right?'

'Yeah, yeah . . . bit tired and emotional.'

'I get it. I'm knackered too. Let's get a few hours' sleep, then reconvene at the mortuary – say, nine thirty.'

'Yep, I'll do that.'

Ten minutes later Henry was back in his car. It was almost two a.m. on Monday morning and suddenly he was feeling famished. His last food had been the quickly shovelled-in roast dinner almost eight hours earlier; nothing since, other than a couple of brews on the go.

With that in mind and an empty space in his belly, he drove out of the police station, swung on to the Whitebirk roundabout and came off at the McDonalds twenty-four-hour drive-through where he guiltily treated himself to a Big Mac Meal but with a bottle of water rather than coffee or a fizzy drink. He drove around to the car park and began to wolf it down.

It tasted much better than it should have done.

Finally, he sat back, replete, and sipped the water, running the images of the week through his brain, visualizing the scene of each murder, the bodies on slabs, the faces of offenders in cells.

As he did this little mental exercise, he saw Jo Howard drive through the takeaway and from his position watched the server hand over two bags of food. Seemingly, the DS was even hungrier than he was. She drove away, Henry thought, without spotting him.

Henry's mind returned to murder.

The men involved – though each would have their own tale to tell (with the exception of Billy Devlin) – were similar to each other. Power-hungry cowards with misplaced self-esteem who resorted to bullying and violence to satisfy their weak egos. He had no sympathy for them. They too had had choices and screwed up big style. Henry felt genuinely sorry for the women – and that included Lauren Devlin as much as the three murdered ones.

He sighed.

Yes, he'd seen enough killing for a week and was glad it would be another eight weeks before he was back on call.

He drank the last of the water, dumped his fast-food packaging into a waste bin, checked the time.

Two thirty a.m.

He had to be in his office at headquarters for eight thirty, then back across to the mortuary at Blackburn for nine thirty. If he was quick enough about it, managed to avoid motorway patrols, he calculated he could be diving into his warm bed in half an hour, even though he had to get across to Blackpool. And if he could purge his mind, he could just about get four hours' sleep, unless he was called out again, because his responsibility lasted until six a.m.

Crossing his fingers – *please, no more deaths* – he set off down the motorway towards Preston, then on to Blackpool.

Since being unceremoniously dumped from his role as an SIO on FMIT – the Force Major Investigation Team – by the new detective chief superintendent who had been brought in from another force (and who had discovered that Henry had once had a brief fling with his wife, before she became his wife, many years before and hated him for it), Henry had been sidelined on to the Special Projects Group based at Lancashire Constabulary Police Headquarters at Hutton, just south of Preston.

In spite of its grand-sounding, slightly sexy name, the SPG (which made it sound even more dynamic) was actually a rag-tag bunch of individuals no one else wanted cluttering up their departments and who had been shunted into a made-up department, then tasked to run dead-end projects nobody else wanted to touch with barge poles.

Henry had had some inkling that his career as a detective was over even before the arrival of the new detective chief superintendent – Dave Anger – who then made almost certain that his career aspirations were reduced to a ground-down paste.

So he now headed Special Projects, although he did still retain the title 'Detective' in front of his rank, supervising a group of people often unfairly referred to as the 'sick, lame, lazy and loony' and realizing that he was now tarred with that same brush. In order to retain some of his sanity and to keep in touch with the real world of coppering and detectives, he ensured that his name appeared on as many call-out rotas as possible. He hoped this would somehow pay off in terms of resurrecting his career, but the downside of it was that he was often exhausted, because even though he might have been out in the middle of the night dealing with some horrendous shit, he still had to run the SPG which, with the staff he had, was sometimes like herding cats.

That was why, later that morning, at eight a.m., after a few hours spent trying unsuccessfully to get some sleep, he rolled into his refurbished office, tucked away in one corner of a much larger open-plan office on the top floor of the headquarters building. There were no windows or natural light, but lots of fluorescent tubes whose constant pinging and flickering gave him a headache and several of his staff migraines, because they were delicate flowers.

When he walked in, the office was deserted, as expected. This was because his staff, in response to their real or imagined bad treatment by the organization, never came in until exactly nine a.m. in protest, unless it suited them to do so.

Henry didn't mind. It gave him the chance to catch up on some of the work the team had planned for the week ahead – thrilling projects such as the feasibility of erecting a ten-foot-high fence around the HQ campus, or investigating the spiralling costs of police canteens, or – more to his liking, but still avoided by others – the health-and-safety state of every police cell in Lancashire. All mind-numbing stuff for a man who had been a detective at the cutting edge for most of his police service.

He ran some coffee through a filter machine after cleaning it first, then sat at his desk behind the glass screen from which he could survey his team at work. When they came to work, that was.

Before he began sifting through the ongoing projects, he called Jo Howard on her mobile, which went straight to answerphone. He left a quick message asking her to call him when she got a chance. He then made a series of calls, first to Blackburn cells to check on the welfare of Lauren Devlin (she'd had a quiet night and had eaten a good breakfast), then all the detectives who were in charge of the other murder enquiries he had attended the week before, to check on the status of the cases. All seemed to be going well.

After this he compiled a brief report for DCS Anger, who, as head of FMIT, had to be briefed on overnight cases, and then sent an email to the inspector in charge of the force comms room about the previous night's murder and asked him to upload it on to the chief constable's daily briefing report which was posted on the intranet for everyone in the force to read.

When all that was done, it was approaching nine a.m. and his less-than-keen staff were all filtering in after the weekend off, not one of them remotely aware he had been on call-out the previous week, never mind having dealt with four murders.

After briefing them, he drove out of HQ, aiming for Blackburn.

The traffic was relatively light for a Monday morning, and less than half an hour later, Henry was making his way through the corridors of Royal Blackburn Hospital to the public mortuary on level zero.

He had tried phoning Jo Howard on his journey across without success and had also tried to reach her via the CID office, but couldn't get anyone to answer the phone. He gave up, once again frustrated at how difficult it was to contact the police anymore – and he was ringing directly to an internal extension in the CID office, which made it even more galling.

However, he still expected Jo to be at the mortuary as per their arrangement before going off-duty.

She wasn't.

He checked his phone to see if he'd somehow missed a message: none.

He tried to ring her again directly: no reply.

In the end, he gave a mental shrug, knowing she would have a very good excuse for not being at the post-mortem.

But he was there and, after signing in and donning a plastic gown and surgical mask, he walked through to Room 2 where Billy Devlin's PM was scheduled to take place at ten a.m.

The Home Office pathologist was busy arranging the tools of his trade on a mobile table next to the mortuary slab, currently devoid of a body.

'Ah, Henry Christie,' the man said, glancing up as the detective arrived.

His name was Baines, now in his mid-fifties, and Henry had known him for a good number of years and to some extent had become a friend; after many a post-mortem, Henry and Baines had downed a pint or a coffee or two to discuss findings and also to give Baines the chance to interrogate Henry about his sometimes chaotic love life. Unfortunately for Baines, this was currently a fairly dull topic as Henry had recently remarried Kate and sworn to be a better man, much to Baines's chagrin.

'Prof.' Henry nodded.

Baines had turned out to the scene of Billy Devlin's murder the previous evening and had already done an assessment. He held up a scalpel and turned it to the light so the blade glinted. It looked extremely sharp.

'Are you alone?' Baines asked.

'It would seem so.'

'Shall we begin?'

'Be rude not to.'

Baines nodded to one of the mortuary attendants who slid open the chiller drawer in which Devlin's body had been stored for the past few hours.

Baines was methodical, painstaking, precise, and the PM examination lasted three hours even though the cause of Billy Devlin's death was obvious: blunt force trauma to the skull and brain.

Although Henry had attended several such post-mortems in his career, he still found the whole thing fascinating, and always asked the pathologist to tell him what he was doing/looking at/dissecting. He had found that showing interest was the key, all those years ago when he was a sprog (as they called young coppers), to not fainting or vomiting. He'd seen many an officer, young and old, succumbing simply because they hadn't involved themselves in the process.

'Remarkable,' Baines mused out loud at one point – clearly, he was still fascinated by what he did for a living. 'The laceration wounds caused by a hammer to the head – bludgeoning – are ragged, and the strands of skin, tissue and blood vessels are deeply impacted into the bone – in this case the skull, which shows many depressed fractures. So many that it is almost impossible to judge the shape and nature of the implement used, even though we do know it was a claw hammer.'

He held up a section of the skull that he had carefully lifted from Devlin's cranium and tilted it for Henry to see.

'However, we can see the shape of the hammer head on this bit.'

Henry nodded. He could see.

'Mostly, though, this is a mush,' Baines continued. 'She has delivered so many blows that it has become impossible to differentiate between them and therefore to count how many were delivered.'

'How many would you estimate?' Henry asked, not having told Baines about Lauren's confession.

'Over forty hard blows; maybe up to sixty.'

Henry nodded at the tally.

'A brutal, frenzied attack,' Baines said, 'sustained by rage.' He sighed and held up more bone and brain matter for Henry to inspect. Henry could see from the hammer blows that splinters of bone had embedded in the brain and a large section of the brain had been pulped by the weapon. Baines went on, 'He died very quickly, and if he was asleep to begin with and under the influence of alcohol, which we will test for, he wouldn't have known anything about it.'

'Pity,' Henry mumbled.

'Why do you say that?' Baines asked, hearing Henry's off-the-cuff remark.

'It's to be investigated, but it looks as though he abused his wife – his killer – over a number of years, big style . . . but that doesn't mean to say I won't thoroughly investigate this and see justice done.'

Puzzled, Henry checked his watch: ten past one.

He was walking back through the corridors of the hospital. Jo Howard was still a no-show and he hadn't had any communication from her. In the car park Henry rechecked his mobile phone and saw no texts or missed calls, so he called her mobile once again but got no reply, just voicemail. Slightly irritated now, he tried the number of the CID office at Blackburn and, to his surprise, managed to get through to a *person*, a DC who happened to be meandering through.

'DC Taylor, can I help you?'

'DCI Christie here. I'm after speaking to DS Howard. Is she there, please?'

'Hi, boss . . . uh, no, not seen her this morning . . . Hang on a sec.' Henry imagined the palm of Taylor's hand covering the telephone mouthpiece as all sound became muffled for a few moments as Taylor probably shouted out the query to whoever else was in the office. He came back on the line. 'Er, no, boss . . . she's not here. Isn't she supposed to be at a PM with you?'

Henry rolled his eyeballs. 'Obviously not.'

'Well, uh, nobody seems to have seen her.'

'Has anyone heard from her?'

'No, don't think so.'

Henry was beginning to get cross. 'Well, where is she?'

'Sorry, don't know.'

'Have you got her home landline, please?'

'Just hang on, boss.'

Henry grunted something in annoyance, but Taylor came back on after a few moments with Jo Howard's home number which Henry then called. When he got no reply, he redialled the CID office and managed to speak to Taylor again. This time Henry got Jo's home address, confirming what he seemed to remember – that she lived somewhere between Blackburn and Preston in a village called Osbaldeston, close to the River Ribble. He thought he would pop by to see if she was in, maybe off sick or something, on his way back to headquarters, as inconvenient as that was.

Henry knocked on the front door of the house, then stepped back to check for some sign of occupancy. He had knocked on a lot of doors in his life, kicked down a good number of them too, and he believed he could intuitively feel if there was anyone to be found inside.

At this house – Jo Howard's nice, old detached one in pleasant countryside – he got the feeling no one was home.

His spidey sense, he liked to think. Not a great one as superpowers go, but it had served him pretty well when hunting down villains.

Nothing moved at any of the windows, no curtain twitches. He glanced down the side of the house along the driveway where one car was parked up, but not the one Henry had seen her driving last night, so probably her husband's, a guy Henry had never met, knew nothing about.

He frowned and phoned the CID office at Blackburn again, which, incredibly, was answered once more by the luckless DC Taylor.

'I'm at DS Howard's address now, but no one's home,' Henry told him. 'Has she landed in work yet?'

'No, boss, her desk is just as it was.'

'Can you just peek in her desk diary?' Henry asked him, referring to the handwritten diary every detective had to keep, literally, on their desk. 'Just see if she has a more important appointment than a murder post-mortem or something.'

'Like a hairdresser?' the DC suggested. When he got no response from that ill-judged quip, he coughed. 'One second.' Henry waited, hearing the sound of the busy office in the background. A few moments later Taylor was back on the line. 'Nothing, boss.'

'OK, no probs.'

Henry hung up, still slightly puzzled and getting miffed. Obviously, there could be nothing in it, but Jo's unusual behaviour did not seem like the person he knew, albeit not well.

He went back to the front door and knocked again while calling her mobile phone from his.

As it rang, he squatted down on to his haunches, flipped up the letterbox and twisted his ear to the hole to listen. He wasn't certain but maybe he could hear a ringing tone somewhere in the house. He let the flap drop back, ended the call and stood up, his bafflement turning to unsettlement. Something did not seem right, but he acknowledged this could just be his skewed detective mind working overtime, imagining something amiss even in the most innocent-seeming circumstances.

Suspicion, Henry thought, is my middle name.

Actually, it wasn't; it was James, and he often cursed his parents for not giving him a real, meaty middle name.

He turned and looked away from the house to the woods on the opposite side of the road, deep, green and lush. Jo's home was in a good location, Henry thought. Better than his estate on the outskirts of Blackpool, even though he loved it. He walked back to his car on the road, unlocking the doors with the remote as he approached, but before getting in and driving away, he took another look at the house. Then, just as he was about to open the car door, he saw a man with a Labrador emerge from a footpath in the woods and turn towards the house.

Henry paused mid-step.

As did the man. For a moment. Actually, just a tad more than a pause – a hesitation, a wariness, an awkwardness. All these things Henry picked up from his body language. Then a decision by the man: to keep on walking towards Henry, smiling as he did.

At that moment Henry recalled something from Jo's promotion board interview. Part of the ice-breaker chit-chat at the start of the interview to relax the candidate before the tough stuff began. The bit where the interviewers asked the subject to tell them a few things about themselves – hobbies, home life, that kind of thing. Nothing that counted for the interview, just an attempt to put the candidate at ease.

'Oh, and I have a beautiful chocolate Labrador called Ellroy – you know, after the American crime writer?' she had revealed with a smile of pride.

Henry didn't really know much about dogs or crime writers, but he knew what a chocolate Labrador looked like – just like the one on the lead next to the man who had come out of the woods. A nice dog.

Henry leaned on his car and folded his arms, watching the two get closer.

The man continued towards him. He was a fairly big guy, at least six feet tall and broad to match, and it was at this point that Henry wracked his brain a little further. Was Jo married to another cop? He thought she might have been. A uniformed PC up in Lancaster division sprang to mind.

Henry was still leaning on the car when man and dog reached the bottom of the driveway.

And as he came into close focus, Henry was reasonably sure this guy was a cop. His face seemed vaguely familiar.

'Can I help you?' he asked Henry, who pulled out his warrant card and held it up for the man to see.

'DCI Henry Christie, from headquarters.'

'Oh, yeah, I think I know you.'

'You Jo Howard's husband?'

He nodded. 'Yep, Robert. I'm a PC up in Lancaster.'

'Yeah, that's right.' His face now slotted into place for Henry.

Robert gave him a curious look. 'Something wrong?'

'I can't really say. Any chance of having a chat with you inside, Robert?'

'Why?'

To be honest, Henry could not really explain why – other than that his cop instincts were beeping like mad and to have Robert in a more confined space seemed a sensible thing to do.

Robert hesitated. 'This sounds like bad news.'

'Not necessarily – but inside might be better to chat.'

He shrugged reluctantly. 'Yeah, OK.' He looked wrong-footed. To the dog, he said, 'C'mon, Ellroy.' The lovely thing looked up at him and Henry could have sworn it grimaced.

'Ellroy?' Henry said.

'After James Ellroy, American crime writer. Jo loved him,' he explained abruptly. He said no more and walked up to the front door which he opened. He unhooked the dog's lead and the animal bounded inside, followed by Robert peeling off his wax jacket and Henry behind him, sniffing the air, picking up the rancid aroma of smoke from somewhere. 'Come in,' Robert said, leading Henry along the hallway to the kitchen at the back of the house. 'Brew?'

'Yeah, sure, thanks. That would be good.'

Robert filled the kettle, put teabags in two mugs. His back was to Henry, who watched him carefully, trying to suss him out.

Physically, he was slightly smaller than Henry, who was six foot two, but Henry guessed he was ten or more years his junior, fitter and stronger.

The kitchen was nice and large. There was a central island with an electric induction hob as its focus, a huge extractor hanging above and a lot of kitchen work surface surrounding it.

Face down on this surface was a mobile phone clad in a protective cover. Henry stepped smartly across the threshold of the kitchen door over to the island and glanced surreptitiously at the phone, registering that the cover was essentially a clear plastic photograph holder which held a close-up headshot of Ellroy the chocolate Labrador and Jo Howard, their heads side by side. She was laughing and Henry was sure the dog was too. It was a happy photograph.

The kettle boiled and Robert poured boiling water into the mugs, then turned to face Henry as the tea brewed.

Robert's eyes narrowed. 'So what's going on?'

Henry saw his eyes glance momentarily down at the phone

on the work surface, then come quickly back up, and just an infinitesimal cloud of concern flitted across his features – there, then gone, but not too quickly for Henry not to notice. It made Henry's bum cheeks tighten and for once that was a feeling he did not like.

'I . . . er . . . turned out to a murder in Bacup last night, and Jo was the first detective at the scene.'

'Not unusual. She's as keen as mustard.'

'However, the post-mortem took place this morning and we'd arranged to meet at the mortuary in Blackburn and she never showed up. I checked the office and she doesn't seem to have landed there either. No one seems to know where she is.'

Robert turned his back to Henry while he dealt with the tea, using a spoon to squeeze the teabags.

'So I thought I'd call round,' Henry said. 'She hasn't been answering her phone either. Just all seemed a bit odd, not like her – what I know of her.'

The pedal bin was next to where Robert was standing. He put his foot on it and the lid clattered open and he dropped the teabags into it.

Henry blinked. Not only did his arsehole contract, so too did his throat.

Still facing away from Henry, Robert said, 'She didn't come home.'

'Really?' Henry said.

'But that's not unusual for her, not with a murder going on. She works some real long hours at short notice,' Robert went on and chuckled. 'Not like me. I do my shifts and that's it, basically.' He poured some milk into the mugs, turned and put one next to Henry on the island worktop. 'Here you go.'

'I assume she told you she would be out all night?'

'Well, no. I just sort of expect it. Goes with the territory, doesn't it? Being a detective. You must know how it is, boss?'

'Suppose. So she's not contacted you?'

'Nah.'

'And that doesn't concern you?'

'Something I've learned to live with over the years.'

Henry saw Robert's eyes dip to the phone again. 'So . . . where is she?' Henry asked.

The dog, which had been lying in its basket in one corner of the room watching the exchange, pushed itself up and whimpered.

Robert tugged at the collar of his shirt. Henry saw the redness of a rash creeping up his neck.

'She could be anywhere. My guess, she just got her head down at a mate's. Does that sometimes.'

'Really?' Henry said without conviction. Then, 'Oh, sorry.' He picked his mobile phone out of his pocket, looked at the screen and said, 'Excuse me, I need to take this.'

'Help yourself,' Robert said.

Henry pivoted away, pretending the phone was on vibrate, then stepped out of the kitchen into the hallway, put the device to his ear and said, 'DCI Christie' to no one. 'Yep, yep,' he said, wandering down the hallway having a very one-sided conversation which he ended by saying, 'Right, thanks, I'll get back to you.'

As he turned slowly, he quickly found the number for Jo Howard's mobile phone and returned to the kitchen with it displayed on his screen.

Robert, seemingly, had not moved.

Henry's eyes quickly took in the scene: the mobile phone that had been on the work surface had gone.

Robert's face had a triumphant, challenging expression on it. 'Everything all right, boss?'

'Yeah, yeah, it is,' Henry answered and pressed the call button on his mobile phone, raised his eyes, smiled and said, 'Do you want to tell me where Jo is, Robert?'

'What d'you—'

It took a second or two for the signals in the ether to connect.

Then they did.

A ringtone began to sound. Robert jumped visibly: the noise was coming from his back jeans pocket. He became very still and slowly extracted the phone between finger and thumb.

Henry pressed the end-call button on his phone. 'Jo's phone,' he said simply. 'Which she had with her last night.'

Robert shrugged. Henry could almost see the cogs in the man's mind whirring like mad as he tried to concoct a story to explain why he'd just lied.

'And the empty McDonald's wrappers in the bin,' Henry said.

'What you on about?' Robert sneered. Suddenly, his affable veneer began to fade.

'I saw them when you put the teabags in. I know she bought two McDonald's last night – well, early hours of this morning after she'd finished work and was on her way home.'

Another shrug. Cogs whirring. The hunted look on his face.

'So where is she? That's her phone, which you've just tried to hide. Those are fast-food wrappers in the bin.'

Henry knew that if Robert was clever enough – or had nothing to hide and there was nothing going on – he, Robert, would have the upper hand in this exchange; however, Robert's problem lay in him telling Henry that Jo had not come home, when she obviously had done.

'I knew who you were when I was walking towards you outside.'

'And?'

'I should've gone back into the woods and waited for you to go.'

'But you didn't.'

'No, I didn't,' Robert admitted.

Silence descended between the two men – but Henry didn't mind that. In fact, he quite enjoyed it. Silence made for discomfort, edginess. Silence made for an urge to fill it, because most people don't like silence. It is unnatural, awkward. But the thing here was that there still could be some simple explanation for this – maybe a sudden family emergency requiring Jo to leave in a hurry. Nothing sinister.

Henry knew this was not the case because of that first big lie: Jo had not come home, when she actually had.

Robert knew he'd made a boob.

And still . . . it could all be nothing.

Except for one additional thing Henry hadn't noticed when he had first walked into the kitchen. But now he had, and Robert caught Henry's eyes seeing that thing – on a door which Henry guessed opened to a cloakroom or pantry underneath the stairs. It was a gloss-painted white door and there was a tiny splatter of blood on the surface, like an elongated exclamation mark as the blood skimmed the door at an angle.

Henry looked squarely at Robert again. 'Are you going to tell me where Jo is, please? And why you said Jo "loved" James Ellroy – past tense.'

It was the moment when several things could have happened. Robert's shoulders could have drooped prior to a babbling admission of something, or flight, or fight.

Robert chose fight.

He flung Jo's mobile across the kitchen at Henry. It zipped across, spinning through the air like a rectangular discus. He threw it fast and hard and, as it happened, with great accuracy.

Henry ducked, but not quickly enough. One corner of the phone glanced off the side of his head.

Robert wasn't far behind.

Emitting an unworldly scream, he came towards Henry, his arms outstretched like a demented Frankenstein monster, his fingers splayed in the 'strangulation' position, and went for Henry's throat. The fingers curled tightly around his windpipe and the momentum of his charge smashed Henry back down through the open kitchen door on to the laminated floor of the hall.

It was a blur and took only seconds. Before he could react to defend himself, Henry found himself pinned down, with Robert straddling his chest and his arms locked at the elbows in an isosceles triangle, with Henry's throat being the sharp point. And Robert was squeezing with great power, his thumbs interlaced over Henry's Adam's apple.

Henry was incredulous at how quickly this had happened: from standing up to being throttled. Life moved in mysterious ways.

In another train of thought, Henry took no crumb of comfort from the fact that if Robert murdered him here and now on the hallway floor, he would be convicted of at least one murder that he would be unable to wriggle out of and spend the next twenty years (or less, depending on the leniency of the judge) incarcerated.

With a surge of his own energy, Henry swung a punch into the side of Robert's head, just as his vision began to swirl like fog.

It wasn't a great punch and certainly didn't put Robert off his stride.

The pressure and tightness increased, as did the pain and wooziness. Henry felt his eyeballs start to bulge, ready to burst, and even though his eyes were wide open, his vision blurred.

And then he became aware of something.

A slavering, slurping noise. He wondered if this was one of those things that dying people heard in that precise moment before brain function ceased.

Then Robert's fingers eased off the pressure. Blood poured back into Henry's brain with a bang, almost too quickly for comfort, making him feel as if the top of his skull might blow off. At the same time, air rushed down his reopened oesophagus, and he choked and rolled sideways, clutching his throat, scrambling away down the shiny-floored hallway before coming up on to one knee to work out exactly why he was still alive.

Robert was sitting on his backside against the wall, his knees drawn up, and Ellroy the Labrador was snuffling him, licking his face. Robert released a deep, painful wail and began to sob, muttering, 'I'm sorry, I'm sorry,' while Ellroy's tail wagged low and uncertain, the dog not understanding any of this.

Henry massaged his neck and stood aside as the crime scene investigators, clad from head to toe in their forensic coveralls, filed past him along the path into Mercyfield Wood, where Jo Howard's car and body had been dumped, set alight and were now both nothing more than charred remains.

Henry followed them but stopped at the ring of police cordon tape strung around the sad scene. He had already been up to the car and body once, before backing off and calling for backup, having seen enough to know there was simply nothing he could do.

Now it was all a case of careful evidence gathering.

On the way back up to the road, he met the chief constable approaching from the opposite direction, the rotund Robert Fanshaw-Bayley, making his way down to the scene, having turned out to the death of one of his officers at the hands of another of his officers.

'Bloody hell, Henry,' he exclaimed, breathing heavily. 'Bit of a trek, this! How the hell did he manage to get a car down here?'

'With difficulty.'

It was a narrow path, only just wide enough.

'This is a hell of a thing,' the chief said. 'I hear he tried to strangle you, too.'

'He had a bloody good go.' Henry raised his chin for the chief to see. It was red raw. 'Fortunately, his dog started licking his face and something must have clicked in his scrambled brain and he stopped throttling me.' Henry coughed and winced. It was sore inside and out, and his voice was raspy. 'Otherwise, I'd probably be charcoal, too.'

The chief sighed. 'What the hell's it all about? How did he expect to get away with killing her?'

'He mumbled something about an affair and a kid as I was locking him up . . . I don't know what it all means but I'm going to try and find out, boss.'

THE PRESENT
Lancaster, Lancashire, England

ONE

It was the longest twenty minutes of Detective Constable Diane Daniels' life.

Up to that point, though, the evening had been run-of-the-mill. It began at five p.m. when Daniels managed to squeeze her battered Peugeot 406 into the last narrow space on the jam-packed lower-level staff car park at Lancaster Police Station and then wend her way through the series of doors and other parking levels to enter the station itself and hop into the unreliable lift up to the second floor on which the CID office was situated.

It was Monday evening, the first of seven as the night-duty detective, the 'night owl' as they called it. She'd just had a long weekend off, mainly decorating her comfortable new apartment in a converted warehouse down on St George's Quay overlooking the River Lune, and was glad to be back at work because she'd been alone, mostly, and needed some human interaction; plus her lower back and almost all her muscles ached like mad after three days of stretching to paint. She would work until one a.m. then go home, but would be on call until six. For a week, it suited her nicely.

She nodded to her detective sergeant, who gave a perfunctory wave and refocused her attention on some serious-looking paperwork on her desk. Daniels entered the CID office proper and was greeted by the two DCs still in there.

Her first port of call was a recce of her own desk and in-tray. The desk was relatively tidy, as left on Thursday evening, but the tray was stacked full of prosecution files requiring some degree of attention. She sat down, had a quick skim through, sorted them into a pile in order of importance – 'must/should/could' was her mantra – then forced them back into the tray, deciding to come back to them later. Being a Monday, being Lancaster, the odds were it would be quiet enough to spend some time scribbling away later. Usually, though this could not be guaranteed, the first three nights of the week were relatively quiet.

This done, she looked over at the chubby detective at a desk in the far corner of the office. His name was Dave Uren. 'Fifteen years a jack and proud of it,' he liked to say. He actually had twenty-plus years in the job, the first seven as a uniformed PC. He was a dependable guy but broke no pots in the pursuit of villains.

He smiled his chubby smile at Daniels.

'What have we got, Dave?' He was the go-to guy for updates.

'Not a lot. One in the traps on a three-day lie-down for a murder in the town centre over the weekend, a few more for odds and sods. You'll need to show your face in the custody office, sweetie.'

'OK.' She didn't baulk at or acknowledge his term of endearment, patronizing though it was, because Uren was one of the harmless ones and she could handle him. Some of the other detectives were worth avoiding and – 'with the new way of thinking about floozies and coloureds', one even confided in her – their approaches and reactions were much more subtle now and consequently a little more dangerous and creepy, mainly because they regarded her as a floozy and a 'coloured', although she was definitely black.

She logged on to her computer and checked the custody system which showed a total of four prisoners in custody – three males, one female. She read quickly through their records and decided to go down to the cells on the lower ground floor later. She logged herself 'on duty' on the computerized duty states, then made her way up to the communications room on the top floor of the building and spent some time reviewing message pads and summaries to see what she'd missed over the weekend.

The standout was the murder Dave Uren had referred to which occurred in the early hours of Sunday morning: a young man kicked to death in the city centre, one arrested for it now held on a seventy-two-hour remand – 'a three-day lie-down', in police parlance – for further questioning. The murder had caused a lot of inter-gang unrest on one of the council estates and trouble simmered, so the Support Unit was drafted in to 'lid it' – keep it quiet. There was the possibility of repercussions and revenge attacks apparently, with lots of threats being made and patrols still out there on this Monday evening.

Interesting stuff – as murders always were – but unless something serious kicked off, it wasn't likely to involve Daniels.

Next she went down to the cells, had a chat with the custody sergeant, PS Bill Heaton, and had a peek at all the prisoners, including the young man suspected of murder. His name was Thomas Costain, and he insisted he was of no fixed address. She peered in through the inspection hatch at him. He was a good-looking lad, just twenty years old, with a shock of red hair and a sneer on his face for her.

'To be fair, he's been a little git,' Bill Heaton said. 'He's admitted nothing, tried to stop us taking samples and fingerprints – we had to hold him down, hard. But he's going nowhere.'

Half an hour later, back in the CID office, Daniels dropped a herbal teabag into her mug – refusing to tackle the precariously stacked, unwashed dishes in the tiny kitchen area – and as she waited for the unreliable water heater to come to a boil, she reconfigured her night ahead. She was mindful of the need for flexibility should anything arise. She was one of the few detectives who liked to jump into a CID car and turn out to assist even low-level crimes. It was very easy for the night-duty detective to remain elusive, but that didn't sit easily with her. She was a doer.

However, for the moment, her desk beckoned and, with the ginger and lemon tea in hand, she swished through the office – now deserted as all the other detectives had gone home – and plonked herself down. She selected the most urgent court file and opened it with a feeling of dread at the multitude of red-pen remarks from the CPS team.

'Mm,' she muttered. She found her PR – personal radio – switched it on, programmed in her location and pressed 'send' to let comms know she was ready for deployment if necessary.

She didn't get a second sip of her brew.

'Patrols – machete attack, Carr Road, Luneside estate, one person severely injured now outside Condor Stores. Patrols to attend, please,' the comms operator coolly relayed over the air.

Daniels reacted immediately.

Scooping up her radio, extendable baton, rigid handcuffs, torch, stab vest and a set of car keys from the board, she sprinted, threading her arms through the vest as she went.

She didn't wait for the lift – too slow, too creaky – but flew down the stairs and crashed out through the back door of the police station on to the ground-level car park and jumped into the complete shit-mess that was the night-duty detective's CID car. She didn't even want to look at the clutter in the passenger footwell, although it was always in the corner of her eye.

With a grunt of exasperation – at the fuel gauge needle which did not even attempt to lift itself off empty and the other two red dashboard warning lights (battery and oil, she guessed – she was no mechanic) – she crunched the dog-eared Astra into reverse and sped out of the car park.

The thing about Lancaster is that it is essentially a one-way system wrapped around the city centre with a few rat runs used by people in the know, such as street cops. Daniels had never been a response officer in the city, having been only transferred there on to CID in the last year, so although she knew it reasonably well, she couldn't yet find her way easily through the back streets without coming to a dead end or finding herself back where she started. Not that such knowledge would have given her much of an advantage that evening because her destination lay on the north side of the River Lune, and she had to cross Greyhound Bridge on the northern edge of the city to reach the small but notorious estate known as Luneside, slotted between the outskirts of Lancaster and Morecambe. This meant looping right around the city before cutting across the river.

Although Lancaster was usually a traffic bottleneck, the rush hour had more or less passed, and by zigzagging through traffic without the aid of a blue light or two-tone horn, just swerving and with accompanying gestures, Daniels pulled on to the estate five minutes later, aiming straight for the address given.

Even the ambulance hadn't arrived, but two police cars had, and a large crowd of onlookers, mostly hostile to any police presence, had gathered around the scene of the incident.

Remembering to lock the car, Daniels threaded her way firmly through the crowd until she found four uniformed constables dealing with the situation. Two were doing their best to keep the crowd at bay while the other two were kneeling over the body of a young man outside the convenience store.

There was a lot of blood to negotiate and it was clear from the trail of it that the victim had dragged himself along the footpath before collapsing outside the shop.

The two cops dealing with him had propped him up against a low wall with his right arm elevated, trying to stem the flow of blood from a vicious wound which, at first sight, appeared to be on his upper left arm around the bicep. The lad – a teenager – looked pale and grey, his eyelids fluttering as the shock of blood loss and agony affected him.

Daniels bent down for a better view.

There was a huge, wide-open gash across the bicep just below the line of his T-shirt sleeve, but there was one, much worse – a slash across the neck just below his chin – which was the true bleeder. One of the officers was trying desperately to plug this with dressings from a woeful first-aid kit out of their car. It looked as though a major artery had been severed.

Over her radio, Daniels prompted comms. 'Gee up the ambulance, please. If this lad isn't in A and E soon, he's going to bleed out. Maybe as well to alert A and E at Lancaster, too. They might want to be ready for this one.'

The comms operator acknowledged this.

In the distance was the approaching sound of sirens.

Daniels bent down again and asked the two officers, 'What've we got here?'

'Machete attack, Diane,' one replied. 'To do with this job over the weekend – the murder. Drugs turf shit, we think.'

'Right – who's this lad?' she asked, looking at the victim whose head lolled as if he was drunk. His eyes rolled back in their sockets. He was very much on the way out.

'Sam Dorner – local dealer and hard man.' The officer looked at him contemptuously. 'Don't look so hard now,' he said, even though he kept up the pressure on the neck wound and he himself was covered in blood up to his elbows. He didn't like the lad but would do anything to prevent him from dying.

Daniels jumped as something hard crash-landed on the pavement next to her: a hefty chunk of house brick, which partly shattered as it hit the ground. It had been pitched from the back of the assembled crowd. Daniels could feel it beginning to get ugly.

'They're very appreciative,' the cop tending the lad commented.

Daniels spun and rose to her feet, hearing a few nasty shouts aimed at her colour, but ignoring them. 'Patrol inspector, receiving?' she asked over her PR.

'On my way, Diane,' the harassed voice of the duty inspector came back. The screaming sound of his engine was in the background.

'Roger that – all getting a bit tense here,' she told him in an understated way. 'Sooner we get the victim into an ambulance the better, then get ourselves out, because they're going to kick off. And where is the Support Unit?' she demanded.

'On their way from headquarters, been delayed for some reason,' the inspector told her. 'I've diverted all other patrols to the scene,' he added.

Which, Daniels thought, probably meant that everyone on duty in Morecambe and Lancaster would be arriving soon.

An arm at the back of the crowd shot up and another half-brick arced through the air.

Daniels saw it and ducked instinctively, even though it crashed against the shop door. She looked at the line of angry faces of the crowd. The cops were fair game in situations like this, but she wondered if their hostility was also aimed at the lad on the floor – maybe he had strayed, intentionally or otherwise, into someone else's territory. Intentionally was Daniels' bet. She knew trouble had been brewing for a few weeks, though the police had yet to get a real handle on it, and maybe this weekend was when the pimple had burst.

The next few weeks, she guessed, would be fun.

For the here and now, though, the issue was to get this wounded lad to hospital and calm the situation down.

The ambulance sirens were getting closer.

Another object landed, having bounced off the arm of one of the officers tending the lad. The crowd was collectively growling, itching to get their hands on him or the police; either would do.

Then Daniels saw with relief two more police cars haring down the road and three officers bailing out and pushing their way through the throng. Although the police were outnumbered – maybe fifty people had gathered – seven cops plus a detective was a different matter to four, and when the inspector arrived, all bustle and authority directing his officers, the mood of the crowd changed as they were hustled back and ordered to disperse.

When the ambulance arrived a few minutes later, with the exception of half a dozen gobby kids, it was all over and the injured lad was rushed to hospital. The remaining officers made a tactical withdrawal and Daniels made her way up to the A&E unit at Royal Lancaster Infirmary.

They nearly lost him. The neck wound was very deep and had severed the carotid artery, and what Daniels had not seen on her arrival at the scene was the spurting fountain of blood the first two officers had faced. Despite the serious health risks, both had tackled it without hesitation, and in so doing had saved the life of one of Lancaster's best-known young villains who, at eighteen, had built up a thriving, expanding drug supply business. Presumably, Daniels guessed, it was the 'expanding' aspect that had caused the furore, led to a murder over the weekend, then retribution by means of a machete.

She thought it was highly unlikely the police would ever truly unravel the web of gang allegiances, which were often complex and deep-rooted, yet flexible, often going where the power lay. They would probably just do well to react to whatever happens, make arrests and quell unrest.

She ensured there were two officers with the lad just in case anyone tried to finish what they'd started. After a quick chat with a consultant moments before he was wheeled into an operating theatre and being told that surgery could easily last two or more hours, and that the patient would probably be too out of it for a coherent conversation for at least a day, Daniels' next step was to inform the family and look at identifying a suspect.

The latter, she guessed, wouldn't be too difficult, but she wanted to get on to it as soon as possible, and also get police back on to the estate now it had calmed down a little to begin work on recovering anything of value from the crime scene.

She would have liked to do things in a more regimented order, but the street disturbance side of it was a curved ball. In an ideal world the scene would have been sealed immediately, but circumstances and safety considerations dictated otherwise. Keeping the police as sitting ducks in fear of being injured was not something she wished to do, and if she was criticized from upstairs for making that on-the-hoof decision, she was prepared to justify it.

After arranging for a CSI to turn out, Daniels set off for Sam Dorner's home on an estate in south Lancaster. She arranged to meet another patrol there because she expected the household would have already heard about the assault and there would be a tinderbox of emotion that might be directed at her. She was no coward, but common sense ruled.

She was right. It took all her effort and coolness to bring the family down and then extract some information from them.

She was good at this sort of stuff.

Several years as a detective on the Public Protection Unit, dealing with child protection issues, had given her a tough exterior and a mushy inside, and one thing she was very capable of doing was mining information from families who were, at best, distraught or, at worst, grieving.

In this case she found that the name of the possible offender was a lad called John Dishforth, who was pretty much Dorner's opposite number in a rival gang.

She passed the information to the patrol inspector and left it to him to put an arrest plan together for Dishforth. Daniels would deal with him if he came into custody, though chances were that Dishforth would be down in the blankets, being harboured in someone else's house. He would probably take some rooting out.

It took over two hours to deal with Dorner's angry family – several of whom were already talking revenge despite her warnings – by which time it was almost two a.m. and Dishforth had yet to be located.

Daniels should have been crawling into bed an hour earlier, but she didn't mind.

When she left the Dorner house and thanked the uniformed PC for assisting her, she suddenly found she needed a coffee.

She drove down the A6 away from the city centre and pulled on to the forecourt of a twenty-four-hour petrol station. It served decent takeaway coffee which she intended to sip on the forecourt before going back to the station to get the paperwork up to date, then heading back to the hospital.

She hoped that everything that could happen that night had already done so.

She was wrong.

TWO

She bought the coffee – a medium Americano, double espresso (she needed the buzz), hot milk – and took it out to her car on the petrol station forecourt, perched half her backside on the front wing and sipped it, feeling it hit the spot almost immediately.

The night was still warm and she knew it would be uncomfortable in bed, so she wasn't in the least bothered about working through. She wanted to make sure that everything was in good order to pass over to her daytime colleagues so they could hit the ground running.

She took in the air, just getting a hint of the smoke from the fires on the moors way to the east of Lancaster. For a couple of weeks now the fire service had been run ragged trying to douse flames sweeping across bone-dry grassland, caused by a lack of rain, lots of sunshine and some fools who seemed to delight in causing mayhem by purposely setting fire to the moors.

Just occasionally, depending on the direction of the breeze, the smell of the smoke drifted across Lancaster.

As she leaned on her car, she went through the tick box in her mind regarding evidence, victims and offenders, because one of the worst things for a detective to do was to leave glaring holes in the handover files.

With the exception of arresting the offender, Dishforth – which she hoped might have happened before the night was over – she was pretty sure she'd covered all other bases, or at least would have done by the time she went off-duty.

She tipped the last of her coffee down her throat and tossed the disposable cup into a bin and turned to her car. As she opened the door, she saw a man run across the A6, Scotforth Road, into Hala Road at the traffic lights. He was running hard as if a devil was behind him, the sort of run that always caught a cop's eye. He also had something in his arms. In the night and under the streetlights it looked as if he was clutching a large kit bag to his chest. Very briefly, Daniels thought he was perhaps fleeing from a burglary – except it wasn't a kit bag, unless it was one with arms and legs.

He had a child in his arms.

The man was gone in a moment, but Daniels knew she had to have a word with this guy.

Before she could twist into the car, there was a deep 'whump' of a noise, followed by a blast of scorching hot air which lifted her off her feet and spun her backwards on to her bottom by one of the petrol pumps. For a moment she was completely disorientated, not comprehending what had happened, but feeling as though she had been standing in front of a massive blast furnace door that had suddenly opened.

Slightly stunned, she pushed herself up on to her feet and regained her balance.

The guy in the petrol station shop had run to the door.

'Fuck was that?' he shouted.

Daniels did not have time to chat. She was already running towards what she knew was an explosion.

Daniels ran to the junction that the man carrying the child had just crossed, glancing briefly to see if she could still spot him. He had gone. But she did not have time to dally because she knew she had to veer in the opposite direction into Ashford Road towards the source of the explosion, at the same time shouting into her PR that something had happened but she didn't know exactly what.

She ran past the first junction – nothing amiss down there – then up to Uggle Lane, which is when she saw it all: a terraced house on the left-hand side with flames spewing out of the ground floor, with a mass of rubble blasted across the street like something from a World War Two photograph, smoke, hot dust rising like angry volcanic clouds from it all.

People in nightwear were out, shouting, screaming, some scrambling across the huge pile of house bricks towards the front of the damaged house.

And screams coming from the house itself.

Daniels ran towards it, trying to get her mind together to fully comprehend what she was seeing: the whole ground floor of the house had been blown out and from the front bedroom window above there was a screaming figure – a woman frantically waving her arms while trying to avoid the flames licking upwards in searing tongues of fire.

For a moment Daniels could not understand why the woman wasn't trying to escape from the rear of the property – but then she got it.

These were late-nineteenth-century back-to-back terraced houses built originally for workers in a local cotton mill, long since demolished. The houses were still lived in, most restored and knocked through, but some like this one – two up, two down – were still basic terraced houses, with no way out from the rear.

The woman was trapped by flames at the front and the adjoining wall of the house behind. She had nowhere to go.

A man stepped in front of Daniels, impeding her path.

'Y'need to get back, love – this has been a gas explosion, could be really dangerous. Could go again!' he shouted.

'Police,' she said. 'It's a chance I'll take.'

She barged him out of the way, scrambling over the debris until she got as close as possible to the damaged house. She was still yelling down the radio, giving a situation report and being informed that backup and the fire service were en route.

That didn't make her feel much better because now she could see that the trapped woman was clutching a screaming infant to her chest.

She was stunned by what she saw – and also amazed that the explosion hadn't completely destroyed the whole of the house. The first floor was intact but presumably precarious and ready to collapse in on itself.

And the flames leapt unchecked, probably from a severed gas main, Daniels thought.

'You've got to get back,' the man shouted at Daniels. He grabbed her shoulder.

Although appreciating his concern, she shrugged him off. 'Can't we get a ladder to the window?'

'Even if we could find one, the heat wouldn't let us get close,' he replied.

'We must try.'

The man gave a despairing gesture as Daniels moved forward again, pulling her jacket collar up around her ears and the back of her head. The heat was terrifying and seemed to draw the breath out of her lungs. She could feel it scorching her forehead. Any closer and her hair would be set alight. She cowered away, a hand covering her eyes.

She had to back off. The man was right.

The woman reappeared at the bedroom window. Her face was a mask of terror as she looked out through the flames. Her child screeched remorselessly.

Daniels was stunned by her own inability to help.

'Oh my God,' she mouthed. Then, into her radio, she demanded to know the ETA of the fire service.

Comms could only confirm they were on their way.

An arc of people began to gather around Daniels, all transfixed by the harrowing scene taking place in front of them.

Suddenly, a giant ball of flame resembling a meteor rolled out of the house, causing all the onlookers to dive to the ground to avoid being incinerated. Daniels was among those, feeling the sizzling whoosh of fire only inches above her.

As quickly as the flame shot out, it retreated like a flame thrower.

Daniels got to her hands and knees, looking up at the house to see that the woman, with her child, was now straddling the window frame, ready to hurl herself off. In her terror, this seemed to be, and probably was, her only option now . . . but another curling lick of intense flame shot up from downstairs, sending her tumbling back into the bedroom.

Daniels tugged her jacket over her head again, knowing that, for her own future sanity, she had to at least attempt to save the woman one more time. She ran low across the road until she was standing just to one side of the house, yelling up at the window. If the woman threw the child, at least she could try to catch it; if they both came out together, she would try to catch them both, such was her desperate mind-set.

Then there was a creaking, tearing sound as the first floor collapsed and fire engulfed everything.

It took twenty minutes for the fire service to arrive, by which time the fire had completely destroyed the house and caused severe damage to those either side, plus the one behind, the occupants of all these houses, thankfully, having managed to flee safely.

Daniels watched from a distance as the firefighters from the two units in attendance doused down the last of the flames after ensuring the gas supply for the whole street had been disconnected. She sat on a kerbstone in a trance. Her hands shook as she took a bottle of water from Brian Uttley, the patrol inspector who was standing alongside her.

'Thanks,' she said. She twisted the lid off and took a gulp of the cold liquid.

'You couldn't have done anything, Diane,' he told her.

'I know,' she said quietly. She ran a fingertip across her eyebrows, which had been singed without her realizing. Some hair above her forehead had also fizzled in the flames. 'I know,' she said again. 'I should have gone after the guy running with the kid in his arms. At least then we might be some way towards getting quick answers on this.'

'Could have been a coincidence.'

She looked him squarely in the eye. 'I know of one very good detective, now retired into oblivion, who believed in coincidences. Coincidences are always clues, he once told me.'

'Who was that?' The inspector wasn't all that curious really.

'Guy called Henry Christie.'

'Oh, yeah – knew of him.'

Daniels plucked a few strands of charred hair from her forehead and rubbed them to dust between her fingertips. 'Jeez.'

She was now sitting on the low wall back at the petrol station, where, even though she had not been in direct line of sight of the blast, she had earlier been blown off her feet. The force had been so huge that it had rushed around and over many houses and along streets. Most of the houses in Uggle Lane had been damaged by the blast, and Daniels knew that within a radius of about a quarter of a mile some houses had their front windows shattered.

The inspector was still with her.

'Anyway,' she said to him, 'we do need to find the guy and eliminate him if he has nothing to do with the explosion. He needs to explain what he was up to running through the streets with a kid.'

She knew that a perfunctory house-to-house was being conducted along Hala Road by a few uniformed PCs, but so far this was not bearing fruit and it would be a job more for the later morning. It was also to some degree dependent on what the fire service and forensic teams found at the scene. If it was down to a faulty gas appliance, then all this could just end up being a Health and Safety Executive investigation, with the police playing only a peripheral role, preparing a report for the coroner.

Her gut feeling, however, was that the man with the child had a part to play and she would not let it go until proved otherwise.

'Have we got anything from the immediate neighbours?' she asked the inspector.

'Just that there was a woman living there who had a few male callers, shall we say? Two kids, but she kept herself pretty much to herself. The voters' register doesn't really help much – says there's one occupant, female, name of Andrea Greatrix.'

'Right.' Daniels checked the Fitbit she wore in lieu of a watch.

It was after four a.m. Dawn was fast approaching, the sky becoming noticeably lighter in the east. She had already spoken to the on-call senior investigating officer who was responsible for turning out to any murders and she had briefed him. His name was Detective Superintendent Rik Dean and he was reluctant to roll out of his warm pit for something that might just turn out to be a uniformed job. He'd been grumpy at being woken and told Daniels to let him know if and when any foul play was suspected.

Even Daniels' sighting of the running man couldn't persuade him to attend the scene. She kind of understood, but if it had been her, she would have been out like a shot.

'Lazy fucker,' she muttered as she hung up.

'And we still have John Dishforth to find,' she mused to the inspector. 'The machete guy.'

'Yeah, this distracted us somewhat, as explosions tend to.'

'So . . . two kids supposedly at the house, but only one woman and one kid at the bedroom window . . .'

'You're not going to let that go, are you?'

'Nope.'

She pushed herself up to her feet.

The inspector moved in closer to her. Under his breath, he said, 'Am I seeing you later?'

'No, Brian, you're not. I'm not just a quick fuck on the side before you go home to the missus. I deserve better than that.'

'I've told you I can't leave her . . . but you have to admit, it is one hell of a fuck.'

'Maybe, but it's destined to become a clusterfuck of epic proportions and I don't want to be in the middle of it . . . so finish your shift and go straight home to wifey, eh?'

Not waiting for a response, she walked across to her car and drove away without a backwards glance at the inspector who remained rooted to the spot, open-mouthed and speechless. She felt some sadness but also stupidity for getting involved with a married man on the rebound from an ugly split from her husband. It was too soon to get tangled up in any relationship, she'd realized, especially one with a man, wife and two kids. It wasn't going to end well.

Five minutes later she was back at the station, sitting at her desk and logging on to the intelligence database to see if she could find out anything about the occupants of a house in Uggle Lane that no longer existed as of one hour ago.

As she searched the database, her tired mind drifted and briefly she got to thinking about the old cop she had mentioned knowing: Henry Christie.

She had met him quite a few years earlier. He had been a detective superintendent and she had accompanied him across to Yorkshire to review two unsolved murder cases at the request of the chief constable of that force. At the time Daniels had aspired to be a murder squad detective, but events on the other side of the Pennines had shown her, by her own admission, to be not quite ready for that. With good grace she had returned to the child protection work at which she excelled, although she did not completely shelve her ambition.

A couple more years had made her feel ready and she transferred into a regular CID role with a view, eventually, to a sideways move on to the Force Major Investigation Team.

In the intervening years, she had never come across Henry

Christie again. She knew he had retired to run The Tawny Owl, a pub and country house hotel out in the wilds of the Lune Valley which was part of the division in which she now worked.

She wondered how he was doing. She'd heard various things about him, including the tragic story about his fiancée. He seemed to be one of those ex-cops who couldn't keep out of trouble – or perhaps it was that trouble in various forms kept rooting him out – but she hadn't heard much of him recently. She hoped he was thriving.

She shook her head and resumed the intel search which was proving fruitless.

Her mobile phone rang. She saw who was calling and answered it reluctantly. It was the patrol inspector. Her lover. She answered half-heartedly.

'You still in work, Diane?'

'I am.'

'You may want to come back to the scene of the explosion.'

Uggle Lane had officially become a crime scene, locked down, closed to the public and traffic, and guarded by a uniformed cop who, as well as preventing unauthorized entry, was also logging the time and date of entry and exit of personnel and ensuring they were wearing forensic suits.

Daniels picked up such a suit from the CSI van and put it on with overshoes and a hairnet, also taking a pair of disposable nitrile gloves and a face mask. She signed in, dipped under the cordon tape and walked towards the devastated house while fitting the mask and pulling on the gloves.

Daniels was irritated to see the inspector was not wearing a forensic suit over his uniform but said nothing as she approached him. He was talking to a woman who was dressed in such a suit but with a fire service logo on the front of it.

This was Janet Keogh. Daniels knew she was a fire scene investigator. They had encountered each other a couple of times previously.

'What've we got?' Daniels asked the inspector, who struggled to make eye contact with her. He jerked his thumb at Keogh and Daniels nodded at her. 'Hi, Janet.'

'Are you in charge, Diane?' Keogh asked.

'From the crime point of view, yeah.'

'Good. I know it's early days, but you'll be wanting to see this. C'mon.' Keogh beckoned her with a twitch of her head. 'Follow me.'

She led Daniels towards what was left of the house, now simply a space of mushy, saturated, burned rubble, a combination of all those things that once made up a house – floor boards, plaster, plastic, furniture, white goods – some recognizable shapes, others not so.

Steam and smoke rose from it all. It was like stepping on to the floor of a tropical rainforest.

It also stank. An acrid blend of smoke, gas and flesh.

Keogh paused to let Daniels come alongside her. 'It's amazing there isn't more damage to adjoining properties,' she told the detective. 'But that's the nature of explosions. No two will ever be exactly the same, and if it did happen again, the result could be completely different – so in some respects, we're lucky. In others, maybe not.'

'I get that.'

'So it is what it is,' Keogh said.

'What have you got, then?'

'This is only preliminary, but I thought you would want to know.' She moved into the house, trudging into the sodden mess. Daniels followed her into the damaged shell of the building. 'These are old houses and the problem is that the gas feed from the mains – which was probably put in forty years ago – is right into a meter in the actual house under the stairs. Real old-school stuff. Wouldn't happen these days, and I'll bet it's not been serviced for years, which means it's vulnerable and deadly.'

'Which bit's vulnerable?'

'The pipe work . . . see.'

Keogh walked into the remains of the cupboard which would have been under the stairs and where the gas meter was located. She bent down next to it and pointed to the ragged remains of the gas inlet pipe which came into the house from under the floor, connected by a flexible hose to the meter itself.

Daniels peered over Keogh's shoulder as she tapped this pipe.

'It's been disconnected.'

'You can tell that?' Daniels asked.

'Uh, yeah.'

'Disconnected, like deliberately, not something that happened because of the blast?'

'No. Disconnected deliberately before the blast. And the cause of the blast.'

'A loose pipe?' Daniels said.

'It's not loose . . . it's been unscrewed,' Keogh said. 'Obviously, just unscrewing a pipe would not necessarily cause an explosion. An explosion needs a spark, shall we say? And I know this is preliminary, but I have already found four seats of fire.'

Stunned, Daniels said nothing as she took in this massive revelation.

Keogh stood up and led Daniels through to the kitchen at the back of the house, which was just about recognizable with the burned black worktops, sink, washing machine and fridge. There was no back door because the back wall was also the back wall of the house behind.

'This is one seat of fire.' Keogh pointed to the charred remains of a two-slot toaster on the work surface which had the charred remains of something in each slot. 'Rolled-up newspaper, I'd say. Pop it in, push down the lever – fire!'

Daniels nodded. Her expression remained neutral, but underneath she was writhing in horror and rage as she began to piece together the timeline of a horrific crime scene.

'There are more seats of fire,' Keogh said. 'Screwed-up newspapers on the stairs, and others.'

Keogh sidled past her again and went into the living room.

Daniels looked up and could see all the way to the roof.

Keogh said, 'You ready for this?'

'Go on.'

Daniels dropped her gaze to see that Keogh was standing next to a strip of tarpaulin.

'The tarp is ours,' Keogh said. She bent down and slowly lifted it to reveal the remains of the woman who had been at the window, the one Daniels could not save. She was lying next to what had been the settee and her body had been burned to a crisp, blackened, awful.

Daniels suddenly felt nauseous. But there was something else to it, and when Daniels worked it out, she let out a whimper.

'She has the child in her arms,' she blurted.

THREE

She had to run. It was the only way. Run hard, run fast, run deep. Chase the demons out of her system.

The River Lune was on her right as she set off. She ran south along its banks by the old railway line for three miles before doing an about-face and coming back up the same route until she was on St George's Quay outside the converted warehouse in which her apartment was located.

She showered for a long time, dried off, then flopped on to her huge new bed, dead to the world for the next five hours.

When she woke, her body felt as heavy as lead and it took a huge effort to motivate herself, but finally she did so, grabbed a banana and a glass of cold orange juice which washed down a couple of paracetamol for a throbbing headache. Then she had another – quick – shower, got dressed and drove up around the city to the rear of the infirmary and the public mortuary.

The post-mortems were scheduled for three p.m. and she wanted to be there for them, even though the case was no longer hers.

The Force Major Investigation Team had finally been roused into action and Daniels handed everything over to Rik Dean, the detective superintendent she'd spoken to earlier who'd declined to turn out. The handover had been just before Daniels went off-duty at seven a.m., at which point her head had become slush and she'd been desperate for the river run, then bed.

Dean was already at the mortuary chatting to the Home Office pathologist, Professor Baines, whom Daniels knew. They were standing by one of the mortuary slabs, wearing medical fatigues. A crime scene investigator was assembling and setting up recording equipment.

They looked at her as she entered. She stopped suddenly when she saw that the PM had not yet started.

'Afternoon, Diane,' Dean said.

Daniels swallowed something that tasted quite horrible in her throat and she told herself to toughen up.

What had brought her to a sudden halt had been the bodies on the slab. Bodies, plural. Both the woman who had died in the fire and the infant clasped to her chest had been carefully transferred to the mortuary as one entity – not separated, but brought here as they had lain in the front room of the fire-ravaged house.

The fact that it was an adult holding a child was even clearer now they were on a stainless-steel slab, their shapes more clearly defined in the terrible death they had endured. It was almost like some modern work of art, a statue or carving from a huge block of charcoal that, if it had been so, would not have looked out of place in a gallery. In that context it might even have represented a celebration of life.

But here, in the mortuary, it was an investigation into brutal death.

Just fucking toughen up, Daniels ordered herself again, got her legs into gear and walked across the space between herself and the men.

'Afternoon, sir,' she said to Dean. Then to Baines, 'Professor.'

Baines gave her a quizzical 'trying to place you' look. 'Have we met?' he asked.

'Over in Yorkshire, a few years back. You came over to help Henry Christie.'

'Ah, yes, I recall; bad cops.'

'That's right. And some.'

Baines narrowed his eyes at Dean. 'And you're his brother-in-law, aren't you?'

'I have that dubious honour,' Dean admitted.

'Is he still running that pub? Shacked up with the landlady?'

'Sort of,' Dean said.

Interrupting the catch-up, Daniels said, 'I hope you don't mind me turning up, boss? I just think I owe it to her . . . I stood outside while she and her kid died.'

'That's fine. I get it. However, Diane, you mustn't blame yourself for this. No one could have rescued her, so don't beat yourself up over it.'

'Thanks, boss.' She was grateful for his words but already knew this would be one of those 'cop things' that would stay with her for the rest of her life. The trick was to keep it compartmentalized.

Baines began to prepare himself to perform the PM. As he did this, he asked Dean, 'Where are we up to with this?'

'Well, the woman is definitely Andrea Greatrix, but we haven't found any relatives yet to formally identify her – even if we had, we wouldn't put anyone through the trauma of seeing this body. Hopefully, we'll have some dental and DNA after this. She's thirty-six, single, we think, and an active member of the drug culture in Lancaster – which, as we know, is very active,' he said cynically.

'I haven't come across her,' Daniels admitted. 'Have we started building a picture of her life yet?'

Dean shrugged. 'Spoken to some neighbours just now. She kept herself pretty much to herself, although there was traffic to and from the house, so it looks like she could have been dealing low-level stuff.'

Daniels nodded. 'And the fire? I know it's early days.'

'Very deliberate, as you know. Gas pipe unhooked, several seats of fire. She was probably rendered unconscious, woke to find the house ablaze, got trapped upstairs and then the house exploded. It's possible there were seats of fire upstairs, but as there's nothing much left of it, we won't know for certain for a while. But that's the hypothesis I'm working on – beaten unconscious, place set ablaze, trapped, explosion – until I'm told different. The pathologist will be able to tell us quite a lot, I think.'

'Neighbours mention kids?' Daniels asked.

'Two – a toddler and a nine- or ten-year-old girl – but all we have so far is the child in her arms. We are still sifting through the debris, but no trace of another so far.'

'So, if there is no other body found, it could fit in with what I saw – a man running with a child.'

'It could,' Dean concurred.

'Have the neighbours mentioned any regular blokes around the house?'

'Not yet. I think we'll find things out in a rush,' Dean said.

'I hope so . . . God, it was a horrible way to die.'

'I think we're ready to begin,' Baines said, turning to the detectives. The CSI had set up recording equipment – four cameras working simultaneously to record the post-mortem from various angles and picking up what Baines was saying, even though he had his own portable recording device fixed to himself. 'My name is Reginald Baines and I am a Home Office pathologist for the North-West Region,' he began, then reeled off his qualifications and experience. They were many and went back a long time. 'I am at the public mortuary at Royal Lancaster Infirmary, together with Detective Superintendent Dean, DC Daniels, a crime scene investigator and a mortuary assistant. I am about to perform post-mortem examination on one female adult and one small infant, gender yet unknown, both of whom perished in a house fire in the early hours of this morning and whose bodies seem to have fused together.'

Baines then walked slowly around the slab, describing his preliminary observations in great detail.

He then reached the point where he looked over at the detectives and announced he was about to separate the bodies.

Daniels had to leave before the post-mortems were completed because she had to book on for her next tour of duty at five p.m.

Before that she nipped home, stripped off, put her clothes into the washing machine to get rid of the reek of the mortuary. Even a couple of hours exposed to the smell of death and burnt flesh meant everything had become contaminated.

Another shower was in order as that same smell clung to her hair and was up her nose.

Those things done, she made it back to the police station in time for her shift. She'd hoped Rik Dean would have asked her to become part of the murder investigation team, but that didn't happen. All he did was ask her to write a detailed statement and forward it to him in time for the first full briefing of the murder squad the next morning.

She was disappointed but not too upset. Dean would have his 'go-to' detectives he knew and trusted, and Daniels knew it was up to her to do this job to the best of her abilities, so that when the next murder came up in the division, he would remember her and give her a chance.

She knew only too well that getting on to FMIT was like eating the proverbial elephant – one bite at a time. You forged a reputation, showed your reliability and some imagination, too. Then you got remembered.

However, as she walked up through Lancaster Police Station, she did wonder, and not for the first time, if she was up to the task.

When she'd worked briefly with Henry Christie as he investigated what should have been a couple of fairly straightforward cold cases, her reaction to seeing a freshly murdered body had been horror and upset, and she knew what she'd witnessed at the scene of the explosion had rattled and disturbed her too.

But she also knew deep down that investigating murder was what she wanted to do more than anything now.

Not because it was sexy or came with kudos, but because she had a desire to be one of those, as Henry Christie had been, who fought for the rights of people who could no longer fight for themselves.

The dead.

The CID office was empty. She sat down heavily at her desk and mulled over what she had seen in the last few hours.

The deaths had moved her deeply; that was very true. But she recalled a conversation she'd had with Henry Christie after they had attended the scene of a particularly brutal murder, when he had admitted to her that, despite his experience, seeing murdered people still had a huge effect on him.

What he'd learned to do was to deal with it and put walls in his mind – sometimes forever.

And that is what she decided to do there and then.

She put all thoughts of a mother and child burned to death to one side and turned her mind to the machete attack from the night before. She skimmed through the paperwork scattered on her desk to see if she had been left some update, but there was nothing to be found. This did not surprise her as most detectives had been pulled into the explosion murder. A fall-out between rival gangs, however serious, would have been put aside for the time being, so her reasoning was that if she could get a result on it, she would start to climb the rankings on the next round of FMIT applications.

Her next port of call was the comms room to check through the day's messages and have a chat with the comms sergeant who would be well briefed on everything that had happened.

Daniels learned that virtually nothing had been done to find John Dishforth, the machete offender, and most free uniform patrols were still deployed keeping a lid on the tinderbox that was Luneside estate.

So a machete-wielding maniac was still on the loose, and DC Diane Daniels made it her job for the night to track him down, lock him up, charge him with attempted murder and get him before court in the morning.

Buoyed by that decision, her next port of call was Royal Lancaster Infirmary to visit the victim of the attack who, apparently, was still in the critical care unit.

FOUR

The fires had been burning for over two weeks, consuming the moors. Dense, acrid smoke hung over the village of Kendleton like an old, choking London smog.

The heatwave had been rare, sizzling and relentless, with temperatures almost touching forty degrees for over a month, and the fires – believed to have been started deliberately or accidentally by human hand and not through natural combustion of the tinder-dry grass – raged out of control despite the best efforts of an overstretched, under-resourced but valiant fire service and volunteers.

Even the one long, almost tropical and very violent thunderstorm and accompanying torrential downpour, lasting over four hours, had failed to douse flames which swept relentlessly as a red-coal carpet over many square miles.

Henry Christie stood on the wide front steps of The Tawny Owl – known locally as Th'Owl – looking intently across Kendleton village green towards the trickle of the stream flowing through the village. Kendleton Brook was usually full and healthy-looking, but this minor tributary of the River Lune, which took its waters from the surrounding hills, was now hardly even a trickle as the fires and scorching weather seemed to dry up and kill everything.

Henry squinted through the unpleasant smoke haze at the steep, deeply wooded area rising from the opposite bank of the stream, checking again for any sign of the old red deer stag he often caught sight of in the woods; since the fires had taken their grip, he had not laid eyes on Horace – as he called him – and he was becoming concerned.

He understood that the beast was free and wide-ranging, so he hoped Horace had not become a victim of the fires as so many other animals had, particularly birds. Henry believed the stag would be fine. He was wily and experienced and could easily have outrun the fires in any direction, maybe never to be seen again in this neck of the woods. That would be sad for Henry who, though hardly superstitious, looked upon Horace as a kind of talisman.

'Still no sign?' came a voice from behind.

Henry felt a hand link into the crook of his arm as Ginny, the young woman with whom he co-owned Th'Owl, tucked up alongside him. She was the stepdaughter of Henry's recently deceased fiancée, Alison, the previous owner of the business that Henry had inherited on her death. He had then split it fifty-fifty with Ginny and in partnership they had carried on running it successfully, very much in memory of Alison, who remained constantly in Henry's thoughts following her brutal death at the hands of vengeful ex.

Henry clasped her hand. 'Not so far. I'm sure he'll be back one day.'

'Let's hope.'

Henry glanced at her and smiled. Ginny was now twenty-four and lived at the pub with her boyfriend, who also worked there. Although Ginny wasn't Alison's blood relative, Henry could see a lot of Alison in Ginny, notably her philosophy of living: *get on with it!*

She grinned back, but their heads turned in unison as a fire tender thundered through the village on the road past the pub, then out towards the moors. Henry and Ginny gave it a wave, then went back inside the pub which had become the unofficial control centre for the area's response to the fires, something that Henry and Ginny were rightly proud of.

When the fires started, it could not have been predicted they would have been so extensive and long-lasting, but Henry had immediately seen that because of the geography of the area – flung way out to the east of Lancaster, bordering on the Forest of Bowland, accessible only via tight, winding country lanes, with Kendleton at its heart – there needed to be some centralized location which could act as the mustering point for all the locals to obtain updated information and somewhere the emergency services and other helpers could simply come to catch their breath.

With that in mind, Henry set up Th'Owl as this unofficial ops centre – using the first-floor function room as a place where firefighters, cops, paramedics and anyone else could bob in, sit or lie down, get a free brew or bottle of water or some food – and as a welfare centre for locals affected by the fires.

People of the village also rallied to the cause, providing free food and drinks.

It was a good community effort in a time of crisis.

Henry and Ginny unhooked arms and went their separate ways, Ginny to the kitchens, Henry into the main bar which was just about ticking over. Local trade had remained steady as the fires burned, but passing trade had dwindled to a trickle. Henry had also taken it upon himself to contact customers who had booked rooms to apprise them of the situation: that staying in the village at the moment was not terribly pleasant and, if they so wished, they could cancel without charge and get any deposits back.

Most cancelled and about £4,000 of business was lost, though in the overall scheme of things this was a minor amount; business was booming and, once the fires were extinguished, it would continue to do so.

Henry spent a few minutes chatting to a couple of the locals propping up the bar, and as he looked around, he noticed a couple of squat, tough-looking young men drinking pints in one corner of the room. He must have been elsewhere in the premises when they had arrived because he didn't recall them coming in.

It was a few years since he'd been a cop. He'd retired with the rank of detective superintendent, joint head of Lancashire

Constabulary's Force Major Investigation Team, and although his whole existence had taken a completely different trajectory since then, he hoped he still possessed a smidgen of the instinct that had once made him a half-decent detective.

So, standing behind the bar of Th'Owl, looking at the pair of outsiders huddled over their pints, talking – literally – through the sides of their mouths, their eyes taking in everything, including Henry who, as soon as they saw his scrutiny, made them clam up guiltily, Henry knew they were double trouble.

Not because they were members of the travelling fraternity: he could tell they were because of their looks, clothing and demeanour. Henry knew this was jumping to a conclusion and he could be accused of stereotyping, but he would have bet a month's bar takings at Th'Owl that he was right. Over thirty years as a cop, he'd come across hundreds of travellers, and travellers were also frequent visitors to Th'Owl because Kendleton was often a stop-off en route to the annual horse fair at Appleby in Cumbria, one of the big events in their calendar. He'd got to know a few and they him, and there was a degree of mutual respect and wariness, but these two guys, he could tell, were not the usual crew.

And not only that, but they were surreptitiously vaping, trying to hide the e-cigarettes under the table, hoping no one spotted the actual vapour coming out of their mouths.

Henry sighed, braced himself and walked over to the men, whose expressions, he would have sworn, became even surlier the closer he got.

'Gents.' He nodded affably. 'Nice to see new customers. Everything to your satisfaction?'

They nodded, said nothing.

'Beer OK?'

'It's OK,' one said grudgingly. His fist was wrapped around his e-cigarette. He had tightly curled ginger hair and a face that looked as if it had been forged by a farrier, and he wore a black donkey jacket with badly sewn on leather patches across the elbows and shoulders. There was a faded business logo on the front of the jacket, the words, cracked and almost unreadable, could have said something about 'ground works'. He wore baggy, moleskin trousers and work boots, the steel toe caps visible. His accent, even from just the two words spoken, had an Irish lilt to it. And his eyes were the colour of flint and just as icy as he glowered at Henry.

Henry smiled. 'You just passing through?'

'And what business would that be of yours?' the other one piped up gruffly. Like his mate, he was perhaps in his early twenties, but his hair was black and ragged, his face round, features soft. He too wore a donkey jacket, jeans and boots.

Henry remained unruffled. 'Just making conversation with my guests,' he said. 'Thing is, though, smoking or vaping isn't allowed on the premises, so I'm going to have to ask you to either put the e-ciggies away or go outside.'

Both men eyeballed him in a way he did not like – dangerously.

'We'll be on us way,' the curly-haired one said.

'Well, you have a safe journey, wherever it may take you.' Henry backed off to the bar.

The two lads dawdled over the remainder of their drinks, eyeing Henry, scowling at him, but not vaping again.

Eventually, they rose to leave. He followed them out and watched them climb into a large four-wheel-drive pickup truck which was parked on the road. As they drove away, the passenger leaned out and gave Henry an extravagant V-sign and blew out a huge lungful of vapour. Henry gave him a nice wave and wondered when they would be back to wreak havoc.

On the off chance, he memorized the registration number and jotted it down on a Post-it note which he stuck next to the landline phone at the back of the bar.

Henry checked his watch – the Breitling Navitimer that Alison had given him as a Christmas present, which he wore constantly now. It was seven thirty-five p.m. He made his way up to the ops room on the first floor and found a couple of people up there he knew well.

One was the Kendleton village bobby PC Jake Niven. Henry had been instrumental in getting Niven the job as the local cop, one of the last good things he'd done before his retirement, and Niven had since made the role very much his own.

The other person was Maude Crichton, a local lady much the same age as Henry who had volunteered to keep the ops centre running during the fires, a role she carried out tirelessly and efficiently. In that respect she had been a godsend, but Henry knew she had an agenda, which was obvious to all and sundry, and that was to get to know Henry on a more intimate basis. Maude was a very wealthy but lonely widow living in a big detached house on the edge of the village and she had set her sights on Henry. He found her funny and attractive, but for the first time in his life he wasn't interested in being with a woman.

Her face lit up on seeing him enter the room and she puffed out her bosom subtly, but not so subtly that Jake Niven did not notice either the look or the body language.

'Hi, folks,' Henry greeted them.

Maude was sitting behind a trestle table on which was laid out a huge Ordnance Survey map of Kendleton and its environs, with areas highlighted in red to indicate the extent of the fires surrounding the village. They were extensive and continuing to spread like an unstoppable blossom.

Stacked behind Maude were hundreds of water bottles supplied by the cash-and-carry warehouse Henry used for the pub, plus boxes of biscuits and a lot of fruit. Next to these piles were two large hot-water urns with supplies of tea, coffee, sugar, milk and disposable cups.

Having seen the fire engine go past a short time ago, Henry expected an influx of firefighters soon, and these supplies would not last long once the personnel launched gratefully into them. Firefighters, Henry had learned, were as voracious as cops when it came to free food.

'Hi, Henry,' Niven said, strolling over to meet him with a knowing look in his eye. They met halfway across the dance floor. 'How's it going?' Then, in a low voice, he whispered, 'She's got the hots for you, mate – better watch out.'

Henry made a show of shaking Niven's hand and patting his shoulder. 'Thanks for that,' he said through gritted teeth, looking over to Maude, whose eyes were wider than normal. She gave Henry a nice little wave. 'Other than that, how's things, Jake?'

They turned and walked to the table, Henry smiling at Maude in an open, friendly way but not one, he hoped, to give the wrong impression.

'Henry, darling,' she said, rising from her chair.

He knew she wanted to kiss both cheeks, so he surrendered but kept the table between them and, despite himself, quite liked the aroma of her perfume.

She held on to his shoulder a second or two longer than necessary, but then they parted and Henry took a step back and looked at the map.

'The fire continues to spread,' Niven said. 'According to the fire service, it's coming this way.' He pointed out the area he was referring to.

'Towards the village now?' Henry asked.

'A change in wind direction.'

'That would account for the smog seeming a bit thicker.' Henry looked at Niven and Maude. 'Not good.' He asked Maude, 'Have you done the ring-round?'

The 'ring-round' was made each day to all the outlying farms and homes just as a welfare check. So far there had been no major problems.

'I have.' She picked up the list from the tabletop. 'Only one no-reply – the York family out on Lowthwaite Fell.'

Henry narrowed his eyes. 'Do I know them?'

'Possibly. They've been in here a few times. Man and wife living in a converted farmhouse – a big one by all accounts. I think they run some sort of financial advice company over Kirby Lonsdale way. Quite well-to-do – he drives around in a swanky Bentley, I think,' she said with a degree of distaste, as if she wasn't wealthy enough to own one herself. Henry didn't know for sure, but the rumour clinic had it that Maude's long-dead husband had been something in import/export in Manchester and left her about ten million when he'd popped his clogs from a sudden stroke about four years ago. 'John and Isobel, they're called.'

'Mmm – yeah, I think I do know them . . . got a Great Dane or something.'

'Yep, that's them.'

'Do we need to worry?' Henry looked at Niven.

'Have they always replied before, Maude?' the PC asked Maude.

'Every time.'

'And you've tried landline and mobile phones?' Niven asked.

'And email, and WhatsApp.' Maude nodded. She had set up a WhatsApp group for people affected by the fire, but there were only about six active members on it, the Yorks among them.

'Call them again,' Henry said.

'OK,' Maude said brightly.

'We should never have gone in there,' Brendan O'Hara said, gripping the steering wheel of the Dodge Ram pickup as he drove out of Kendleton, west towards Lancaster along the narrow, smoke-filled roads. He'd lit a self-rolled cigarette which dangled from his lips and jigged up and down as he spoke. He was the red-haired one of the pair.

'Killing's a thirsty business, Brendan,' the other lad replied. His name was Cillian Roche. 'We needed a pint, only right. We didn't do owt wrong in the pub, 'cept vape.'

'I knows – but that guy made us for what we are, Cillian.'

'Gyppos, you mean?'

'Exactly.'

'So? That's what we is.'

'No,' O'Hara said, 'we's much more than that, my old mate. Much more.'

'Maybe so, but we drew attention to ourselves without tryin'. He'll remember us, that guy, and that might not be good.'

'Maybe we should pay him another visit and make 'im forget he ever saw us?' O'Hara suggested with a dangerous glint, more than half meaning it.

Then Roche screamed, 'Holy shit – mind out!'

O'Hara had been glancing at Roche as he drove, only partly concentrating on the road ahead, but when he turned to face forwards, he too screamed and jerked the steering wheel down to the right as the biggest red deer stag he had ever seen – and he had poached many in his short life – leapt over the hedge from the right and landed almost slap-bang in front of the Ram.

Time seemed to slow right down for him as he slammed on the brakes, veered right and skidded, his eyes growing to double their size. The magnificent animal stopped momentarily, straddling the centre of the road and appeared to glare directly into his eyes. Then, as it seemed the Dodge could not miss crashing into the beast's flank, the animal tensed its huge, powerful hind muscles and bounded in a single leap across the road and cleared the high hedge on the opposite side, leaving what looked like a cloud of silver dust behind it.

The Ram slewed to a stop on the exact spot where the stag had stood, and the engine stalled with a loud juddering of gears mashing together.

'Holy fuckin' Jazus and the saints,' O'Hara gasped, slowly uncurling his stubby fingers from the rim of the wheel. 'See the size of that mother?'

'Nearly fuckin' killed us, it did.' Roche was as still as a block of stone, shocked to his core. 'It was grey, not red . . . it was like a ghost.'

O'Hara twisted the ignition key and the engine purred back to life. 'Ash from the moor fires,' he said.

'Fuck – you know, it was like one o' them big birds that comes outta the fires,' Roche said, still in awe, still seeing the image in his head.

'A phoenix?'

'Yeah, yeah, that's it – a phoenix. We was nearly killed by a phoenix.' He looked sideways at his friend and blew out his cheeks.

Then they started to laugh, hesitantly at first, then hysterically.

'Take more than a phoenix to fuck us,' O'Hara said.

'Yeah, yeah.'

Finally, their laughter subsided. Roche genially punched O'Hara's upper arm. 'C'mon, man . . . more people to kill tonight.'

FIVE

'Diane? This is Emma on the front desk.'

Daniels had been about to leave the CID office and head off on foot up to the infirmary, less than half a mile from the station on the road south out of the city. Wanting to clear her head again, she looked forward to an evening stroll and almost did not answer the phone.

'Hi, Em.'

'Sorry to bother you. I've tried the Major Incident Room, but there's no reply.'

'OK.' Daniels knew that an MIR had been set up by Rik Dean on the top floor of the nick to handle the investigation following the explosion, but also knew it wouldn't be fully staffed and up and running until the following morning, so there was every chance no one was there yet and any detectives on the job could well be out and about, knocking on doors.

'It's just that there's a woman rolled into the front desk – looks a bit of a druggie, to be honest, and stinks of booze and won't give her name, but she says she's a mate of Andrea Greatrix . . . isn't she the woman who died in the blast last night?'

Almost before Emma had finished talking, Daniels blurted, 'I'll be down in a minute. Keep hold of her.' She hung up abruptly, grabbed her PR and shoulder bag, and rushed out of the office, threading her way through the corridors and down the stairs to the tiny office behind the front enquiry counter where she found Emma, the PEA – public enquiry assistant – at her desk.

'Hi, Em, what've you got?'

'Hi, Diane . . . well, this youngish woman came in and said she had some information about Andrea Greatrix.'

'Did she say what?'

'Didn't ask. I've sat her down in the waiting room just off the foyer, but she looks jumpy, so if you want to see her, I'd grip her now.'

'Great, brilliant job . . . you all right, mate?' she asked Emma quickly. She was one of the small posse of women from the station that Daniels occasionally went out with and was probably on the cusp of being a friend. They certainly liked each other.

'I'm good, thanks.'

Daniels smiled and nodded, then reversed back into the corridor and made her way around to the secure door that opened into the waiting room. Daniels smiled at the waif-like woman sitting at the table. She was stick thin, pasty-faced, with darkly ringed eyes sunk deep in their sockets. Her badly dyed red hair was scraped back off her face into a straggly ponytail. Her ears, nose and eyebrows were festooned with rings, her skin a landscape of bad tattoos. She was probably in her early twenties but looked a decade older. Drugs, Daniels thought sadly, because behind the frailness of the woman she detected a pretty girl.

'Hi, I'm DC Daniels, Lancaster CID.' She held out her hand, a gesture not reciprocated. Daniels took no offence. She sat down opposite, placing her bag and PR on the table, still smiling reassuringly at the woman who was clearly on edge. 'What's your name?'

'That's not important.' Her voice was like gravel.

'OK, no probs. How can I help?'

'My mate was killed last night – in that explosion.'

'Andrea Greatrix?'

'Yuh.'

Daniels remained quiet, wanting her to carry on unprompted for the moment.

'She was worried about stuff.'

'What kind of stuff?'

'Boyfriend stuff.'

'Worried in what way?'

The woman shrugged.

'OK,' Daniels said. 'How do you know Andrea? Let's begin there.'

'We were just mates, I suppose. Used to hang around the town centre together, y'know? Drinkin' and that. I met her way back at the drug clinic. We were both tryin' t'get off H, y'know? With methadone and other shit. We both just took it from there. You kinda know a mate when you meet one, yeah?'

'Yeah, I get that. Sometimes you just hit it off.'

'Well, yeah, me and Ands – Andrea – were like that, round town, always bobbin' into each other's houses, like.'

'So you've lost a good friend?' Daniels probed.

The woman's watery eyes misted over. 'I did. My best mate.'

'How horrible, I'm so sorry. And by such a terrible accident.'

Daniels purposely used the word 'accident' because it wasn't well known yet that a fully-fledged murder investigation was about to kick off. She also wanted to see this woman's reaction to the word – and she got it, like pushing the right button.

'Wasn't an accident.' She bristled.

Daniels played dumb. 'How d'you mean?' she asked, getting that shimmer of excitement all cops got, usually in the form of a ring-piece clench, when they realized they might just be prising open a can of worms.

'Like I said, she was worried. Shit-scared, actually.'

'About the boyfriend?'

'A real nasty cunt of an ex-con who'd manipulated the shit out of her,' the woman said vehemently.

'Manipulated how?'

'Over his kid.'

'His kid?'

'I mean, she fucking knew he was a violent fucker when she got into him years back. Nasty piece of work, but she fell in love with the nasty twat and she thought he'd be all right cos of his job 'n' that . . . well, this is the story she told me, I didn't know her back then. But he got her pregnant, then he got sent down, then he comes back out and he wants his twopenn'orth – his kid. It was just a fuckin' mess.'

Daniels held up the palms of her hands in a 'let's pause' gesture.

'Can we get to the point here . . . You're saying you think this boyfriend murdered her?'

'Yeah, in't that what I said?'

'Yes, of course it is . . . Look, before we go on, why don't you tell me your name, love? I'll get us a brew and some biscuits, and it'll make conversation much easier, then we'll get the story down on paper.'

'Do I have to?'

'It'd be really helpful, and I'll look after you. I can see you're a bit worried by all this.'

'You would be too if you knew him. He's out for revenge, that bastard, and I don't want him coming for me as well, cos I've talked to you lot.'

'As I said . . . I'll look after you . . .'

The conversation was interrupted by Daniels' PR on the table.

Patrols, urgent. Royal Lancaster Infirmary, report of men armed with handguns running through the corridors. I repeat, report of armed men with handguns running through the corridors, threatening staff. Believed shots fired . . .

At first, of course, no one knew O'Hara and Roche were armed with anything. They parked the Ram in a dark recess at the rear of the hospital in an area reserved for staff, knowing the chances of being challenged for this transgression within the next ten minutes or so – which was all they needed – was unlikely.

Nor did it really matter if they were caught on CCTV because the Dodge Ram they were in was displaying false number plates and they were both wearing silicone face masks that clung to their features, distorting them, but not so much that anyone would scream at their appearance. They just looked like pug-ugly blokes.

Nor did they streak through the infirmary carrying sledgehammers, jemmies or machetes. These items were in the holdall carried by O'Hara.

In fact, they sauntered through the corridors unhurriedly, having previously studied a floorplan downloaded from the internet. They knew exactly where they were going: to the critical care unit on the ground floor.

When they arrived at the entrance to the CCU, they knew this might be the hardest part: actually getting through the door – hence the sledgehammers.

Entry to the unit was through a door controlled by an intercom and buzzer release on the inside, policed by nursing staff, and it was rare that anyone other than close relatives to the patients was allowed access. But buzzing was O'Hara's and Roche's first roll of the dice, and if that didn't work, then they would simply bludgeon the door off its hinges, something they were highly skilled at, having demolished many things in their time. A locked door into a hospital ward wasn't going to slow them down much.

As it happened, they didn't even have to try to blag their way in or force entry, because a woman was just leaving as they arrived and kindly held the door open for them to slip through. She was diverted because she was deep into a mobile phone conversation about the critical health of whoever she had been visiting and did not even glance at their veneered faces as they ducked in behind her.

Once inside, there was an office with a desk to the left, then beyond that eight open-ended cubicles in each of which was a bed. Such was the nature of the CCU – it was either jam-packed or almost empty – that only two patients were being cared for at that moment, so it took only seconds for the two intruders to locate their target: a young man called Sam Dorner who had been lucky enough to survive a machete attack the night before.

O'Hara and Roche fully expected that Dorner would not be so lucky tonight.

'Please stay here,' Daniels pleaded with the woman. 'Will you? I really must go to this.'

She waggled her PR at the woman – the radio now a mass of voice traffic as patrols were deployed or called up to say they were on their way to the infirmary.

'It's an emergency,' Daniels said. She gave the woman her best puppy eyes and the woman nodded reluctantly.

It was a tough one to decide to leave her. Daniels could probably have got away with not turning out to the infirmary, but there was no way she could let her uniform colleagues pile into a job that could be very dangerous without her backup.

'Thank you,' she said genuinely. 'I'll arrange for the lady on the front desk to sort a brew out for you.'

'Whatevs . . .' The woman shrugged, unimpressed.

Daniels gave a quick nod and scurried out of the waiting-room door into the foyer. She was almost sent flying by two uniformed PCs who launched themselves across the enquiry desk like characters from a 1970s American cop show and ran through the door to their car parked out front. This was not the usual way out for police personnel.

From behind the counter, Emma shouted, 'Careful, guys!'

'Sort a brew out for this lady, will you?' Daniels said to her, gesturing to the waiting room. 'I'm going too . . . and try to keep her from leaving.'

'OK, yes – and you be careful too,' Emma responded.

Daniels pushed her way through the front door and ran into the police parking area to the CID car, which was in the same horrific mess as always. Tonight she didn't have time to dwell on it.

She skidded across the car park, out under the barrier, but was forced to slam on for another vehicle turning on to the public apron of the car park – but then she was on Marton Street where, at the next junction, she had to brake hard again as a blue-lighted traffic car, two-tones blaring, shot past her nose on the one-way system, heading south towards the infirmary . . . and then she was in its slipstream, driving one-handed while reaching over the back seat to grab a stab vest someone had left in the car.

'Sit-rep, please,' one patrol called up. Daniels recognized the voice of the patrol inspector.

Comms replied, 'Just trying to piece this together, sir. Calls coming in thick and fast on the treble-nine system, but it looks like two masked men, armed with handguns and machetes, have burst into the critical care unit, forced staff and others on to their knees, and attacked the victim from last night's knife attack who was in the unit.'

'What's his status?'

'Unclear as yet, but first reports look bad.'

'OK, roger that. And the offenders – update, please.'

'Again, sketchy at the moment. Two males, fairly young, tight-fitting masks, armed with handguns and machetes. Made their escape running towards the rear of the infirmary.'

'Vehicles?'

'Just come in – two men seen getting into a large four-wheel-drive pickup of some description at the back of the building. Nothing more than that at the moment.'

'Roger that.'

He sounded stressed, Daniels thought, and she wondered what had happened to the police officers who'd supposedly been guarding the lad. Perhaps they'd been stood down for some reason. That was a question to be asked.

Just ahead of her, the traffic car swerved across South Road and pulled up outside the A&E unit at the front of the infirmary. Daniels kept going up to the roundabout at Pointer Island with the intention of nipping on to the A588 and then turning right, almost back on herself, on to the road that would take her to the back of the infirmary, which seemed like the route the offenders might have used to escape.

As she circumnavigated the roundabout, something clicked in her mind with a heavy clunk and her guts tightened.

She went all the way around and accelerated back towards the city centre and to the police station, hoping like hell she was wrong.

Of course, the police station had been reconnoitred prior to this visit. Observations had been kept, notes taken, numbers of officers recorded, and decisions made at the very highest level within the organization. They were decisions not taken lightly, but decisions which, if translated into action, would not actually result in too much collateral damage for the organization if things went awry.

O'Hara and Roche were possibly the best duo operating at that moment – trustworthy, usually professional, courageous to the point of stupidity, but they got jobs done. Plus, ultimately, they were also expendable if it went shit-shape.

They knew and accepted that.

They also knew that, if successful, the rewards were good, but even if they were unsuccessful, and they kept their mouths shut, they would be looked after. However, if they blabbed anything, they would also be looked after – just in a different way.

Having almost collided with a car rushing off the police station car park, they drove on to the public apron, spun the Ram around and left it facing outwards at an angle, the engine ticking over. Both disembarked and walked into the public foyer after courteously stepping aside for the skinny, red-haired, obviously drug-addled women hurrying out with the look of a hunted rat.

The waiting area was empty – but it would not have mattered if it had been packed with people, because nothing would have stopped O'Hara and Roche from carrying out their last task of the night.

As they stepped across the threshold, they were still wearing the flesh-coloured silicone masks that had hidden their identities at the hospital and would continue to do so here.

There was a youngish woman behind the sliding screen at the front desk. She watched them approaching with a smile on her face and slid the screen open to welcome them.

Emma's first impression was that they looked like twins, although one had red curly hair and the other's was black and straggly. It was the faces – so similar. Yet as the two men got closer, they looked very weird indeed.

Roche was carrying a holdall which he dropped at his feet as he reached the desk. O'Hara was standing just to his right.

'Hello, darlin',' Roche said.

He smiled and the clinging mask moved with his lips – which was the moment that Emma realized the men were wearing masks.

She began to close the screen. Quickly.

Both men bent down out of sight for a moment, then stood back up, each brandishing a sledgehammer. In unison, they brought the sledgehammers up and, emitting murderous screams, began smashing them into the toughened glass.

The first couple of blows bounced off.

Then the screen disintegrated, falling in a shower like snow from a roof, and suddenly, other than the width of the counter, there was nothing protecting Emma as the men clambered across, one of them discarding his sledgehammer.

Emma cowered away in terror and shock. O'Hara grabbed her by her uniform blouse, dragged her to her feet and spun her round in front of him. Holding and manoeuvring her by her shoulders, and with a hand gripping her neck, he shoved her through the inner door into the ground-floor corridor that ran most of the length of the police station and bundled her along it. At the far end was the door that gave access to the custody office, on the lower ground floor below.

O'Hara forced her along the corridor, jamming something hard into her ribs – the muzzle of his revolver. Roche followed.

'Go, go, go, bitch,' he screamed, rushing her along the corridor, keeping her off balance.

On reaching the custody office door, he slammed her up against it and shouted into her ear, 'Open this fucking door – now!' Then he slammed her against it again and jerked her back a foot.

Inside the station, access to the custody office from this direction was by a simple four-digit code on a keypad. With a shaking finger, Emma entered the digits and the door clicked. O'Hara grabbed the handle and wrenched the door open, bundling Emma on to the small landing, then forcing her down the iron steps.

Roche came in behind, using the handle of his sledgehammer to wedge the door open, just in case it was less easy to leave.

The three virtually tumbled down the steps into the area in front of the custody desk on the lower ground floor that could be accessed from an underground car park where police vehicles delivering or collecting prisoners parked up.

Roche and O'Hara would have preferred to use this as a way into the police station because of the direct access to the cell complex, but it would have been impossible for them to burst through because the door was made of steel. All access and egress was controlled from inside by the custody sergeant who also had a view of people coming and going through the security camera over the door.

Instead, they came in through another route.

As they herded Emma ahead of them, the custody sergeant looked up from whatever paperwork he was concentrating on at the desk. He looked as if he was about to smile at Emma, but then took in the whole scene and instinctively reached for the alarm strip along the wall.

O'Hara shunted Emma aside, brought his handgun up and fired at the sergeant before the man's fingertip touched the rubber strip.

The .38 slug slammed into his right shoulder, shattering the joint, spinning him off his chair, back towards the wall, which he thumped against and slid down, leaving a thick bloody smear.

Emma screamed.

O'Hara sideswiped her with his gun as Roche dodged past and went around the custody desk.

The cell keys were attached to a long chain fastened to the injured sergeant's belt which simply needed unhooking. The sergeant himself, already in deep shock and agony, blankly watched Roche, unable to react as the colour drained from him and blood spouted from the shoulder.

'Male cell two,' O'Hara said. He was standing behind Emma, holding her hair in his fist, almost tearing it from her scalp.

'I know,' Roche said.

This was just another part of their research.

Roche stood up with the keys and hurried down the cell corridor, turning first right, where he faced a locked gate.

There were only two big chunky keys on the chain, one each for the male and female cells (cell doors did not have individual keys), plus two smaller brass ones for the gates at the entrances to the cell corridors. There were other smaller keys for offices and desk drawers.

Roche slotted one of the brass keys into the gate with a fifty-fifty chance of getting it right first time.

He did. He was through.

In the corridor he stopped outside cell two and slid down the hatch.

'We're here, boss.'

A face appeared at the hatch with a big grin on it.

Roche again opened the door with the first key he tried. He and the prisoner legged it back into the custody reception area where O'Hara was standing over Emma and the injured sergeant. He still had Emma's fine hair wrapped up in his fist. When he saw Roche and the prisoner, his face beamed and let he go with a rough shove. She sank to the floor, cringing in fear.

'Gun, gun.' The prisoner waggled his fingers at O'Hara, who immediately handed the weapon over. He pushed O'Hara aside and stood threateningly over the custody sergeant whose eyes were starting to glaze over but who managed to look up at him. The prisoner brought the muzzle of the gun around and aimed it at the sergeant's face.

'For calling me a gyppo.'

He pulled the trigger.

Sometimes cops get feelings based on absolutely nothing really. Something that, like a crazy itch, has to be checked out.

Daniels knew she could check this one out within a minute, and if the feeling turned out to be nothing, she could be back at the infirmary two minutes later, nothing lost.

This particular feeling was caused by a combination of the vague description of the vehicle that might – possibly – be being used by the offenders at the infirmary and a brief glimpse of a similar vehicle turning into the police station car park as she herself had accelerated off to go to the incident.

She knew it could be nothing.

There were lots of big four-wheel-drive monstrosities knocking around these days.

In which case, so be it.

No one would need to know that she'd had a look just for her piece of mind . . . to scratch that feeling.

She gunned the CID Astra back down South Road and cut slightly right into Penny Street, then careened sharp right into Marton Street, with the police station on the left just after the turning for the police garage.

The big four-wheel-drive was there – and three men were scrambling into it.

She slammed the accelerator down as the vehicle began to move, drove across the front of it and stopped, preventing it from going any further. The huge bull bars that curved around the front grille rocked just inches away from the passenger door of the Astra.

Daniels jumped out, hoping she was completely wrong about this, quite ready to eat humble pie.

As she did, the Dodge Ram reversed a few feet, then, with a roar from its massive engine, surged forwards and smashed into the side of the CID car, buckling the door and forcing it almost halfway across Marton Street with a loud tearing, screeching, metallic sound.

Daniels leaped aside to avoid being crushed.

She raised her arms in a 'What the fuck?' gesture.

The Ram drew back. Stopped. Revved. Then leapt forward to smash into the Astra again, pushing it even further across the road, making Daniels jump away.

The Ram reversed and, having cleared enough space, swerved to the left, but then suddenly stopped once more.

The driver leaned out of his window, pointed a handgun at Daniels – and fired.

She threw herself down with a yell, aware the Ram was moving away. She took a moment just to check she hadn't been shot – no – then rolled up on to one knee, bringing her PR up to her mouth and cutting across all the other transmissions on the frequency as she ran around her mangled car and tried to yank the driver's door open.

'Urgent assistance needed at Marton Street outside the nick. Shot fired at me by occupants of a big four-wheel-drive pickup, now made off towards Thurnham Street, three males on board. Not sure if linked to the infirmary job, but possibly.' She kept her voice as cool as possible as she tried to pull the door open – not easy as the whole of the car had been crippled by the impact. She kept watching the pickup – although she had no clue as to its make or model – which had reached the Thurnham Street junction. She expected it to go right into the one-way system. Part of her was thinking this was good because it would mean the vehicle was heading up to the infirmary, towards which every other cop was currently hurtling. Her other thought was about the police station connection. Only two men were on board the pickup when she'd seen it arrive. Three had left in it. What did that mean?

'Bravo Three – are you hurt, Diane?' the patrol inspector shouted up.

'All OK, but my car's been rammed . . . bloomin' 'eck, the car's turned left into Thurnham Street against the flow of traffic,' she said hurriedly.

'Lancaster comms interrupting – request a patrol to divert to the custody office, personal attack alarm sounding.'

'Can you cover that, Diane?' the inspector asked her.

Her intention had been to chase the four-wheel-drive in the CID car, if possible. Instead, she said, 'On my way,' and left the damaged car abandoned skew-whiff across Marton Street, though not totally blocking it.

Most of the rest of the radio transmissions were lost on Daniels from that moment as she boxed off the thought that if she'd been hit by a bullet, she could have been dead or dying on the street right now. If she'd had the chance to dwell on it, she might have had a meltdown, but that was often the nature of police work. If there was time to stop and consider what the hell you were doing, you'd pack up and head for home. The time for analysis would come later, at leisure or in some counsellor's office.

When things were happening, the job and others came first.

So she didn't really hear that two officers had arrived at the critical care unit or that an armed response unit had been diverted to search for the pickup truck.

She was too busy bustling in through the front door of the station, immediately seeing the smashed screen at the desk and no sign of Emma, but she could hear the piercing shriek of the personal attack alarm from the custody office which was programmed to be heard throughout the station.

She clambered across the desk, skidding in the glass fragments, shouting Emma's name over the alarm, getting no reply.

She dropped down the other side, then stepped into the inner corridor and sprinted towards the custody office entrance, noting the sledgehammer wedging open the door.

On reaching the door, the alarm ceased, but its echo carried on reverberating through the corridors and in Daniels' cranium.

She left the tool where it was, shouldered her way through the door, not touching the frame with her hands, already automatically thinking about securing evidence, even though she wasn't yet sure what she was stepping into as she descended the steps.

She crossed the custody office floor towards the high reception desk, seeing no one until she spotted a shoed foot sticking out from behind the desk. The shoe was black, spit-polished to a glass-like shine, and she already knew it belonged to PS Bill Heath, the custody sergeant. His shoes were his pride and joy. Daniels had known him for several years, well before she came to this division. It wasn't only the shoe she recognized, but also his sock with the head of a white West Highland terrier embroidered on to it, a breed of dog Bill owned and adored.

Daniels slowed her approach, then stepped cautiously around the end of the desk.

Emma was sitting there with her knees drawn up to her chin, arms wrapped around her shins and an expression of trance-like terror on her face as she rocked rhythmically back and forth. She didn't even look up at Daniels.

Next to her, slumped sideways, was Bill Heath.

Although she did it anyway, Daniels knew there was really no point checking for a pulse.

She swallowed and raised her radio to her mouth and said calmly, 'Urgent assistance required in the custody office. PS Heath has been shot and seriously wounded. He may be dead. Please call an ambulance and get a high-ranking CID officer to the scene, please, and also inform the divisional commander.'

She knew there were a lot of 'pleases' in there but she didn't care.

She bent down next to Emma and drew the PEA gently towards her, holding her tightly as she burst out of the trance and began to sob with body-wrenching gasps.

SIX

Now that Henry Christie lived permanently in the countryside, he had decided it would be a wise investment to buy a four-wheel-drive vehicle. He didn't fancy anything ostentatious, so he shelled out for an ancient 'K' registered (that would be 1972) short-wheel-base Land Rover. The odometer said 72,000 miles, but Henry was sure the mileage had been fiddled; from the state of it, he guessed that maybe even 144,000 miles was a modest estimate.

He had decided to make it his little project and had lovingly refurbished the interior and restored a good proportion of the engine himself, slaving over a Haynes Manual and lots of nerdy motor vehicle restoration magazines as he did so, steam often hissing out of his ears.

He was no mechanic and generally hated working with his hands, but he'd stuck at it, did some bodywork restoration and ended up with something that worked, mostly, and of which he was mighty proud.

However, to be on the safe side, he kept his convertible Audi as well.

He was leaning against the Land Rover, arms folded, waiting for Jake Niven. The plan was that they would drive out in Niven's police vehicle – also a less than new Land Rover – to check on the York family who still had not responded to Maude's contact calls or WhatsApp messages.

Henry did not expect to find anything amiss, but the Kendleton community had pledged to keep everyone safe while the fires continued to burn.

Plus it gave Henry the opportunity to stay out of Maude's clutches. She was starting to make him feel nervous.

The smoke from the fires still hung over the village like a veil, making day-to-day life pretty unpleasant for folk at the moment, but there was no easy answer to the problem other than torrential, sustained rainfall, which the weather forecast suggested was unlikely.

'C'mon, Jake,' Henry said under his breath.

His plea was answered when he heard Niven's Land Rover on its way down the hill from his police house on the opposite side of the village. A moment later, headlights cut through the hanging smoke and Niven came to a halt beside Henry and slid open the driver's door window.

'Sorry mate, gotta go,' Niven called. 'The town's kicking off big style.' He held up his PR and Henry fleetingly heard words spoken by someone he knew – Diane Daniels.

'What's going on?'

'Not sure – some big incident at RLI, shot fired at a detective, something grim in the custody office. Headless chickens are on the loose – gotta go!'

And with these words Niven released the clutch and accelerated away in the stately manner in which only a Land Rover could.

Henry shrugged. Although Niven's beat was supposedly all the rural areas surrounding Kendleton, he often got called in to help the police in Lancaster and Morecambe, especially at weekends. His supervisors tried to keep these requests to a minimum, but they were becoming more frequent as police numbers continued to fall and having a rural beat bobby was becoming a luxury. Henry guessed Niven's tenure in the role was in jeopardy, despite the very vocal wishes of the parish council. It would be a shame to lose him. He was good, effective and well liked, but when the city was in battle mode, he had to go.

It was the way of the world – irreversible, it seemed.

Henry was actually glad to be able to give his own Land Rover an outing, so he got in and fired up the reconditioned engine, listening to the clatter of the cold tappets with a nod of pride – a noise no longer heard on modern cars.

'I did that,' he said to himself.

He found first gear with a forceful push and started to move, glancing sideways when a movement at the pub door caught his eye.

Maude, leaning seductively on the door frame, looking slim and elegant, had come to wave him off.

He gave her a quick waft of his fingers and said to himself, 'Do not be tempted, my old son, not even for ten million quid.'

Henry drove off the car park of Th'Owl, turned left and then picked up the road to the moors.

The man sitting in the driver's seat of the old Transit van in the small public car park by the village green slid a little lower in his seat as the Land Rover trundled past, but he knew that Christie had not spotted him, wasn't even looking, had probably not even given him a thought for years.

The man's throat was dry and he swallowed as an awful feeling of rage enveloped him at the sight of Henry's profile. He half considered following, but that wasn't his plan.

Behind him, in the back of the van, there was a whimpering sound.

The man inhaled a deep, steadying breath, then turned his head slowly with a large smile on his face to look at the young girl on the floor.

He was sorry he'd had to bind her wrists and ankles, and stick a strip of duct tape across her mouth to keep her quiet, but she had become a hysterical ball of fire, the exact opposite of what he expected when he'd told her who he was.

Instead, she had screamed and screamed to be released, and he'd had to resort to his standby tactics, which made him feel bad.

That said, it was early days. Given time and love, she would come to accept her new way of life with him. Of course she'd be upset at first – that was only natural – but kids were adaptable and resilient, and blood was thicker than water and in time she would realize this was all for the good.

'What's to do, darling?' he asked her gently. The look of terror in her eyes and the rolling tears upset him. 'You've nothing to worry about. Not long now and we can be together for the rest of our lives. It's sorted, honestly. You'll love it all.' He paused and gave her a reassuring nod and arch of his eyebrows. 'I just have something to do first, and in time you'll understand all this. Honestly.' He pursed his lips into a kiss. 'Love you.'

He faced the front again just as the rear lights of Christie's car disappeared over the brow.

'Just this one more thing,' he said.

SEVEN

Daniels had to move into automatic mode. She had to accept that for the time being, until people were mobilized, she was the one in charge and had to make all the early decisions. The crucial ones.

There had obviously been a serious occurrence at the infirmary, followed a very short time later by the horrific incident at the police station. In her mind, the two were connected by the vague description of the vehicle used by the offenders at the infirmary, which matched the one she had seen leaving the cop shop.

Her responsibility at that moment was to secure and preserve evidence at both scenes and initiate the beginnings of a wide search for the offenders until the big guns could be prised from their comfortable homes to take over and no doubt sideline her.

That didn't bother her much. She was a long way down the food chain, but her efficiency and professionalism in this immediate aftermath of the crimes was crucial to them being solved. Any cock-ups now would seriously affect everything to come.

No pressure.

Daniels' here and now was the custody office. She had radioed the patrol inspector to ensure that a proper job was done at the infirmary. His natural instinct was to rush back to the station: a cop was down, dead, and suddenly no one cared about a dead drug dealer.

The inspector was arguing the point.

She was talking to him via the mobile phone facility which was an integral part of the personal radio system, and at least no one else could hear their discussion taking place as she stood looking at Bill Heath's bloodied, unmoving body.

'You need to make sure everything's done up there,' she told him.

'Don't you frickin' tell me what I can and can't do,' he replied, verging on hysteria.

She got it. She was also verging on the hysterical, just keeping a lid on it.

One of the members of his shift, who was also a good friend, was lying dead in the police station. Daniels felt for the inspector but did not want grief to cloud his judgement. It was imperative he did his job first.

'Look, I've got this side under control,' she assured him. 'I've closed the custody suite down and I'm going to do the same with the police station – it's all one big crime scene now. The ambulance should be here in a minute. They're not really necessary, but Emma needs checking over. She's a wreck – and also the main witness, so I want her looking after. The infirmary needs more cops up there to seal the scene because it's so fluid and harder to control . . .'

'I know, I fucking know,' the inspector said. 'But Bill . . .'

'Brian, there's nothing you can do for him . . . he's dead,' she said bluntly, not wanting to mince her words, although her voice cracked as she spoke. 'Please – just lock down what you can up there . . . it must be linked to what happened here. Then come down here. Please, Brian . . . I know it's hard.'

'OK, OK, OK,' he gasped. 'I will.'

Daniels breathed a sigh of relief. He was an experienced inspector but he could lose it just like anyone else.

She ended the call and stood for one long moment looking at Bill Heath's body. Then she ground her teeth and got to work.

The moors above Kendleton were some of the highest in England, some of the most beautiful, yet desolate. And vulnerable.

Since moving to The Tawny Owl, Henry hadn't really spent as much time exploring them as he should have done, but he knew how fabulous they were. Hugely popular with walkers and bird-watchers and people simply driving across them, in extremely dry and hot weather they became brittle and prone to ignite. The last two weeks had been awful and a huge challenge for the fire service.

Beating out a fire with nothing more than a paddle was no joke, especially when the wind direction suddenly changed and the fire began chasing you like a dragon. But they had to keep on top of it because there was a real danger of the fire moving into the woods surrounding Kendleton, which could result in injuries or even fatalities. So far, they had been lucky.

It was like driving through a grainy fog which became more intense the higher he got, and although Henry had fitted a very macho bar of extra lights across the roof of the Land Rover, even their piercing beams struggled to make inroads. His journey was slow and precarious as the twisting roads began to narrow even more.

He gripped the steering wheel tightly, hoping not to come face-to-face with a fire truck emerging from the gloom, taking it very gingerly in case he went off the road and plunged into a ravine – something he had done once and survived, and not something he wished to repeat.

At one point, where the road clung to the hillside and way down to his left at the foot of an almost perpendicular drop was the River Roeburn, he came across a landslide which he had to delicately circumvent, aware that the edge of the road was likely to crumble away.

He made it and not far beyond he found the turning signposted to Hawkshead Farm, which he knew would lead him up the narrow driveway towards the converted and restored farmhouse where John and Isobel York lived in fairly isolated splendour.

Henry bounced the Land Rover through an open five-barred gate, which made him think the Yorks were out; that was probably why they weren't responding to Maude's calls.

The drive wound up around the hill, and Henry passed through another gate, also open, and clattered over a cattle grid. The way ahead was still shrouded in smoke from the fires, but he could just about see the dark outline of the farmhouse.

Then, just ahead, there was a dark shape across the driveway.

He stopped abruptly and peered through the windscreen at the mound. At first he assumed it was a dead sheep, something not unknown in this area. But as his eyes began to work in conjunction with his brain cells, he realized he was staring at a dead dog.

A very large dead dog, bigger than a fully grown sheep, but slimmer and lankier.

Henry pouted. He reached across to the passenger seat and picked up a disposable face mask with elastic ear loops, which he fitted before leaving the vehicle, grabbing his rubber LED torch. For a moment he stood still by the door.

He listened, could hear nothing – literally nothing. He looked around, seeing very little in the gloom, but already feeling the grit in his eyes from the ash in the atmosphere, making him blink, making him want to rub them.

He approached the dog, flashing his torch on its body, recognizing it was a Great Dane, the dog owned by the Yorks, which they had brought into Th'Owl on their visits. It was a lithe, tall dog, and he remembered it being a genial giant.

Getting closer, though, he fully expected the animal to leap up, attack him and rip out his throat because he was an intruder.

However, it did not move.

Standing over it, he saw why, and behind his mask, Henry's face dropped in shock.

The dog was certainly dead. Henry knew enough about gunshot wounds to recognize one when he saw it and, in particular, the devastation caused by a shotgun.

The dog's brains had been blown out.

Henry swallowed and swore. He was no animal lover but he

despised anyone who hurt or killed anything for no reason. He fumbled for his mobile phone in his jeans pocket and tried to call Maude, scowling angrily when he saw the signal was, at best, intermittent. Although he did make a connection, the signal dropped and cut him off.

He returned to the Land Rover and drove carefully around the dog towards the farmhouse, which he still could not see clearly until he was almost upon it. It seemed to loom out of the darkness. He drove on to a wide parking area at the front and stopped. Lights were on inside, but all the curtains and blinds were drawn.

There were three cars side by side in a line outside the house. One was an Aston Martin, the other a McLaren and the third a Bugatti. Unlike dogs, Henry knew his cars pretty well – from being a cop for thirty-plus years as well as having an interest in them – so he had no trouble identifying the make of cars he was looking at, even though each one was just a smouldering burned-out wreck with smoke still rising up from them.

Henry tried his phone again. The call went through, but he got no reply.

He walked around the trio of cars, still able to feel the heat from the fires, which must have been quite recent. He could also smell accelerant.

At the side door of the house, he knocked and also rang the doorbell, which he could hear chiming inside. There was no reply.

His next knock was harder and louder and his doorbell ring more insistent. As he rapped his knuckles on the door, it moved slightly and he realized it was only pushed to. Keeping his knuckles on the wood, he opened it further.

It led into a vestibule area. To the right was a door to the downstairs loo and shower room, then next along was an open door to a utility room. Straight ahead of him was a wall with hats and coats on hooks and pairs of wellington boots on the floor.

Just down the vestibule, to the left, was an open archway directly into the kitchen. From that angle, he could see an Aga and a large, American-style fridge.

'Hello? Anyone home?' he called into the house, lifting his face mask up on to his forehead so as not to muffle his voice. 'Mr York? Mrs York? It's Henry Christie from The Tawny Owl in Kendleton.' His voice seemed to echo into the house. 'Hello?'

He stepped on to the intricately tiled floor of the vestibule, now starting to get that age-old sensation that he was entering a place where something dreadful had happened, hoping the feeling was wrong, but knowing full well it wasn't.

The circumstances were starting to pull together.

No response from phone calls.

A dead dog on the drive.

Three burned-out cars.

Not to put too fine a point on it, he was now expecting to see dead people.

'Shouldn't we cover him up or something?'

Daniels helped the quivering PEA to her feet and steered her away from Bill Heath's body towards the stairs leading out of the custody suite. But Emma, in spite of the fact she had become a mass of mush, could not tear her eyes away from the dead sergeant and plainly did not want to leave him. It was Daniels' intention to manoeuvre her up to the inspector's office on the ground floor, sit her down and tell her to stay put until things got sorted.

'No, no, we shouldn't,' Daniels said.

'I don't want to leave him,' Emma said firmly and stood her ground, extracting her arm from Daniels' grip. 'He shouldn't be alone, not for one moment,' she insisted. She looked into Daniels' eyes. 'I know what you mean about evidence, but I want to stay with him and hold his hand. Surely that can't do any harm?'

She faced the detective defiantly – even with the tears streaming down her face and the bash she'd had to the side of her head.

'I won't touch anything. Just want to hold his hand. Please, Diane.'

Daniels felt herself welling up and she had to fight to stop her own flood of tears. She looked at Heath's slumped body, weighed up the pros and cons, and relented with a nod.

She and Emma returned to him.

'You must keep out of the blood and all you can do is hold one of his hands,' Daniels instructed her.

'I know.'

Emma knelt carefully beside him and slid one hand under and one hand over his right hand and clasped it between them. She glanced at Daniels through her streaming tears.

'He was a nice man,' she whispered.

'Yeah, he was . . . Look, when people start arriving, Emma, you will have to back off. You know that?'

She nodded. 'Now you go and do what you have to do.'

The first thing was to throw the 'off' switch on the cell buzzers. There were three males in custody, who had been disturbed by the events. They had all pressed their call buttons, and the custody area was filled with the high-pitched screech of each one – not as intense as the personal attack alarm had been – but still annoying. The override switch was on the wall behind the custody desk. Daniels flicked it off and the whole place fell silent.

The prisoners would have to be attended to somehow, and Daniels added that to her 'to do' list. Even though they had been behind locked doors, one or more of them could be a good witness in terms of what they had either seen through their peepholes or heard.

At least they weren't going anywhere for the time being.

'Emma – I'm going to dash up to the enquiry office and make sure the front door is locked, OK? I'll be straight back.'

A look of horror passed over Emma's face, but she nodded.

'Two minutes,' Daniels said. She quickly ran her eyes over the 'In Custody' board on the wall and saw the four names of the four male prisoners listen thereon. She turned to Emma. 'Which prisoner was it?'

'I don't know the name – he was in cell two.'

On the board, cell two showed the name 'Costain' – the lad who'd been arrested over the weekend and was on remand for murder. She hurried down to the male cell corridor just to check. It consisted of eight cells all down one side of the corridor. Five of the doors were open – including cell two.

'Fuck's goin' on, love?' one of the remaining prisoners asked through his cell door.

She didn't bother with a response but glanced quickly into cell two, from which Costain had been liberated. There seemed to be nothing of interest in it; it was bare, with just the thick plastic mattress and blanket strewn on the floor.

The key was still in the door.

She touched nothing, but carefully nudged the door shut with her knee, then ran back into the custody office where Emma was still kneeling with Bill Heath, holding his hand. Daniels dashed past and ran up the stairs to the ground floor, ensuring she did not dislodge the sledgehammer still propping the door open. She stepped over it and ran down to the public enquiry counter, glancing at the smashed safety screen. She let herself out, went to the front door and bolted it from inside. Aware she was compromising part of the overall crime scene by treading on the tiny shards of broken glass that had once formed the screen, she tiptoed carefully through before running back to the custody office.

As she hurtled back down the steps, she was on her radio to comms, giving them the name of the escaped prisoner and also asking if there was an ETA for a senior investigating officer.

She got a response over the radio – 'Detective Superintendent Dean interrupting, just pulling on to the lower-ground-floor car park of the station, seconds away from the custody office.'

Daniels ran to the desk and stretched over it, getting her fingers under the edge and finding the button release for the back door. She twisted her head so she could see the screen of the CCTV monitor, giving her a view over the rear door where Rik Dean was already standing, looking up at the lens.

She pressed the button, the buzzer sounded and he entered.

Daniels then slithered back off the desk, propped herself on it and took a deep breath to steady herself so she could report professionally and succinctly to Dean.

As he came through the door, she was glad to see him. She then exhaled the breath and fought with her knees to keep them from folding underneath her.

Henry stood in the kitchen, announced himself again and was again greeted by silence.

He licked his lips.

He noticed the upturned kitchen chair on the floor next to the island in the centre of the room, which in itself meant nothing.

He swallowed, his throat dry, and took a few steps over to the island on which were two bowls containing salad, both meals partly eaten. A glass of wine stood by each bowl, one with a smudge of lipstick on its rim. Across the kitchen, on a long, wide worktop next to the Aga, was a large, military-style holdall, unzipped. He went to it and opened it wide.

'Um,' he allowed himself to say.

The bag was packed full of bank notes in maybe a hundred (he estimated) vacuum-sealed clear plastic bags, all about the size of house bricks. Just from that first glance he could see there was a mixture of currencies – sterling, euros, dollars and others that could have been from the Middle or Far East. Without counting the number of bags, he could only guess at the amount of money he was looking at. Definitely in excess of £2 million.

Further along the worktop was a vacuum money-packing machine, about the size of a large digital printer, which would have done the packing and sealing of the notes. It was essentially a laminator into which a stack of money in a pouch would be fed, the air sucked out, the stack compressed, the pouch sealed.

On the worktop next to the machine was a stack of about twenty sealed blocks of money.

Henry had seized a few similar machines in his time and they were usually found during raids of premises used by organized criminals.

He allowed himself another, 'Um.'

On the floor was another holdall, yawning open, three-quarters filled with loose notes of all denominations and currencies. If he was playing a guessing game, he would say there was at least £750,000 in it.

Further along the worktop, up to where it abutted the wall, there was a money-counting machine and, next to that, several large supermarket carrier bags full of even more notes.

Henry took all this in, spun on his heels, then spun back and took his mobile phone out of his pocket and took a series of still photographs of the money, the machines, the salads and the wine glasses, before setting the camera to video mode and taking an unhurried, 360-degree scan of the whole of the kitchen.

He touched nothing, sidestepped past the island and walked to the double doors leading from the kitchen into the house.

They were slightly open, but he shouldered his way through into a large lounge with a huge TV affixed to the wall and an extensive library of DVDs on shelves underneath it. Opposite was a long, comfortable settee with a coffee table, next to which was a very expensive-looking hi-fi stack with hundreds of CDs beside it.

What might once have been called a rumpus room, he thought. The place where chilling-out took place.

No sign of the Yorks, though.

He drew back then and went through another door which took him into a wide hallway with the actual front door of the house straight ahead of him. To his left was a staircase, and there were three more doors off this hallway. He crossed the plush carpet and opened a door into a study with two laptops on a desk; next was an old-fashioned dining room. The third door opened into a modern, well-appointed lounge, the sofa of which looked as if it had never had a single backside on it. It all smacked of two people living in a house that was far too big for them, he thought.

All the rooms were empty, so Henry went to the foot of the stairs and looked up. They led to a landing, and then dog-legged up another flight to the first floor where Henry assumed the bedrooms would be found.

'Mr York? Mrs York?' he called. 'John . . . Isobel?'

His voice simply disappeared up the staircase. He placed his right foot on the first step and started to ascend cautiously, wishing he had an extendable baton and maybe CS spray. Neither offered much protection but they were a comfort.

He reached the first landing, turned and looked up the next set of stairs and saw they opened out into a broad hallway, and then turned up again to another floor. Trying to recall what the outside of the building looked like, Henry guessed this next floor would be the attic.

As he took another step, he saw the first smear of blood on the wall.

'Shit.'

It was a big smear along the wall on the right at the top of the steps. It looked fresh.

Henry reached the top step where he paused again, listening, taking in what he was seeing, assessing, wondering what story the blood splattering on the wall would tell.

Just for the moment he was trying not to jump to any conclusions, though he did glance up the next set of stairs to the attic and saw more bloody smears and handprints on the walls.

He still had his phone in his hand, so he took stills of the blood, then made his way across the hallway towards the doors at the opposite side.

He chose his route carefully because he now saw blood stains on the plain beige carpet, lots of them. He tried to avoid putting his size elevens in any.

Four doors faced him.

The one directly in front was slightly open and had a bathroom sign on it. The door to the right of it was also just open. His eyes flickered from door to door and to the blood, trying to work out its trail, but it wasn't immediately obvious.

There was a smear of blood on the bottom of the door to his right, so he carefully toe-tapped it fully open and saw a large bedroom beyond.

It was a nice bedroom with a wide, expansive, unmade bed and beyond that a French window opening out on to a small balcony. Henry tried to recall seeing the balcony from the outside, but as he'd worked his way through this unfamiliar house, he had somehow lost his bearings. He went over to the window and peered out, but it was quite dark now and he wasn't completely sure in what direction he was looking. He checked the en-suite shower room and a big walk-in wardrobe – empty – before returning to the hallway and moving to the door to his right which he knuckled open.

The door swung easily open to reveal a wash basin, loo and bidet, shower cubicle and a long, wide, deep, free-standing bath.

All the fixtures and fitting were pure white, including the tiled walls and floor and the fluffy towels hanging over the tall radiator.

Very white.

Which highlighted the blood.

In his very early days as a cop, in a training session on blood delivered by an old dinosaur of a CID officer (who had shown slides of busty naked women during his presentation, claiming females were the deadliest thing known to man), the youthful Henry had been chosen to come to the front of the class to help with a demonstration.

Happily, Henry had obliged.

At the age of nineteen he was keen, naïve, and he'd charged to the front of the class to help out.

The point had been to show what a pint of blood really looked like. Most students in the class, back then predominantly male and white, were of the opinion that a pint of blood wasn't all that much.

'I mean,' one had declared, 'I must lose a pint when I have a nosebleed.'

Most agreed with this estimation, even Henry.

He stood grinning at the front – immature, yes, but also cocky, and intent on catching the eye of the prettier of the two female recruits in the class, very much hoping to impress and get into her knickers later.

He certainly made her laugh, though perhaps not for the right reasons.

Secreted behind the instructor's desk was a pint of milk in a bottle which the CID man proceeded to tip over Henry's head – an embarrassment which remained with him to this day, though not one of those incidents to fill him with bleak thoughts and depression. It was just one of those 'done' things in those days – ritual humiliation – which most people took in good humour.

However, it did prove its point.

A pint of blood, when spilled, is actually an awful lot of blood.

From that point in his career, Henry had seen a lot of blood, and as he stood at that bathroom door, several years beyond his service, he knew he was seeing much, much more than a pint.

The bathroom was covered in it – and its source was lying in the Victorian-style bath: the headless body of a naked woman.

Her head was in the wash basin, twisted up, eyes staring, hair matted in drying blood.

Mrs Isobel York. He recognized her.

Henry swallowed and licked his lips again.

Yes, he had seen death in many forms. Mangled, beaten bodies; stabbed, shot, kicked to death. If he was honest, sometimes he wasn't shocked enough and, up to a point, he had grown immune to the sight and smell of death.

But this one hit him in the solar plexus and he had to take a grip of himself mentally and physically. From the moment he saw the dead dog he had known that something horrible had happened in this house. He had thought it would be some sort of domestic thing.

He was half expecting a shotgun death, as per the dog. Possibly a murder-suicide.

That would have been bad, but expected. However, a beheading was something else entirely.

He had seen people decapitated in road accidents; that was not particularly unusual. He had seen people dismembered, too, but for a domestic incident to end up like this, he thought, was pretty much off the radar.

He exhaled slowly, walked up to the bath and looked at Mrs York's body, her legs akimbo, splayed up and hanging down from the knees on either side of the bath, her arms folded across her stomach, one on top of the other.

Then he looked at her head in the wash basin.

There was no sign of her husband.

Henry reversed out and turned on to the landing where he looked at the blood smears and splatters across the carpet, spreading across to the next set of stairs. He decided this looked like a route taken from the bathroom.

Henry followed the trail to the stairs where he stopped and called up again. 'Mr York? This is Henry Christie from The Tawny Owl. Are you up there?' If he was, Henry wanted him to know that he was coming up.

He was imagining Mr York up these steps, cowering in a corner, horrified by what he had done – cutting his wife's head off – and still gripping the weapon he'd used, sitting up there, gone to pieces, shaking, afraid, yet quite capable of going off the rails again and attacking the next poor soul who popped his head around the corner. Henry didn't feel like being sliced by a machete, or whatever the choice of bladed weapon was, so he needed to warn of his approach. That was if Mr York was up there.

Maybe he wasn't.

Henry dithered.

He wasn't a cop anymore, so this wasn't his responsibility.

Yet it was.

'Mr York,' he called again, 'I'm coming up, OK?'

No response.

Henry took each step slowly, finally reaching the small landing where the stairs turned back on themselves in another dog-leg. He stopped, looked up and could see the pitched roof of the farmhouse.

This was definitely the last floor and, from where he stood, it looked to be one huge space running the whole length of the house.

One more step and his eyes came up to floor level and he could see the bulbous legs of a full-size snooker table in the middle of the attic, with plenty of room around it for elbows, leaning and stretching.

Another cautious step and he could see the full length and width of the attic, but no sign of Mr York.

A moment or two later and he was standing on the floor, looking down the length of the snooker table which, indeed, was full-sized championship specification, six feet wide by twelve feet long. A good, expensive table which must have been a nightmare to get up here.

It was easily long enough for the body of a man to lie on.

Or, in this case, the dismembered body of a man.

John York's torso filled the central part of the table, covering the spot the blue ball would have occupied.

His severed arms had been shoved into the centre pockets and his legs had been laid side by side in the baulk area of the table behind and parallel to the line where the yellow, green and brown balls would be placed at the beginning of a game of snooker.

York's head had been positioned upright on the black ball spot. It was tilted at a slight angle. One eye was closed, the other partially open as though he was giving a salacious wink, and his tongue lolled out of his distorted, open mouth.

The green baize had not done a great job at soaking up the blood.

Henry took all this in. He did not move for many moments, just looked, feeling his heart beating, aware of the rise and fall of his chest.

Then he got out his phone again and started to record the scene in still photos and video images.

His instinct as a member of the public now should have been to flee and call the cops. However, that instinct was pretty dormant.

He edged carefully around the table, recording the gruesome image, before noticing a gun cabinet tucked away in one corner of the attic, bolted to the wall. It was made of strong steel and the door was open. Henry crossed to it, seeing two shotguns and two .22 rifles clipped and padlocked to the back of the cabinet. On the floor by the cabinet was a sawn-off shotgun, broken at the breech with several cartridges strewn around.

Henry's mind reconstructed this aspect of the crime scene.

John York had witnessed his wife being murdered. He had raced up the stairs to the gun cabinet in order to arm himself and take out the killers, but he had not been fast enough. He had been pursued, overpowered and hacked to pieces.

Time to call the real cops.

EIGHT

With Daniels alongside him, Detective Superintendent Rik Dean took overall charge of the incidents currently overwhelming the police in Lancaster. As much as Daniels had done her best, Dean's rank was the key to calming the whole thing down.

He continued the lockdown of the custody office and the murder scene at the infirmary, calling out one of the FMIT detectives to go to that location as soon as possible, then he turned out the local DI to take control of the scene at the custody office.

With the assistance of the Operations department, a huge search and locate operation was put in motion, with roadblocks and the helicopter looking for the four-wheel-drive vehicle believed to have been used in both crimes. Daniels had managed to see a partial of the number plate and the Police National Computer was being searched for possible matches.

Dean turned out crime scene investigators and forensic teams and also began to call in intelligence analysts.

Daniels was as happy as she could be to sit alongside him as he pulled all this together from his mobile phone. In just a few short minutes, she learned a lot; during that time she also managed to calm herself down as everything that had happened in such a short space of time began to sink in – not least that she had been shot at too.

Dean reached a point where he finished a phone call – to the chief constable, as it happened – took a breath and looked squarely at Daniels.

'You did really well,' he complimented her genuinely, then looked at her more closely. 'But are you OK? I need to ask, and I'm not being funny – peculiar, that is – because this whole thing looks like we're going to need everyone operating at the top of their game, and being shot at isn't something you just shrug off. I've been there; I know.'

'I'm fine. Mad as hell – but they missed me; they didn't miss Bill. I want to be part of this now.'

'You got it.' Dean seemed convinced. 'So, right now, two things we need immediately are your statement and Emma's statement. They need to be as detailed as possible as both of you saw the offenders, Emma in particular. I want a blow-by-blow account from her of everything that happened, from the two guys entering the station to leaving and everything in between. Your job, Diane. Not sexy, but crucial – and if she says things you think the investigation needs to know, you keep us bang up to date, OK?'

'Got it. She's going to need some handling.'

'You can do it. Every detail. You know the score.'

Henry picked his way carefully around the snooker table again, this time just using his eyes and brain rather than his phone camera to see the body of John York, which is when he began to feel slightly anxious. Whoever had done this – and he guessed two, maybe three people were involved – had come very prepared to kill.

As well as the state of the bodies, he could conclude this by looking more closely at the handprints in the blood splashes. He was no fingerprint expert but he could tell from the smudges that gloves had been worn, and the footprints in the blood showed that the footwear worn by the offenders had probably been encased in elasticated overshoes which disguised any patterns on the soles.

In his mind Henry saw the killers wearing protective suits, no doubt similar to the ones used by cops and technicians at crime scenes to avoid contamination of evidence.

He completed his circuit, then made his way slowly back down one flight of stairs to the first floor and had another look in the bathroom, just to confirm to himself he wasn't seeing things.

Next, he went down to the kitchen on the ground floor where the money was stacked and bagged.

Had the killers come simply to murder but not to steal?

That seemed unlikely to Henry.

Maybe there had been even more money; maybe they had taken only what they physically could and what he was seeing here was just a fraction of the total. And if that was the case, were they due to revisit to get the rest?

He took a last look, then stepped outside. He would have liked to take a long, deep breath to clear his lungs and nasal passages of the reek of death, but the smoke-laden atmosphere was not conducive to that.

Instead, he looked at his phone, held it up, twizzled it around and tried to find a decent signal.

Emma sat silent and pale in the inspector's office. She had a mug of tea in her hand, but it was cold now. She had not drunk any of it. She clutched a tea towel packed with ice to the side of her face, which had swelled from the blow she received. She looked up when Daniels entered, but there was no smile on her face, simply pain lines and tears.

Daniels sat next to her. 'How are you doing?'

'Not good, Diane.'

'Up to talking? We need to get a witness statement from you, sooner rather than later, while it's still fresh in your mind.'

Emma's mouth turned down at the corners and her chin began to wobble.

'You saw something terrible,' Daniels said softly. 'Nothing can prepare you for that. But you did brilliantly and now it's vitally important we get down everything you saw, heard and felt. You and me, Emma – we're the keys to catching these evil men.'

'I know . . . but I . . .' She found herself lost for words. 'I just want to go home and get my husband to hug me for a while. I know it sounds utterly pathetic . . .'

'No, it doesn't. It's what husbands are for. So I'm not going to force you to make a statement just now, but we do need one as soon as you're able.'

'I understand.'

Daniels' PR blared out her name. She'd had the volume turned low and she could just about hear what was going on – it was the busiest she had ever heard, with the exception of a football match – and she managed to hear her name as comms shouted her up.

'DC Daniels receiving.'

'Diane – I need to put a call through to you. What extension are you on?' the comms operator asked.

She gave him the internal number and asked who was calling.

'A guy from up in Kendleton village out in the sticks – a Henry Christie? He's asked to speak to the night-duty detective. Says it's urgent.'

'That'd be me . . . put him through.' She sat back and wondered what Henry could possibly want. The phone rang. 'DC Daniels.'

'Hello, Diane, how are you? It's Henry Christie here, retired and loving it. Long time no see.'

'I'm good, Henry and it's nice to hear from you. Unfortunately, I haven't got time right now for a catch-up.'

'I believe it's all kicking off in town.'

'Understatement, Henry.'

'Well, I don't want to add to things but I need to send you some photographs and three short video clips.'

'Eh? Why?'

'Look, I'm out doing a welfare check because of these moorland fires and I've come across a couple of dead bodies – murdered dead bodies.'

'You are kidding me!'

'Nope . . . look, I've got a mobile number for you on my phone from years back. Is that still your current one? If so, I'll send the photos and vids now, then you call me back if you're interested.'

'My number's still the same. Send them to me.'

'OK. Gonna hang up now. But prepare yourself . . . it's brutal stuff.'

'Whatever,' she said. 'I've been shot at tonight, so not much is going to faze me.'

'These will,' Henry assured her bleakly, then cut the connection.

They did.

It seemed to take forever for the photographs to arrive on to her phone, but as soon as she clicked on to them she could hardly believe what she was looking at: they reminded her of photos she had seen of cartel-related deaths in Mexico – beheadings and horrific mutilations.

She was still sitting with Emma when her phone pinged to announce their arrival and she opened them, not sure of what to expect after Henry's slightly enigmatic phone call. She was sucker-punched by their violence.

Emma watched Daniels' face change as she thumbed through the stills. Daniels looked at her. 'You go home to your husband. We'll catch up later.'

'What is it?'

Daniels blew out her cheeks and shook her head. 'You don't want to know.' She stood up and left the office but once in the corridor she leaned on the wall and forced herself to click the video link and watched them all again, her mouth agape.

'DC Daniels receiving?'

She answered her PR. 'Go ahead.'

'Diane, it's Jake Niven from the Kendleton rural beat. I just half heard you got a call from Henry Christie. Is there something I need to know?' Niven had heard the earlier transmission from comms to Daniels.

'Where are you, Jake?'

'I got called in from the beat. I've just been deployed to the infirmary.'

'OK. Just stand by a few minutes, will you?'

'Roger that.'

Daniels pushed herself away from the wall and hurried to find Rik Dean who had gone up to the comms room. Daniels found him there in a heads-together cluster conflab with two detectives. All three watched her approach.

'Boss?'

'What is it?' Rik asked.

'Sorry to interrupt. Just take a look at these, will you?'

She held out her phone with the photos from Henry ready to be looked at. As Dean took the phone and began to swipe through them, she explained their origin.

'Are these for real?' Dean asked incredulously.

'According to Henry, they are.' She took the phone, found the video clips, then gave it back. Dean watched with his mouth as wide open as hers had been a few minutes before.

'Shit, that's all we need,' he said. 'Do you know where these were taken?'

'No, but Jake Niven's in town – he got called in to help. He'll know.'

Dean knew Niven well. 'OK – sack taking that statement. Get Jake to pick you up and take you to see Henry, find out what this is all about.'

Henry's mobile rang, the display showing Rik Dean to be the caller. Henry was still outside the farmhouse, trying but failing to inhale fresh air.

Henry knew Rik Dean very well. He'd been instrumental in getting Dean on to the CID many years before, when Dean had been an eager uniformed PC who also happened to be a brilliant thief taker, a skill Henry, then a DI, had been keen to get on to the branch. Dean's subsequent rise through the ranks had been his own doing. He was as good a manager as he was a detective, which was a rare combination. Nor was it Henry's doing that Dean (who was a serial womanizer) had met and subsequently married Henry's wayward sister Lisa (who was a serial manhunter). Their marriage was the first ever to be held at The Tawny Owl, when Henry's fiancée, Alison, had still been alive. Henry had never expected the union to last because they were too much alike, and sparks certainly flew, but they seemed to have settled into contended marital harmony, if not bliss. Henry was happy for them.

However, there had been some professional disharmony between Henry and Dean when the latter stepped into Henry's shoes at FMIT in the fraught months leading up to the messy end of Henry's career. He couldn't entirely blame Dean for accepting the job as FMIT superintendent, and he did get over it, but he hadn't seen Dean for some time.

'Ahh, the student calls the master,' Henry answered his phone.

'No pleasantries,' Dean said in a clipped tone. 'Those pictures you sent to Daniels – are they real?'

'No, I found them on the dark web and sent them for fun. Of course they're real.'

'So what the fuck are you doing there?'

'Just a welfare check. We're all keeping an eye on each other because of the fires.'

'Very cosy. Look, stay put, don't touch anything. I've told Daniels to get up there with Jake Niven. They'll be a good twenty minutes.'

'OK, I'll get myself a brew.'

'Don't touch a fucking thing!' Dean hung up.

Henry frowned and thumbed the end-call button on his phone, then grinned. What stress does to a person, he thought.

In the distance, he thought he could hear a car approaching up the drive but paid no particular heed to it.

His phone rang again: Daniels.

He answered it, but as he did so, he heard the engine of the approaching vehicle get louder and saw a set of bright headlights appear over a slight brow on the driveway.

'Henry? Diane. I think Rik Dean's just spoken to you.'

'He has.'

'So you'll know I'm on my way up with PC Niven. I'm just waiting for him to arrive from the infirmary, so we're maybe twenty-five minutes away at most.'

'So it's not you driving up to the farmhouse right now?'

'Nope.'

'Oh dear.'

'Henry, are you all right?'

'Yeah . . . got some company, that's all.'

Henry ended the phone call and suddenly realized what stress really could do to a person.

He turned and ran.

NINE

Henry's first instinct had actually been to reveal himself and walk towards the car coming up the drive, but as he came to the end of the phone call to Daniels, wariness and suspicion flipped uppermost in his mind . . . Who could be coming to the house?

Maybe it was friends or relatives, and possibly he was being mega-cautious, but with two dismembered bodies in the house and a ton of money, there was every possibility the killers could be paying a return visit to pick up the cash, taking a chance because of the remote location, and until he was certain there was no threat, he decided on discretion, not valour.

He ran to the front of his Land Rover in order to shield himself and hide, yet still be able to watch the progress of the car creeping closer and closer. And as it came out of the smoke with its headlights on full beam, he knew it was some sort of four-wheel-drive pickup, but because of the bright lights in his eyes, he couldn't quite identify a make or registration number – it was just a huge silhouette.

He ducked, keeping hidden at the front of the Land Rover.

The vehicle stopped about thirty yards short of Henry's car.

Suddenly, every front light on the pickup came on in a blaze and a crackle of electricity, including the four spotlights on the light pod fitted to the roof and four fitted to the bull bars. The intense white light bathed the whole area in front of the house, making Henry shade his eyes and squint. There was a loud tapping noise and then a voice over the PA system fitted to the vehicle.

'Show yourself; otherwise, we're coming for you and we're gonna kill you dead as fuck!'

The front doors of the vehicle swung open and two men climbed out.

By this time Henry had dropped to a crouch by the front nearside of the Land Rover, hoping he was completely out of sight. He swivelled on his heels and looked to see what was behind him. To his right was the house and the open door leading to the kitchen. To the left was a large quadruple garage – four roller-shutter doors – with what looked like a flat or an office above; behind that was a barn with its front doors wide open. Beyond all the buildings was open ground, rising up towards the higher moors and crags, now all in complete darkness.

'One more chance, matey,' the voice over the PA offered.

Henry glanced. The two men – just shapes and silhouettes – had shotguns in their hands and Henry, even over the purring sound of the big engine, heard the distinctive noise of the two weapons clicking shut. He heard and felt the guns being fired at the back end of his Land Rover. There was the loud crack of the shots themselves, then the metallic peppering splat as the cartridges pebble-dashed the car and the right rear tyre deflated instantly with a loud hissing sound, making the vehicle sag.

He winced and ducked, though none of the shot hit him.

'There's more,' the voice over the PA announced.

Henry braced himself, sure they hadn't actually seen him and these were just flushing-out tactics.

He heard another sound he recognized which seemed to travel on the night atmosphere: the metallic 'snick' of an automatic weapon being cocked.

Then fired.

A fusillade of bullets pounded into the back of the Land Rover, punching holes in it and puncturing the other rear tyre, which deflated with a whump.

Henry closed his eyes and waited to be hit. He knew that car bodywork offered no real protection from gunfire. Bullets simply sliced their way through the thin sheet metal. He had known several unfortunate people who'd died thinking that ducking down behind a car would save them from a gunman. In movies it did. In real life, not so much.

He heard the hammer slam against the empty chamber as, finally, all the bullets from the weapon were discharged.

Again, none had hit him.

He saw his chance to run.

Presumably, the shotguns would need to be reloaded, as would the automatic weapon, so, depending on their skills, the men could be looking down at their weapons for a second or two at least.

Crouching low, he spun around and, using the damaged Land Rover as some sort of cover, he scampered away like a baboon and headed towards the garage block, keeping going until he was past the building before turning, pulling himself up and flattening himself against the back wall and peering around the edge of the brickwork. He had a view of the side door of the house, his car, the burned-out shells of the other cars and the big four-wheel-drive beyond, where he could now see three men walking cautiously towards the Land Rover, shadows back-lit by the light pods, crouched like soldiers.

Each had a weapon – two with shotguns and the other with a machine-pistol of some sort, which is the one that must have been used to spray his car with bullets.

They crept to the Land Rover, two edging down the left side, the other down the right.

Henry tried to control his breathing and his rising panic as well as his shaking hand as he looked at his mobile phone and twisted down behind the garage.

First thing he did was put it on silent mode. There was nothing like a jaunty ringtone to bring bad guys with guns running.

That done, he had another peek around the corner.

The men had reached and gathered around the kitchen door, whispering to each other, getting their tactics together.

Then one of them shouted into the opening, 'This is your last chance. You come out or we come in – firing and killing!'

Obviously, this was met by a resounding silence from inside, because there were only dead people in the house.

'And I know who you is,' another shouted.

A shroud of dread rolled through Henry on hearing this revelation. How the hell could they know him?

He took a chance to peep around the corner again. The men were still in a huddle, then two of them broke away and entered the house, leaving the third one outside holding a shotgun.

Henry's mouth was popping open and closed like a goldfish as he desperately tried to think his way out of this. As soon as the two guys swept through the house to find nothing but dead bodies, they would realize that the owner of the Land Rover wasn't inside and they would come searching, firing and killing.

Henry looked at his phone. The screen lit up showing him – silently – that a call was coming in: it was Jake Niven's number.

He thumbed the dismiss call button and began to scramble quietly along the back wall of the garage block, thinking he might leg it across the lawned garden to the fields beyond, though the prospect of running into a pitch-black, smoke-filled void filled him with dread. He would probably break his ankle vaulting over the first low wall only to find a ten-foot drop on the other side of it.

As he reached the far corner of the garage, he saw Niven was ringing again; again, Henry dismissed the call.

He also found a door into the garage. He reached for the handle and pulled it down, expecting it to be locked but finding it open. He contorted through it into the garage when a movement sensor flicked on the lights.

I'm dead, he thought.

He was relieved to see the garage did not have any windows and that the bottom edges of the four roller doors were flush with the ground. There was every chance light was escaping through minute cracks and he had to hope that the attention of the man left outside the house was concentrated on the house itself.

Henry braced himself for the shout of discovery. It did not come.

He exhaled, looked along the row of four cars side by side in the pristine garage, their noses facing the garage doors. The York family's private, mothballed collection of very expensive classic models, all beautifully maintained, shining.

Henry was a bit of a car buff up to a point. He took a quick inventory of the four vehicles. The one that struck him most now was the newest of the set, the one that made him wince to look at, probably the least valuable, but which, under the circumstances, was like a present from the gods: a Hummer, fitted with very macho, wraparound bull bars.

Henry moved along the row of vehicles until he reached the Hummer, listening all the while for the voices of the three men and then the shout when – if – they spotted the sliver of light under the garage doors.

The Hummer was an H1 Alpha and was the last model manufactured around 2006 when all production ceased. Although Henry knew his cars, the Hummer wasn't really on his radar, but he knew they were four-wheel-drive vehicles based on American military off-roaders.

He opened the driver's door silently, only to find the steering wheel was on the opposite side because it was an imported car, so he walked around and got in, relieved to see the ignition key in place.

His next problem was whether it was fuelled and would fire up.

All the cars looked well cared for, so he assumed they would all start.

He turned the ignition key one notch. The vehicle began to hum with the air-con unit and the fuel gauge indicated half a tank of juice.

He did not start the engine.

Next he had to deal with the garage doors and figure out the best way of escaping.

There was a remote-control fob on the passenger seat of the Hummer with a figure '1' inscribed on it, leading Henry to assume the door in front of the Hummer was that one and each door therefore had its own controller. You wouldn't want all four doors opening every time just to get one car out.

He slid out of the Hummer and dashed along to an Aston Martin, also unlocked; on the passenger seat was a fob with a '4' on it. He grabbed it, then went back to the Hummer and quietly closed the door as he sat in.

He knew that as soon as the garage doors began to rise the men would be on him; the door would no doubt open with painful sluggishness, and he could well find himself trapped – but leaving via the garage now seemed the only option for him.

He aimed the remote-control fob at door number four.

It began to open, smoothly and more quickly than Henry would have anticipated.

He started the huge 6.5-litre diesel engine of the Hummer.

Then he held his breath and his nerve because he knew none of this was likely to go particularly well.

His right hand hovered over the gear shift.

Door number four had risen about a metre.

He pressed the button for door number one, which started to open.

He put his right foot on the brake, released the handbrake and slotted the gearstick into drive.

The big vehicle lurched slightly as the power connections were made, but his foot remained firmly on the brake pedal.

The door in front of him continued to rise, but the one away to his right reached its full height and stopped.

Henry couldn't wait any longer. He put his phone between his clenched teeth and held it there.

His plan – not well thought out, he admitted – was to lure the guy at the door of the house across the front of the garages to see what was going on but that did not seem to have worked so well – as no one appeared, poking their head around.

Henry lifted his foot off the brake pedal and slammed it hard on to the accelerator just as the opening door in front of him reached about a third of its ascent.

The Hummer's huge engine gave a roar like an angry grizzly

bear and the 77-inch-high vehicle smashed into the garage door, tearing it off its fixtures as it powered through with a sheet of ribbed metal twisted across the bull bars.

Henry's spectacular exit worked better than he'd hoped because the guy who'd been guarding the kitchen door was standing directly in front of the car as it burst through and the Hummer's sudden, violent appearance caught him completely off guard. Even over the crumpled remains of the garage door, Henry briefly saw the guy's eyes widen and his mouth open as he tried to bring the shotgun round instead of leaping to one side, which is what he really should have done. But he was too slow and Henry powered straight into him without a qualm.

The bull bars connected with his thighs, just above his kneecaps, breaking both femurs, and as Henry continued to hold the power on, the guy disappeared from Henry's view as his whole body went under the radiator grille. Even though Henry did not know this at that moment, the bottom edge of the front registration plate caught the man's chin as he seemed to be sucked under, jerked his head back and snapped his neck at the nape.

The car bundled over him and he was already dead when one of the back wheels ran over and crushed his right leg, then right arm and shoulder.

Henry didn't even register the bump of the wheel going over the man's limbs, but kept his foot down, swerved around his shot-to-pieces Land Rover and raced down the drive, aware from a glance in the rear-view mirror that the other two men had run out of the house.

He did not stop. He knew he had to put as much distance between them and him as possible.

He saw the men dash across to their fallen colleague.

Henry's phone was still clamped between his teeth and he was aware that the screen had lit up again as a call came in. Steering with one hand, he took the phone with his free hand and glanced at the screen. It was Daniels. He answered.

'Henry, what's going on?'

'That company I mentioned – they had guns. I've done a runner in one of the Yorks' vehicles . . . I might've knocked one of them over.'

'Where the hell are you now?'

'Getting as far away from them as possible.' He steered the Hummer around a kink in the driveway. 'Shit!' Now he had to swerve again to avoid the dead dog on the driveway.

'What?' Daniels demanded.

'Nothing. Where are you?'

'We haven't even reached Kendleton yet.'

'Well, you're going to need armed backup here, Diane. Not that these guys will be here when you land, but you never know.' Henry was trying to think fast, something he'd not really had to do since becoming a landlord. 'We need an RV point,' he said.

'RV point?' he heard Daniels ask Jake Niven.

Henry cut in with his suggestion. 'Gallows Hill crossroads.'

'Got it!' Niven shouted.

The Hummer zinged across the cattle grid, and Henry was thankful he wasn't too far away from the end of the drive. However, this relief suddenly evaporated in the glare of a huge bank of headlights behind him and the rear window of the Hummer shattering.

The remaining pair were coming after him and shooting at the same time.

Henry dropped the phone, grabbed the wheel with both hands and tried to see if he could get more speed out of the beast he was driving. At the same moment the wing mirror disintegrated as a bullet hit it.

From the phone, which now slithered around the footwell under the pedals, out of reach, he heard Daniels screaming his name but then the signal must have been lost because the phone went dead and Henry realized he was way out on his own here.

Tommy Costain had relished – *savoured* – two things in the last few days.

The first had been ambushing and then kicking to death a young man called Damian Medway in a Lancaster side street. It was one of those things that had to be done personally, this revenge killing, and Tommy had not entrusted it to anyone else. He had kept the whole thing to himself, his intention, and then delivered it himself, which he believed was a much scarier way of doing things: if you worked for Tommy and the Costains, ripped them off, did not heed warnings, tried to take over their turf, then it was only right and proper you should live in abject fear of reprisal stepping out of the shadows and killing you.

That was why Medway had to die in a sordid back alley in Lancaster in the early hours of a sultry Sunday morning in the trash heap from an upturned wheelie bin and split-open rubbish bags.

Medway had been doing all those things Tommy had warned everyone who worked for him against. He'd been playing a dangerous game of drug-turf chess in the mistaken belief that Tommy didn't even know moves were being planned against him.

But Tommy Costain knew.

He also knew that Medway was having a quiet night out for once with one of his girlfriends. A bit of a pub crawl, on to a club, then a takeaway. A normal sort of night that normal people had, which, if Medway had been normal, would probably have ended up in his girlfriend's bed.

Medway did not get that far.

Tommy had brought in someone Medway would not recognize. A lad from Blackpool whom Tommy kept under wraps. Throughout the evening this lad had discreetly tailed Medway from pub to pub, finally to a nightclub, reporting to Tommy just before chucking-out time that Medway and his girl were on foot in the city centre, having just left a kebab shop.

That was when the very patient Tommy Costain emerged from hiding in the squalid bedsit he'd had on rental for several weeks. He quickly caught up with his lad who was following Medway along Church Street as he made his way to the taxi rank on Cable Street for that last bit of his journey.

Tommy signalled for the lad to move in on the couple, which he did quietly and effectively at the entrance to an alleyway running behind New Street and Sun Street. He grabbed the girl and dragged her away as Tommy took a stranglehold on Medway and dragged him into the alley as he throttled him.

Tommy was big and strong – a legacy from working on building sites and laying tarmac on driveways that never really set properly – and his biceps were too large and rock solid for the more scrawny Medway to peel away with his fingers; all Medway could do in those opening moments of the assault was dig his nails into Tommy's flesh.

When Tommy started to punch him in the side of his head with his big, hard, calloused hands, Medway's brain blacked out, his knees buckled, and from that moment he was as good as dead.

Tommy hurled him to the ground in among a stack of burst bin bags and overturned a wheelie bin on to him in a last display of disrespect, its evil reeking contents covering the stunned young man.

Tommy had come prepared. He was wearing steel-toe-capped work shoes, ideal for protecting feet, but also ideal for kicking a man to death with a ferocity he could barely control.

It was only the 'Boss – cops!' shout from his lad that broke into his violent concentration.

Two officers had been routinely patrolling the city centre on foot. They had turned into the street and immediately seen something odd happening in one of the doorways – a girl being held by a lad. They acted immediately, with the effect that the girl was thrown across the street, pirouetting like a drunken dancer; the lad shouted something down an alley, then scarpered.

The officers raced to the girl who was on her hands and knees, screaming, 'They got Damian!' gesticulating towards the alley.

The cops stood side by side at the entrance to the grim alley, lit only by a flickering sodium streetlight which was just enough for them to see a body and a man standing over it, breathless.

They took a step towards him, one cop ordering Tommy, 'You stay there and do not move, pal.'

Tommy turned and fled – but only as far as the dead end of the alley. He was trapped by an unscalable wall and doors into backyards that were locked, so finally, after trying to scramble up the wall and shouldering each door, he faced the two cops with a feral snarl. 'Come on then, you twats.'

The officers sidestepped the body – which was not moving – and drew their batons.

'Hands on your head, fingers interlocked, down on your knees,' one ordered him. 'Otherwise, this will get nasty.'

'Up yours,' Tommy replied. His blood was still pumping hot, adrenaline surging through his system, and he was very much on a natural high from killing Medway, feeling he could take on anybody, especially two pasty-faced coppers who looked shit-scared of him.

He ran towards them, screaming.

What he did not expect was a face full of CS spray which had an instant effect on him. The searing irritant invaded his nasal passages, his eyes and the back of his throat and took all his breath away. It was as if he had smashed into a brick wall, and the next ten or so minutes were a haze for him as he was cuffed, arrested and conveyed to Lancaster Police Station with his eyeballs on fire and razor blades down his throat.

He was brooding in a cell not much long after, having been stripped of his clothing, searched from head to toe and everything in between, given a forensic suit and told he was under arrest for murder.

In the following hours he said nothing, made no reply to any questions and had to be held down by four hairy-arsed cops who forced his mouth open to take a DNA swab and then his finger-prints, at which point his ID was revealed.

He remained a nightmare prisoner – uncooperative, rude, always threatening violence – but even nightmare prisoners had rights and he was able to ensure he got the solicitor he desired to represent him at interview. Their confidential chats allowed a flow of infor-mation back and forth. This meant Tommy could still control his ever-expanding drugs empire – now with its tentacles firmly squeezing Lancaster and causing mayhem – and also resulted in a call for Brendan O'Hara and Cillian Roche, Tommy's top enforcers, to carry out certain tasks, one of which included busting him out of police cells, once they were told which cell he was being held in.

Before doing that, though, O'Hara and Roche were required to pay a visit to Mr and Mrs York – which they did with fervent brutality (as ordered by Tommy) – then make the trip to Royal Lancaster Infirmary to take care of some local business by killing Sam Dorner.

The last job – the cell break – gave Tommy the opportunity to kill a cop, which was one of the things close to the top of his bucket list. Custody sergeant Bill Heath was the unfortunate officer to bear the brunt of that, which was especially sweet for Tommy, who felt he had been insulted by Heath during his stay in the cells by his gyppo comment. Tommy had almost turned the gun on the blubbering PEA but had decided to spare her for reasons not even he understood.

A potshot at the black woman was just an added bonus, but by that time all Tommy had wanted to do was escape and seeing her cowering was buzz enough for him.

He was bouncing with delight in the back seat of the Ram being driven by O'Hara as they sped out of Lancaster – after having first caused bedlam by driving the wrong way on the one-way system – and were soon up in the hills to the east of the city. Roche and O'Hara were bringing him up to date, including a blow-by-blow account of their visit to the Yorks, which Costain listened to with grim satisfaction.

'You did good, boys,' Tommy congratulated them.

'Cheers, boss,' they replied in unison, their retelling of how they had butchered the Yorks leaving them completely unmoved.

'How much money did y'get, y'reckon?'

The look exchanged by the two hitmen told Tommy all he needed to know. They hadn't got any money.

He leaned forward between the front seats. 'I told you to take every penny.'

'Uh, we didn't get that bit of the message,' O'Hara whined. He was peeling the clinging face mask off as he drove.

'There was money there, I take it?'

'Tons o' the feckin' stuff,' Roche confirmed.

'And . . . where the fuck is it?'

'Uh – still there.'

'It didn't dawn on you numbskulls to grab it?'

'You didn't say.'

'Feck me, fecking idiots. That was the whole point, wasn't it – kill 'em, grab any money lying about, wipe their snotty noses in shit!'

'It'll still be there,' Roche promised. 'I'll bet it's still there, one hundred per cent. No one'll've been up to the place yet . . . the whole area is covered in smoke from the grass fires. Nowt's moving.'

'Then we go get it,' Tommy said.

'Go back up there, y'mean?' O'Hara said.

'No, we'll ask 'em to send it to us by Western Union . . . Yes, go back, get it, do the car swap, disappear . . . There is another motor lined up, isn't there? You didn't forget that bit?'

'Sorted, boss.'

'Feck! Summat right at last!'

O'Hara drove the Ram recklessly along the quiet country lanes, fortunate no one was coming in the opposite direction on any of them as he blasted the big vehicle at high speed, frequently clipping the hedges and working his way through the maze of back roads around the Trough of Bowland, across and emerging in Kendleton, barrelling through the quiet, smoke-hazy village without pausing at any junctions. He slowed down a little for the landslide and turned into the driveway up to Hawkshead Farm, over the cattle grid, avoiding the dead dog, then realizing there was an extra vehicle at the farmhouse and that the side door was open.

O'Hara said, 'I closed that door.'

'And that ain't one o' their motors,' Roche added, peering at the Land Rover.

'That,' O'Hara exclaimed, pointing, 'belongs to that guy at the pub in the village.' He pulled up a good twenty metres behind it. 'Him who threw us out. I remember seeing it.'

'What d'you mean, threw you out?' Tommy demanded. 'You bin in a pub between jobs?'

'Yeah, we needed one; we were parched,' Roche admitted.

'But he chucked us out cos we were vapin' inside,' O'Hara said.

'Feck! Let me get this right – you do the job here, forget the money – *somehow* – but you's still got time for a pint before the next job?'

The two remained uncomfortably silent. Although they were men of extreme violence who killed without compunction or conscience, Tommy Costain terrified them. He was far worse than them, but his additional attribute was that he was more intelligent too. He knew his Western Union quip was wasted on them.

'Yeah – he were called Henry Christie. I saw his name over the front door o' the pub,' Roche said. 'And he had a watch on that I want.'

'Now looks like your chance to get it, then,' Tommy said.

They grabbed their weapons, then stepped out of the Ram.

For a couple of stunned seconds, Tommy Costain and Brendan O'Hara stared at the devastated body of their colleague in crime, Cillian Roche, who had been mown down by Henry Christie at the wheel of the Hummer that had burst out of the garage like an enraged bull.

It was clear he had suffered extensive, traumatic injuries, smashing the front of his face off and mangling the rest of him as if he'd gone through a clothes wringer – and that he was very, very dead.

'Get him! Get the fucker!' Tommy screamed. He grabbed O'Hara's shoulder and both men sprinted back to the Ram and, with O'Hara behind the wheel again, spun the car round and went in pursuit of Henry Christie, intent on having fatal revenge on behalf of Cillian Roche.

'What did you say his name was?' Tommy shouted.

'Henry Christie.'

Tommy frowned. 'I know that name.'

The Hummer careened out of the gate and Henry had to fight with the wheel to turn the vehicle left and not plough straight on to pitch down the almost vertical drop opposite into the River Roeburn. He was already beginning to regret his hasty choice of vehicle and thought maybe he should have gone for one of the sports cars instead. The Hummer was a monster to control, and it was difficult to get any real acceleration from it, which confirmed its origins as a military workhorse. It was designed to deliver soldiers over rough terrain.

The Hummer swerved from side to side as Henry tried to keep it on the straight, and therefore lost speed, which allowed the Ram, newer, faster, to make up ground easily, the piercing lights strung across its roofline completely overwhelming and intimidating Henry, making driving and concentrating difficult – like having a jet fighter on his tail, veering from side to side, disorientating him.

Henry ducked as a blast of bullets smashed into the rear bodywork, making him jerk the beast from side to side in reflex. He clipped a low wall and ricocheted off, forcing him to fight harder to stop plummeting off the road and making him doubt his ability to get out of this predicament in one piece.

Daniels glared at Niven.

'Won't this heap go any faster?'

'Foot's to the floor.'

The police Land Rover that Niven had been provided with when he took over the rural beat of Kendleton and District had been discovered decaying in an unused garage somewhere in the wilds at the back of police headquarters. It was just about useable but, like most old-style Land Rovers, performance was not one of its strongpoints.

The plus point was that Niven now knew these roads intimately and that knowledge meant he could make up time by positioning and late braking – but it was going to be a bumpy ride.

'Just hold on,' he told her, moving the vehicle close to the road edge for an upcoming right-hand bend and finding the racing line.

Daniels clung on to her seat belt with her left hand while trying to make a phone call with her right, hoping to reconnect with Henry.

Straight to voicemail.

'This is bad. I can feel it,' she said.

'Don't worry, we'll be at Gallows Hill crossroads in a minute.'

Henry's head jolted back as the Dodge lived up to its model name and rammed him from behind.

He fought to control the Hummer as it swerved nastily from the impact, veering from one side of the road to the other, and then rounded the next right bend as more bullets slammed into the back of the big Yankee car. He tried to shrink himself in size, hunching his head down between his shoulders as another bullet hit the dashboard and yet another ripped a very big hole through the passenger seat, making him realize that if the car had been built to British specifications, that would have translated into one big, bloody hole in him.

Another tup flicked his head back again, causing him to wobble and swerve across towards the precipice down to the river. He managed to keep control, then rounded the next bend which was a tight left-hander. Ahead of him was the landslide he'd been forced to drive carefully around on his way to the Yorks' house initially.

In his own Land Rover he'd had to take it slow because any misjudgement would have resulted in a rolling tumble down into the water – but seeing the landslide in his sights now, he knew it gave him the best chance he had of outmanoeuvring the vehicle behind.

The Hummer was between the Dodge and the rocks, maybe seventy yards ahead, giving Henry little time to react, but now that his brain had picked up speed and, conversely, time began to slow right down to a crawl, he knew he could do this – if he could get it right.

The rocks covered about seventy-five per cent of the narrow road, from left to right, leaving just enough room for normal-sized vehicles to pick their way around at slow speed.

Henry glanced at his speedometer: fifty miles per hour.

Not too fast under normal circumstances, but on this narrow road at that time of day, with the additional vision-blurring smoke particles in the air and a Dodge Ram right up his backside, what Henry had in mind in those nanoseconds available to him would take skill, precision, a degree of bottle he wasn't sure he possessed, and luck.

He didn't need to check his mirrors to know the Dodge was still right there.

Instead, he took an even firmer grip of the steering wheel, hunched his shoulders tight, gritted his teeth, tensed every muscle and sinew in his body, then pressed down hard on the accelerator just to coax a touch more speed from the Hummer, so that what was basically a wall of rock grew bigger and bigger until Henry was almost at the point of crashing into it. But before that very last moment he swerved right and aimed the Hummer at the narrow gap between where the rock ended and the edge of the road and, holding his breath, gabbling some sort of prayer in his brain, he squeezed through, not even sure the huge car would fit.

Then he was through, out the other side. With great satisfaction he heard the squealing of brakes behind him and the sound of the Dodge crashing into the rock fall simply because the driver hadn't seen it ahead of the Hummer. Henry's last-gasp evasive tactic had worked a treat.

The Dodge would have to reverse to extract itself from the rocks, and those precious seconds meant Henry could put more distance between him and his pursuers and, he hoped, escape with his life more or less intact.

TEN

'Am I, or am I not, under arrest for murder?'

Detective Superintendent Rik Dean sort of shuddered when Henry Christie asked this direct question. He swallowed and Henry watched his Adam's apple rise and fall with an audible clunk.

'Thing is, Rik – may I call you Rik?' Henry said, feeling irritated. 'I'm tired, and a bit dithery because I'm getting old and frail. I've just killed a man, which doesn't make me proud, or sad, because he was trying to kill me. I've seen some terrible sights tonight, the likes of which I thought were consigned to my history. I've been chased by some – I don't know – rednecks, maybe, who shot at me and tried to kill me. You now tell me my lovingly restored Land Rover, which also got shot up, has been torched and is now a black, burned, smoking shell. So, unless you're going to feel my collar and tell me I'm locked up, then I'm going to stand up and walk out of this cop shop, somehow get a ride home, where, despite the time of day, I'll pour myself a pint of Stella from the pumps I cleaned yesterday, and a very large JD chaser, sit down by myself and drink these drinks with a microwaved Holland's meat and potato pie, because as well as being thirsty, I'm also fucking famished!'

'Where will you get your pie from?' Dean asked idiotically.

Henry blessed him with the hardest, most patronizing stare left in his arsenal (though he doubted its effectiveness) and said, 'We have some in the freezer. I run a fucking restaurant.'

He didn't add the word 'Dickhead'.

The two men regarded each other.

Henry could see the strain on Rik Dean's countenance, the result of one outrageously busy night in Lancaster, but Henry had little sympathy. He might have said, 'Been there, done that, got the T-shirt,' but couldn't be bothered.

They were sitting in an interview room at Morecambe Police Station as Lancaster nick had been effectively shut down for evidential purposes. Following Dean's instructions, Henry had been conveyed to Morecambe by Jake Niven – not under arrest as such, but more by polite request, even though Henry's journey had been in the locked cage in the back of PC Niven's Land Rover.

Henry had gone along with it.

He had sat there patiently as a young cop swabbed his hands for firearms residue, swabbed the inside of his mouth for a DNA sample, taken his fingerprints and photograph, then stood there naked as his clothes were taken from him for evidence. Finally, he had given a blood sample to a very nervous on-call police surgeon who had probed inefficiently to find a vein, leaving his inner arm looking as though he'd been mainlining.

Fortunately, Niven had traipsed all the way to Kendleton and back again to get a fresh set of clothes for Henry from Th'Owl, so at least he had fresh underwear, jeans, T-shirt, trainers and a wind-jammer to change into.

All these things had been done willingly by Henry, who understood what was happening.

In the past, he would have done just what Rik Dean was doing.

But now, several hours into this game and only having been provided with a mug of stewed tea for sustenance, it had become increasingly like an arrest-interview scenario and Henry was beginning not to like it.

Rik Dean's lips went tight. 'You see, Henry, you deliberately mowed someone down . . . which is tantamount to murder.'

'Correct, and given those circumstances, I'd gladly do it again. In a heartbeat.' He sighed. 'Look, you have my story on tape under caution; you've never formally told me I'm under arrest or that I'm free to leave at any time. You've never offered me a phone call or a brief. You're just taking advantage of my good nature – which is wearing thin.' It was Henry's turn to give him a tight-lipped smile. 'So you're on a sticky wicket here, Ricky boy. Procedurally, at least, and if I pushed it, I'm pretty sure I'd get you on the ropes for false imprisonment.'

Henry watched/heard him gulp again.

'I'm pretty sure things haven't changed so much since I left and you stepped into my shoes.' Another tight smile at the dig. He was now mentally and physically exhausted and in dire need of the nourishment he hadn't been offered. 'So, Rik, I know you've had a tough night, but nothing like as tough as mine. I've given you all I can and now my patience is see-through, so I'm going to stand up and leave this police station and wander down to Morecambe town centre and see if I can find a cab as, clearly, you aren't going to sort a lift out for me . . .'

Dean began to say something in protest.

Henry held up a hand to stop him. 'Don't bother; honestly, don't bother. I won't leave town. You know where to find me.'

He gave Dean a wink, then pushed himself up using the flat of his hands on the tabletop.

Dean didn't move, just watched him. 'Anyone else would be in a cell while we got this sorted.'

'No, Rik.' Henry leaned forwards to make his point. 'Anyone else would be in the same position as me – caught up in a load of shit they didn't ask for, like a householder knifing a burglar and going to jail for it. So don't bullshit me, OK?'

Henry made his way out, unmolested, unchallenged. He knew Morecambe Police Station well, had run a couple of murder investigations from it years before and it hadn't changed much. The cell complex was now mothballed and no comms room operated from it. Once it had been a major cop shop; now it was little more than a satellite, a place where patrol officers took their refs and a front desk only opened on restricted hours.

He was truly seething with suppressed rage. He knew Rik Dean had a job to do, but he could easily have done it by more subtle means. Still, at least he hadn't been properly arrested. In truth, he could have been lodged in a cell until later in the morning and he tried to be thankful for that small mercy.

He walked out of the back door and turned right in the direction of the town. At the gate he stood and took a breath – the breath he'd been trying to take since discovering the bodies of the Yorks and all that money.

Down here on the coast the air was fresh, cool and clear, not mixed with cloying smoke, and as it went down into his lungs, he could feel its zesty chill.

It felt good and revitalizing, even a bit dizzying.

Because of this little shot of energy, he decided to walk down to the seafront and then stroll along the promenade towards town, knowing he had a good chance of hailing a taxi on that stretch.

He reached the point where the central pier had once jutted out across the sand – it had completely burned down one night years before – and was quite impressed by the improvements being made on what had been a shabby seafront.

A car drew in alongside him.

The passenger-side window opened. The driver leaned across. 'Get in.'

Daniels and Niven reached Gallows Hill crossroads at almost exactly the same time as Henry slithered to a halt in the Hummer coming in the opposite direction.

Although Daniels had spoken to him via mobile phone in the last few minutes, it had been a long time since their joint investigation into two seemingly unconnected murders in Yorkshire which uncovered a miasma of police corruption that had nearly cost them their lives. Although they had got on well back then, they had not seen or communicated with each other since – until today.

Henry was very shaken by the experience up at the farmhouse and it showed as he breathlessly briefed her and Niven, succinctly but with a quaking voice.

As he spoke, Daniels watched him carefully, noting that the intervening years had not been good to him. His face looked gaunt and his short-cropped hair was very grey at the temples. She knew he'd been through some trauma and it looked to have taken its toll.

After he had told her and Niven of the events at the farm, the two cops had a quick look at the Hummer. The missing back window, shattered wing mirror, holes in the passenger seat and dash all confirmed the 'I've been chased and shot at' portion of his story; as, very gruesomely, did the ripped-off ear dangling underneath the front bumper, found by Niven as he inspected the underside of the car with his torch.

'Seriously,' Henry warned them, 'I wouldn't be going back up there without an ARV behind me.'

Then, as if his words were magic, an Armed Response Vehicle with two cops on board came tearing up behind, skidding to a dirt-throwing halt. The ARV had been released by Rik Dean from the infirmary when the threat there had passed, and ordered to get to Gallows Hill and liaise with Daniels and Niven. In the way that such patrols were capable of getting from A to B in the quickest possible time, they probably broke every speed limit en route.

Daniels turned to Henry. 'I'm going to have to ask you to stay with Jake, please. I'll get in with these guys' – she indicated the ARV officers who were eagerly checking their weapons not for the first time that night – 'and go with them to the farm.'

Henry opened his mouth to protest.

But Daniels said, 'Please, Henry, you know the score.'

He wanted to go back, but grudgingly retreated. 'Be careful,' he said, 'these guys mean business.'

'We will.' She looked at the armed cops, one of whom handed her a spare ballistic vest. They looked the business too. She got into the back seat of their Ford Galaxy and they set off at speed along the road until they reached the landslide, which the driver gingerly circumnavigated, then they turned slowly into the long driveway up to the farmhouse, avoiding the mess that was the Great Dane and illuminating the police signs on the car as well as switching on the blue lights as they crossed the cattle grid.

None of them expected the offenders to still be at the scene, but they were ultra-cautious in their approach and very open about who they were, so there could be no misunderstanding: the police had arrived. There was no chance anyway of doing a discreet or tactical approach because of lack of resources.

So if being all lit up scared the bad guys off, then so be it.

The search light on top of the Galaxy came on, its direction controlled by a joystick on the dashboard, and swept across the tableau in front of them, confirming Henry Christie's description of what they would see – although he hadn't expected that his own car would be engulfed in flames.

'He's not going to be happy about that,' Daniels commented.

In front of the house were the three other burned-out black shells that Henry had described. The side door was still open and to the left of the house, slightly set back, was the four-car garage with the right-hand door twisted and mangled, the far left-hand door fully open and the middle two doors still closed, again confirming details of Henry's story – plus a body in front of the broken door.

There was no sign of any other vehicle.

Daniels leaned forward between the front seats of the ARV. 'They've been back and set Mr Christie's car on fire by the looks of it.'

'It's possible they're still here,' one of the PCs said. 'Their car could be out of sight around the back.'

'Possible,' Daniels agreed, but she thought it doubtful. It looked as if they'd returned just to torch Henry's car out of spite.

The PC in the passenger seat unhooked the microphone connected to the vehicle's PA system, clicked it a couple of times to check it was working, then spoke clearly over the system, warning that armed officers had arrived and anyone in or around the farmhouse should show themselves with their hands in the air, then await further instructions. He repeated this twice more.

Daniels knew this had to be the approach, but also knew the PC was talking to no one – no one alive, that is.

The armed cops got out of the Galaxy with all their kit on, stood behind the open doors of the car and repeated the warning.

No response.

With a nod between them, they armed themselves with their Heckler & Koch machine pistols, cocked, ready for use, and began a slow approach to the house, one down either side of Henry's smouldering vehicle, then taking cover at the side of the house.

Daniels watched nervously from the Galaxy.

After further shouted warnings, the two cops crossed to the body at the front of the garage. One knelt by it, quickly checking for any signs of life while the other covered him.

Daniels saw the cop by the body shake his head.

Next they moved to the side door of the house, warnings still being called, until they finally entered the vestibule.

Daniels walked slowly towards the door but stayed short of entering, wanting to allow the cops time to complete a preliminary search and not wishing to surprise them into shooting her by mistake.

From inside she heard voices. 'Clear,' then again, 'Clear,' as they moved from room to room.

Until she finally heard, 'Oh, fucking Jesus Christ!' from one of them.

She jumped aside as one of the cops thundered through the house, exited and sagged to his knees, vomiting copiously, completely emptying the contents of his stomach. Finally, standing upright and wiping the back of his mouth, he said, 'That is gross.'

The other officer came to the side door. He too was affected by what he had just seen but not so much as to be sick.

'You sure you want to see this?' he asked Daniels.

She nodded. As if she had a choice.

She followed him up to the first-floor main bathroom, then up to the attic snooker room, bracing herself as she surveyed the worst murder scene she thought she was ever likely to see.

There was a moment when she could have fled, never returned and handed in her warrant card, but she held it together. Fortunately, the photos and videos Henry had sent managed to shave some of the edge off her horror, but not all. Seeing the dismemberment for real was far worse, but she was better prepared to look at the headless, desecrated bodies of the couple from all angles, even if it did test her inner steel.

Next, she went to look at the mashed-up body in front of the garage doors.

Henry peered into the car that had pulled up alongside him on Morecambe prom.

'Get in.'

'I was going to catch a cab.'

'Up yours, then.'

Henry's face cracked into a smile. 'If I was a superintendent, I'd have disciplined you for saying that to a superior officer.'

'But you're not, you're a civvy with no powers whatsoever, so get in,' Daniels said.

Henry did so and sank into the soft, spongy passenger seat of the ancient Peugeot. 'You still got this thing?'

'It was my dad's, as you know. Can't seem to let it go, even though it costs more and more each year to run. Comfy, though.'

'Some things are like that.' Henry sat back. 'Well, nice to see you after all these years.'

'Yeah, and in such pleasant circumstances.'

She did a U-turn on the quiet prom and headed north, intending to cut inland at the Broadway junction towards Lancaster, then drive out to Kendleton to get Henry home.

'I'm sorry we had to do what we did . . . to you, if you get my drift.'

'You mean, semi-arrest me? I get it – people died, and even though I did what I had to do, I know I still might end up with my name on a murder charge sheet.'

'Not if I have a say.'

'Justice moves in mysterious ways,' Henry said enigmatically. 'And to be honest, I did lay it on a bit thick with Rik. Enjoyed seeing him squirm a bit.'

'You're still cheesed off he got your job!'

'I don't hold grudges, honest. Not for more than ten years, anyway.'

Daniels snickered and drove on, cutting across on the new by-pass road before joining the A683 away from the city out into the Lune valley through Caton, then taking the right turn that would put them on the road to Kendleton.

'How are you with dead bodies these days?' Henry asked her.

'Better. Not brilliant, just better.'

'And with what you must have seen at the Yorks' place?'

'Pretty grim – but it's been like that for a couple of nights now in Lancaster, though beheading and dismemberment does take some beating. And, yep, despite it all, I still want a crack at FMIT. I suppose I'll always be like a sailor who's seasick. You learn to manage it. How about you? Must have been a shock, even for a grizzled old curmudgeon like you?'

'More upsetting to get shot at.'

'Well, I've been there tonight, too.'

'So what's going on? Rik Dean was playing his cards close to his chest, not very forthcoming about anything.'

'I don't think we're all that sure at the moment. The stuff over the weekend seems to be drug-related power plays, but we're not certain how they all interlink, tit for tat, if you know what I mean?'

Henry nodded, glad it wasn't something on his plate.

'It's something the murder squad will begin to look at in depth in the morning,' Daniels went on. 'I've got my own thing to sort, which, as horrendous as it was, probably won't get the attention it deserves now, especially with Bill Heath's death being part of the picture.'

'What is your thing?'

Daniels explained the house explosion and the two deaths from that, the mother and daughter.

'Sounds particularly nasty,' Henry said.

'I was just about to interview the friend of the woman who died when the infirmary thing kicked off. She was a reluctant witness to say the least and disappeared pretty quickly from the nick, so I'm going to have to find her again, which might not be all that easy.'

'DC Daniels receiving?' her PR piped up. Rik Dean.

'Yes, boss.'

'Did you pick up Henry Christie off the streets by any chance? Against my specific instructions?'

Daniels looked sideways at Henry, half grinned like a naughty kid and shrugged. 'Yes, boss.'

'Are you still with him?'

'Yes, boss, on our way to Kendleton.'

'Any chance of checking out something in that neck of the woods?'

'Of course.' She rolled her eyes. What she wanted to do was drop Henry off, then race back to her flat in Lancaster and crawl into bed.

'Comms have just received a report of a car on fire in Hornby village . . . I know it might not be connected – we have no details as yet – but it's possible it's the one we have an interest in, so just take a look, will you?' He gave her directions.

'Roger that.' She turned to Henry, now slouched a long way down in his seat like a grumpy teenager. 'Do you mind?'

He folded his arms and closed his eyes. 'Wake me when we get there.'

Daniels took the next left turn, not really sure if it was the right road, but knowing instinctively she was heading in the direction of Hornby, a picturesque village straddling the A683 to the north-east of Lancaster.

Eventually, she passed a Hornby sign, then she was in the village and crossing the bridge over the River Wenning. A quarter of a mile further on she came to a lay-by where a fire tender was just pulling away, leaving a marked police car and one bobby parked behind the remains of a burned-out vehicle.

Daniels parked behind the police car and the lone PC got out of the car and sauntered up to her as she climbed out. They both walked to the wreck.

The PC explained, 'A guy driving past saw it up in flames and called it in.'

'Anyone with it?'

The PC shook his head.

Daniels walked around the vehicle. It was definitely a big four-wheel-drive utility vehicle – similar to the one reported at the hospital and the one used by the guys who had invaded the police station and shot at Daniels. It was a blackened mess, hardly recognizable. The windows had all blown, the tyres burned away, and there was nothing remaining of the interior except the springs of the seats. She saw Henry get stiffly out of her car and amble in her direction.

Daniels saw the rear number plate was charred and unreadable, so she walked to look at the front one. That too was burned, but she bent down and gave it a swipe with her fingers.

As she did this, Henry caught up with her.

This plate was readable.

She said, 'I'm no car freak but I'm bloody sure this is the one I saw at the nick . . . and that number . . .'

Henry stood behind her as she tried to relive the incident. She had been crouched down – yes, cowering – watching the vehicle drive away. The rear plate had been square, this front one was rectangular, but she remembered the top line of letters and numbers – 'BN12' – but not the bottom line because of everything else that was happening. She thought she'd done pretty well, bearing in mind her first consideration was to stay alive.

The first four letters and numbers on the plate she was now looking at were 'BN12'.

Coincidence? she thought. Until that moment she'd suspected the incidents in Lancaster and up at the farm might be linked – if only because of the terrible violence used – but she hadn't been a hundred per cent certain. Now she was ninety per cent of the way.

She did another circuit of the car, more and more convinced of her beliefs.

Henry followed her. She checked the car number on PNC but it came back as an invalid registration number and no registered keeper, which did not necessarily surprise her. When she had done that, Henry started talking over her shoulder.

'I do know my cars, pretty much, but I have to admit, while it was happening, I couldn't have told you what kind of motor those two guys who were after me had or what the number was. All I know is that they were in a big thing with lots of lights and it was like being chased by a monster truck and I didn't really have time to appreciate it. But I do know this is a Dodge Ram.'

Daniels was distracted by her thoughts and said, 'Fuck.'

'It is,' he said, mock-hurt.

'I don't dispute that, Henry.'

'And I'll bet it's the one that came after me.'

'Thing is, the first four letters and numbers on the plate match the ones I saw on the car at the police station,' Daniels told him.

'BN12?' Henry asked.

Daniels nodded.

'So it's more than likely that the car you saw at the police station then went to the farmhouse, where I encountered it.'

'Yeah,' Daniels said to that. Her mind was almost out of control now.

'And prior to that, the occupants paid a visit to the infirmary,' Henry said.

Daniels nodded again.

'So it's highly likely the occupants also paid a visit to the farmhouse even before all that to kill John and Isobel York,' Henry suggested. 'Except when they killed the Yorks there were only two of them, and they came back with a third one – the man they broke out of the cells.'

'Yeah, yeah.'

'Which makes it all very, very interesting,' Henry said. 'Because I saw this car earlier yesterday.'

Daniels came to a grinding halt and turned to him, stunned. 'You what?' She gave him a 'spill the beans' gesture.

'At The Tawny Owl,' he said casually.

Daniels, as exhausted as anyone could be, was suddenly as alive as a mad springer spaniel. 'Henry, my arse is twitching here.'

'Two men were having a drink at Th'Owl late afternoon yesterday. They weren't causing any problems, but they were vaping, so I asked them to leave, which they did, reluctantly. They got into a Dodge Ram and I clocked the number . . . it's in here.' He tapped his head. 'Also on a Post-it note by the till. And, uh, this is the number on the front of this car.'

'You saw two men? You spoke to two men? Yet there were three at the farm?'

'Yep.'

'You spoke to two men without masks on?'

'Yep.'

'Why didn't you say before?'

He shrugged. 'No one asked and, up to this moment, no connections were being made.'

'Guess what, Henry Christie? You ain't going to bed. Oh no, man, we've got so much to discuss.'

ELEVEN

There had been plenty of times in Henry's past as a detective when he'd spent countless hours on the go, fuelled by coffee, adrenaline and the hunt for a killer, but that was no longer his domain.

Not only did he have a busy country house hotel and pub to run, but he was now exhausted and wanted to get some sleep. His desire for a pie, beer and bourbon had gone, but he still needed a mug of tea and probably a bacon sandwich just to tide him over.

He could also see that Daniels was flagging and she needed both sustenance and rest, so he made a suggestion.

'Take me back to The Tawny Owl. Let's have a brew and some food, get Rik Dean to come and join us – if he can. We can talk and then crash out for a few hours.'

'Crash out? How do you mean?'

'I'll give you a room and you can get your head down before

returning to the fray. How does that sound? And you can keep an eye on me, see I don't leave the country.'

'It sounds good – but I don't have a change of clothes and that is something I desperately need because I'm sweaty and beginning to reek a bit. I know,' she said off Henry's look, 'women don't reek.'

'I didn't want to be indiscreet,' Henry grinned and feigned a duck just in case she slapped him. 'If you can't do it, just drop me off and we'll meet later. If I recall, you live in Preston, don't you? Bit inconvenient just to nip and grab some clothes.'

'We really haven't spoken for a while, have we? I have a flat in Lancaster now – which is in nippable distance. I could grab a few things, then we could head over to Kendleton.'

Henry yawned like a very big, lazy cat. 'Let's do it.'

Daniels called Rik Dean on the journey back to Lancaster. Her phone was connected to Bluetooth and the conversation was on loudspeaker for Henry to listen in, something Dean was initially unaware of.

'Do not let him go home,' he said firmly to Daniels. 'We need to pin him down and get everything he knows on paper and tape with regard to these toe-rags. This is a hot investigation and we need to push forward with it, give it momentum and, clearly, what he knows is vital.'

'I think he just wants to go to bed.'

'Silly old fuckwit – don't let him. Bring him to Lancaster nick, arrest him if you need to, and let me speak to him even if I have to shake him awake.'

Daniels grimaced at Henry.

There was a slight pause before Dean said, 'He can hear me, can't he?' Then quickly added, 'I'll come and see him.'

The wind had changed direction. By the time Henry and Daniels returned to Kendleton, dawn was well on course, the sun rising slowly through a cloudy haze. Much of the smoke from the fires had blown away, the air was fresh for a change and it was a proper daybreak, the sort Henry had grown to love and appreciate.

There had been a shift change of the fire service and a tender was parked at the front of Th'Owl with half a dozen or so soot-faced firefighters milling around on the car park, supping tea and breakfast sandwiches provided by the pub.

Once more Henry thought how this was all costing him a small fortune; on the cynical side, he hoped his generosity would ensure that if he ever needed the fire service in a hurry, they would come running.

As Daniels pulled up, Henry got out of the car and had a chat with the senior officer present, who told him that the wind direction had indeed changed, become quite strong up on the moors, hence the clear sky. Rain was actually forecast but he did warn Henry that the fire had come dangerously close to the woods surrounding Kendleton overnight and it was only the wind that had helped prevent it from entering the trees. He also told him that a helicopter had been contracted to drop water later in the day, which should help matters.

The officer thanked Henry for the food and brews, then rounded up his crew, and Henry watched them climb wearily on to the tender and drive away.

Daniels watched the exchange.

'You're doing a good thing,' she said to him.

'At great personal cost,' he grumbled. 'It will bankrupt me.'

She giggled. 'You don't take compliments well, do you?'

He shrugged. 'Only when they come with pay rises.' He turned to the pub.

He was then met by a series of individuals.

Ginny rushed out and hugged him so tightly he couldn't get his breath. 'We've been so worried about you.'

'I'm fine, sweetie.' He kissed her cheek.

Next in line was a rather sheepish Jake Niven.

Henry dealt him his famous hard stare, then smiled and winked at him.

'No hard feelings?' Niven tested him.

'You mean for basically arresting me?'

'I never!'

'OK, obliging me to "help with police enquiries",' Henry said, doing the air quotes thing.

'You know I had no choice under the circumstances.'

'Well, don't worry – I got police bail,' Henry teased him.

'No! You fucking . . . Oh, I see, you're just fooling with me.'

Henry gave him a slap on the shoulder, maybe a touch too hard as it almost knocked him over, but Niven let it go. 'Just don't do it again, hear?'

Next in line was Maude Crichton. She was standing at the top of the steps, waiting for him with her best alluring stance, wearing a light, chiffon summer dress through which he could see her flimsy underwear. Very flimsy, almost non-existent underwear.

Despite the time of day and the fact she had probably been up most of the night fretting, she looked immaculate.

Henry was quite impressed, but the naughty twinkle in her eye was really a warning signal to him, plus the open arms which he felt obliged to enter for the hug – tight up against her soft bosom and slim but curvaceous body. She did smell very nice too, but she frightened him somewhat.

'We were all really worried about you, Henry,' she whispered into his ear.

'I'm fine, Maude.' He extracted himself as delicately as possible. 'Is everything OK here for today?'

'Yes.'

'You're doing good work.'

She opened her finely lipsticked mouth to say something that Henry assumed he did not want to hear, so the sight of Rik Dean striding towards him from inside the pub with a mug in his hand gave Henry an excuse to pat her shoulder – much more softly than he'd whacked Niven – and meet the detective superintendent halfway.

The two men faced each other.

Henry's tired countenance had become granite-hard. 'Silly old fuckwit, eh?'

Dean emitted a strangled chuckle. 'Didn't mean it.'

'Whatever,' Henry said petulantly.

'Look, I've brought the e-fit artist along with me. I've got access online to a load of mugshots . . . Could we sit down, get an additional statement from you, get you to look through the faces, then do the e-fit thing if you can't nail anyone?'

'No,' Henry said.

Henry lived in the owner's accommodation in the old part of The Tawny Owl, accessed through a door off the main public bar. It was spacious, with a large living/dining room overlooking the rear gardens, plus a kitchen and three large en-suite bedrooms.

One was Henry's, the other occupied by Ginny and her boyfriend, and the remaining one was a guest room. It was to this one he showed Daniels. Then he went into his own bedroom where he looked longingly at the bed – very tempting – before stripping off and going into the shower which was hot and refreshing.

He could hear the shower running in the en suite next door and tried not to think too much about the proximity of Diane Daniels because, he told himself harshly, he was far too old for such things. And knackered. Instead, he concentrated on his own hygiene, shaved in the shower, put on a new set of casual clothes, then made his way back to the bar area where he caught up with a glum Rik Dean sitting in the dining area, morosely sipping coffee.

The e-fit artist sat primly alongside Dean, pretending to be busy on her laptop.

Dean rose awkwardly.

Although the two men had a long professional and personal history between them, Henry was actually fuming by the off-the-cuff remark Dean had made about him. He knew he should have to let it go, but for the moment he could feel himself tensing up about it.

'Look, Henry,' Dean began, steering Henry away from the police artist who was trying to give the impression she wasn't listening in. 'I'm sorry. I'm under severe pressure. It's like Lancaster city's been set on fire. Murder at the weekend, the explosion, the kids on the estate kicking off, people being hacked to pieces; then the murder at the infirmary, the breakout and Bill Heath's death . . . fuck! Then you find some of your neighbours chopped to bits, you run over someone, kill 'em, get shot at . . . y'know?' he said helplessly. 'It's enough to try anyone.'

Henry looked at him and gave a long, heavy sigh. 'Then, then, then, then,' he mimicked. 'Boo-fucking-hoo!'

'Right, right, you're right, mate.' Dean gave Henry a gesture of submission. 'Sorry, OK. Look, I think this explosion thing Diane attended is its own thing, but it looks like the infirmary, the police station and the dead couple are all linked – and you're the glue in it. You are the only person to have seen the two guys' actual faces. They were wearing masks made of something like latex or nitrile when they did the jobs . . . The other thing is, because the guy who was sprung out of the cells was in custody for the murder over the weekend, it all links to him, too.' His expression became contrite. 'So, yeah, really sorry, really would like your help on this . . . melting pot of violence . . . mate.'

'Pretty please,' Henry teased him.

'Up yours, Henry.'

'That'll do.'

'There's another thing . . . the guy from the cells, his name . . .'

'Is?'

'Thomas – aka Tommy – Costain.'

Henry considered the name for a moment and burst out laughing.

Henry sat alongside Daniels on the low wall outside Th'Owl, looking across the village green to the stream.

It was the first time he'd sat out here for a while. It was his place for any 'me' time he cared to have. Though not a greatly introspective person, he did like to spend a few occasional minutes out 'on the stoop' as he called it, coffee in hand, thinking about Alison and his late wife, Kate. It was a good place to sit, usually pretty peaceful, even though the main road through Kendleton ran just in front of the pub.

He and Daniels had a coffee and bacon sandwich each. She had showered and changed too and seemed ready to go.

Henry could not stop chuckling and shaking his head.

'What is so funny?' Daniels demanded.

'Tommy Costain.'

'You know him?'

'No, no, I don't think I do.'

'And yet . . .'

'I'm laughing, yes. I don't know him, but I'm pretty sure I know a lot about him . . . in a roundabout way.'

Daniels waited, taking a bite out of her sandwich which, under the circumstances, tasted amazing. She was on the verge of becoming a vegetarian, often went weeks without eating meat, but the rare bite of something as delicious as this made her wonder what she would be missing.

Next to her, Henry took another bite of his.

He was nowhere near becoming a vegetarian.

He chewed thoughtfully, swallowed, then said, 'Ironically, one of the last things I promised myself I would do before I retired was bring down the Costain family. Without doubt, they are evil beyond belief and were Blackpool's foremost crime family.' He shrugged. 'But I failed – obviously – retired, and such is life. Crime groups carry on.'

'I've heard of them,' Daniels said.

'I even once had one of the family as an informant – on the QT, that is. Totally against procedure. I used him mercilessly.'

'You must have had something on him.'

'Not specially. I arrested him once for something and nothing and discovered he had raging claustrophobia and was terrified beyond logic of being in a cell. He'd be crawling the walls within a minute, would have coughed to anything . . . it was a hell of a thing to have hanging over him.' Henry gave a wicked smile. 'Cells terrified him.'

'What happened? Presumably he's still around. Could we tap into him?'

'He . . . er . . . came to a sticky end.' Henry clammed up, recalling how he'd overused Troy Costain and eventually put him in a situation that led to his demise in a drainage gulley. He coughed. 'But the Costains . . . they went from strength to strength, a bit like that fairground mole game, the one where you bat one down and others appear – "whack-a-mole", that's it! They expanded across the county, violently and with intimidation. They even claim their heritage is from Romany gypsies. In reality, they're just a crime family with travellers' roots. I can only assume that Tommy is the latest incarnation, and even without knowing much about him, I'd guess everything that's happened over the weekend revolves around him. Otherwise, why bust him out? That is one very, very serious undertaking even for a top crime family – followed by the other, very scary stuff, the killing at the infirmary and the job up at Hawkshead Farm which,' Henry mused, 'if they were carried out by the same pair, now minus one, as seems likely, means you are hunting some very dangerous people who are scared of nothing. Killing a cop just seems like a bit of fun for them. They're feral, Diane, and I don't envy you.'

'And I don't envy you, either,' Rik Dean said.

Dean had walked up behind Henry and Daniels without either noticing and earwigged the last bit of the conversation.

Henry looked over his shoulder. 'Why would that be?'

'You saw them, Henry. They could come back to haunt you.'

'Thanks for that thought.' Henry finished his sandwich and washed it down with the coffee which was now only lukewarm. 'I'd better make sure the e-fits are nothing like them and I don't pick out any mugshots.'

Dean joined them on the wall, rubbing his weary face with the palms of his hands. 'I've just got off the phone with the chief constable.'

'Nice,' Henry said. He did not have one pang of jealousy about that one. Over the years, his relationship with chief constables was variable at best. Even as a detective superintendent, there are always others above, and as much as those of lower rank believed that supers wielded great power, the truth was they didn't. There were three or four tiers above them who they were answerable to and usually made their lives very uncomfortable.

'I've run a couple of things past her,' Dean said.

Henry glanced at Daniels and raised his eyebrows.

'First off, your involvement in the York double murder and that you are going to provide some valuable evidence of identity that could make you a target.'

'Right,' Henry said cautiously.

'It's true, isn't it? You're the only one who's seen their actual faces.'

'OK,' Henry said, curious as to where this was going.

'So, I've come up with a plan,' Dean said, rubbing his hands together. 'Now hear me out, Henry,' he went on as Henry's mouth opened in protest. 'It's a two-fold plan. First is this: we are really short-staffed at the moment. Government cuts, people off sick with stress – duh! – all that kind of stuff. For example, FMIT. Down to one detective super – me – to run the whole shebang, while my opposite number is off with anxiety issues, for fuck's sake! We have no chief super, the ACC Ops is off sick or suspended – I forget which – hence my direct line to the chief.'

'Rik, this is a very long set-up and I'm not looking forward to the punchline, but I do want you to get to it before I doze off. Today. Sometime soon.'

'OK, OK, I put it to the chief that, based on your past experience as a detective super in FMIT, plus your intimate knowledge of the Costains and, of course, the vital evidence you can provide . . . we take you on as a consulting detective, part-time investigator, consultant – whatever you want to call it – to help out with the York murders.'

Henry blinked. 'Did you run that past me?'

'N–no.' Dean became flustered. 'It's a chicken and egg thing. I thought you'd be pleased.'

'An assumption, Rik boy. I have a business to run for starters.'

'Well, surely Ginny and her boyfriend can run the place? They're quite capable.'

'Not the point.'

'Look, hear me out at least, yeah?'

Daniels said, 'Should I make myself scarce, boss?' She was feeling the tension between the two men.

'No, Diane, you stay. You're part of this,' Dean said, much to her surprise.

'Now I am intrigued,' Henry admitted.

Dean faced Henry square-on. 'I want you to run this side of the investigation – the York bit. And the chief's agreed to a generous remuneration package at the end of which you'll probably be able to afford a new old Land Rover to restore.'

'How long, how much? And even though I ran one of them over?'

'One month, twenty working days, two fifty per day. Five grand, Henry – less tax, obviously. Say three and a half in your back pocket? And we'll work round that.'

'I don't get out of bed for less than a grand a day.'

'You've got to be bloomin—'

'A thousand a day and that's my final offer,' Henry said, teasing but also meaning it. 'Just remember, you're the one who came to me. And I thought the police were cash-strapped, so where did that money come from anyway?'

Henry said that knowing there were hidden coffers all over the place. You just had to know how to find them and then twist the arm of the finance manager to access them. Money, or lack of it, had been a driving factor when he was in the job, as it became more and more apparent that central government did not really want a police service in the traditional sense anymore. But when money was needed, it could be found, and even though what Henry was demanding seemed high, it was probably a cheap fix in the overall scheme of things.

'Seven-fifty,' Dean counter-bargained.

'One thousand per day.' Henry knew he was on to a winner by the harassed look on Dean's face. 'You've got big, interlinked, complex jobs going on, so if you get me, cheap at the price, you'll be able to stand back like a good manager should and have a strategic view of things, which you will need.'

'OK, a grand a day, twenty days,' Rik agreed, although Henry could see it stuck in his craw.

They shook hands. Henry refrained from saying, 'Sucker.'

'But don't let on. If anyone asks, it's a hundred quid a day, OK? That goes for you too,' he added, glowering at Daniels. 'Say nothing!'

'OK,' Henry said. 'You mentioned Diane was part of this.'

'Yeah. Diane, I want you to chaperone him. I remember you worked together once and did a good job, and you have some sort of relationship. He'll need someone to advise him about current policy and procedure and hold his hand, et cetera.'

'But boss, I'm involved in the deaths following the explosion. I need to get back on track with that.'

'Leave it. I've allocated it to DI Simpson. He'll be running a small team on it. You forget it for the time being.'

'Not sure I can,' Daniels said truthfully.

'Well, you're going to have to.'

Daniels sighed. 'I'm not being funny, Henry – this double murder and all the Costain stuff is all very well and sexy, and normally I'd want to be part of it. But that explosion left a mother and child dead in each other's arms and they *were* murdered. I don't want them to get forgotten in the rush to do the fun stuff, shall we say? And you never know, there could be some connection to all this . . . the mother was a druggie.'

'What was her name?' Henry asked.

'Andrea Greatrix.'

Henry frowned on hearing the name. Daniels picked up on the look.

'Does that mean something to you?'

'Not sure. Rings a bell, but I don't know why. My cop brain has been asleep for a while and needs a service. On which note, if you are going to chaperone me, you might have to get used to me taking naps to recharge the batteries.'

'I've had a pensioner foisted on me.' She laughed.

'A wealthy one, though.'

'Which makes all the difference. Now all I have to do is get you to change your will.'

They were in her car driving out to Hawkshead Farm on a day that was turning out to be quite pleasant as the breeze managed to lift the smoke haze away, though the fires on the moors still burned ferociously.

Daniels edged the car around the rock fall and congratulated Henry on somehow managing to drive a Hummer around it at fifty miles per hour and not end up submerged in the river.

'If I'd stopped to think about it, that's where I would be.' He looked down the slope. 'Pure instinct, backed up by terror.'

It was only a short drive further before Daniels turned into the gate, then on to the drive leading up to the Yorks' place.

There was now a small crime scene tent erected over the body of the dog and Daniels had to drive on to the grass verge to get around it before re-joining the drive and heading up to the house, now a bustle of police activity. She was waved to an area on the lawn now designated as a parking spot by a uniformed PC. Henry looked at the cars, one of which was clearly not a cop car.

It was an old Jaguar XK150 Roadster in burgundy, which was totally out of place. He knew it belonged to Baines, the Home Office pathologist who had a penchant for old Jags and had restored a few in his time. Daniels parked next to it and gave it a wistful look.

Daniels had to explain Henry to the constable, who was booking people in and out of the crime scene, and next stop was a CSI van where she and Henry were given forensic suits which they stepped into, plus latex gloves and face masks.

On the way to the house, Henry spent a few minutes looking over his Land Rover, the first time he'd seen it since it had been set on fire. He felt quite emotional seeing his first ever vehicle renovation project now just a blackened hulk and beyond any sort of repair. It probably didn't even have scrap value now.

Daniels had to drag him away.

The body of the young man Henry had mown down was still in situ outside the broken garage door. He was not covered by anything, the body just cordoned off while a tent was being erected. Henry walked up to the barrier and looked.

The kid – because that's all he was – was a terrible mess, as Henry had imagined he would be. He kept his distance but circled the body to get a better look at the face.

'Not good,' he said, remembering the impact, seeing him disappear under the front grille of the Hummer. However, he was glad to see that the sawn-off shotgun was there and he hadn't imagined it in the lad's hands. It looked as though the rear wheel of the Hummer had gone over it, crushing it. 'It's one of the lads from The Tawny Owl,' he confirmed. 'I can tell, even though he's a mess to look at.'

'You OK?' Daniels asked him.

'Checking up on the pensioner already?'

'Something like that.'

'I'm fine,' he assured her. 'Let's do a walk-through of the crime scene. I'd better start earning my money.'

TWELVE

'We've got to leave him, Bren,' Tommy Costain had said urgently to O'Hara as they'd inspected the fatally injured body of Cillian Roche that lay mangled and unmoving in front of the garage door. 'We haven't got time to be dragging him round with us . . . we'll claim him back and cause some shit with the cops, but for now we have to move.'

O'Hara nodded, unable to rip his gaze away from the corpse of his best friend and partner in crime. His face was set like concrete as he accepted the words of Tommy Costain, his boss.

'C'mon.' Tommy shook him back into the reality of the situation.

After hurtling in pursuit of Henry Christie – O'Hara at the wheel of the Ram – with Costain leaning out of the front passenger window firing shots at the Hummer ahead and O'Hara doing the same when he could from the other side using a pistol, he just hadn't seen or remembered the landslide on the narrow road, so its sudden appearance as the Hummer swerved and skewed around it left him no room or time to avoid smashing straight into it, screaming curses. Both men were thankful they had not been hurled through the front window; it was like driving into a brick wall and they had hit so hard that the back wheels of the Ram lifted up.

By the time O'Hara managed to reverse out of it, the Hummer had long since gone and they decided not to chase it any further. O'Hara backed all the way to the farmhouse gate and gunned it up the drive where, on closer examination, his fears had been confirmed: Cillian Roche was as dead as they came.

Overwhelmed with grief, O'Hara had to drive himself through the next few minutes back in the house as they collected all the money and heaved the holdalls into the Ram.

Before leaving, O'Hara had tipped half a can of petrol from a jerry can strapped to the back of the Ram over Henry Christie's Land Rover and lit it.

There'd been a certain grim satisfaction as the flames shot high in his rear-view mirror, but the sight had also made him feel so much more than just rage. Vengeance was now in his mix of emotions.

At the gate, they'd turned right and cut across the moor on a tight, bumpy track over to the northern side of Salter Fell, keeping on it until joining Hornby Road, eventually bringing them out at Hornby village where they found their onward transport waiting in the lay-by just beyond the River Wenning bridge.

After a quick transfer of the money into the new vehicle, O'Hara had doused the Ram with the remaining petrol from the can and shoved a burning rag into the petrol tank.

It had burst into spectacular flame as they drove off.

In the back of the new vehicle, Tommy Costain smiled widely while O'Hara sat brooding ominously.

He had definitely not finished with Henry Christie.

* * *

Henry and Daniels did a long, slow walk-through of the scene of the double murder. Henry had brought a portable digital voice recorder with him and made observations and also recorded any of his conversation with Daniels when they shared some insight or other.

After over two harrowing hours of observing minute details, they returned to the kitchen where just the counting machine sat on the worktop, all the cash having gone.

Henry, still recording, said, 'They came back for the cash, which begs the question: why didn't they take it in the first place? There is always a risk in returning to a crime scene. So, they came back for the cash and not to gloat, which is what offenders have been known to do.'

'Perhaps they were acting on orders and misunderstood them,' Daniels ventured. 'Orders from Tommy Costain, maybe?'

'Good punt,' Henry agreed. 'But there is also another question to be asked . . .'

He took out his mobile phone, opened the photo file and watched the mini-panoramic video he'd taken of the money in the kitchen before it disappeared. He paused it, then using his finger and thumb, expanded the view and showed it to Daniels.

'There was easily over a million quid here – sterling, dollars, euros, other currencies – and that's a conservative estimate – maybe even two. Those cars out there, the burned-out ones – one was an Aston Martin, one a McLaren and the other a Bugatti. I know we've yet to positively say what they were, but I'm pretty sure I'm in the ballpark. Then in the garage, there's a classic Aston, a Ferrari, a Bentley and the Hummer. I reckon, collectively, they'd have been worth what, four or five million?'

'You're jesting!'

Henry shook his head. 'On the right day, in the right salesroom, I know I'm right. So, the question is' – he gave Daniels a stupid grin – 'who were John and Isobel York when they were at home? That nice couple who occasionally popped into Th'Owl?'

'A fine question,' Daniels agreed.

'Cash, expensive cars, a bath in the middle of the bathroom floor, fancy pad – and very violent death . . . More than a robbery gone wrong, Diane. What say you?'

'I don't want to jump to any conclusions. There might be a

legitimate answer for all the wealth . . . but I'd like to work on the hypothesis that there isn't.'

'Same here. Mr and Mrs York were concealing secrets.'

'A whole shitload, I'd say.'

The travellers' site was in the Marton area of Blackpool, close to junction 4 of the M55 in an area known as Lower Ballam. It had been in existence for over twenty years and was probably one of the most settled, peaceful sites of its kind in the country. There were good water, gas and electricity supplies, and the community living on it kept a low profile, rarely interacted with neighbours – mainly farmers – and had little hassle from the authorities.

There had been moments, but, generally speaking, these travellers were at peace with the world, kept themselves to themselves.

Which is how Conrad Costain liked it.

Most of the static caravans on the site – over twenty of them – were new, spacious, pristine, lovingly cared for. As was Conrad's, but his was undoubtedly the biggest, most luxurious on site, tucked away in one corner with its own well-tended little garden, security cameras and a rangy, dangerous-looking Doberman Pinscher, which kept station at the open front door of the caravan, hardly ever moving, other than his all-seeing eyes. His name was Satan, although Conrad usually shortened that to Stan. Satan – Stan – had once shaken a baby in his jaws, but the severe, almost fatal beating he received from Conrad after that event meant that the dog had become a pussy cat other than when responding to Conrad's orders, and then he became a murderous killing machine.

The baby had lived, the family taken care of, the whole incident covered up, the authorities none the wiser.

Conrad Costain was eighty years old – or so he thought. As far as he knew, he did not have a birth certificate, but his calculations put him about that age. Not that it worried him unduly. A piece of paper to say you had been born really meant nothing to him. He'd been born free and would die free.

Unless the cops got him, in which case he would undoubtedly rot in a cell for the remainder of his life.

He did expect to live quite a bit longer. Despite a couple of health scares, he was in good fettle and his body was as lithe and muscular as someone thirty years younger, if that someone had kept in shape.

That morning, as Henry Christie and Diane Daniels walked their way through the brutal crime scene, Conrad Costain was waiting patiently, slowly lifting a dumbbell with his right hand as he sipped sweet tea from a metal mug with his other.

It was Conrad who kept a lid on this travellers' site, and the other residents, though under his strict orders, were glad of it, even if most did not work directly for him. They were a mix of people – couples with kids, a few older widows and just a few obnoxious teenagers who had started attracting the attention of cops and whose tenure on site would shortly be terminated. On the whole, though, most people lived in peace and harmony with their immediate surroundings and took their business out of the area.

And that was how Conrad liked it.

A life under the radar.

Which was always a good thing when you are the head of a vast organized crime gang and you did not want cops to come knocking in the early hours.

Not that they would have found him at home if they did.

The site was secure and difficult to access – unless law enforcement arrived by helicopter and abseiled down – with high corrugated walls topped with razor wire and only one entrance through a ten-foot-high steel barred gate kept locked at all times and guarded by one of Conrad's grandsons who lived in a tiny caravan by the entrance. The grandson had quick access, if required, to a sawn-off shotgun and a revolver, both always loaded and ready for use.

The name of that grandson was Tommy Costain.

And if the police did ever breach the gate, other than with Conrad's permission, and there was someone or something to hide, his caravan had a trapdoor in the floor which dropped into a tunnel that led a hundred yards into the field behind, coming up into a small copse of trees where, under a camouflage tarpaulin, a carefully maintained getaway vehicle awaited.

He had never had cause to use that escape route in anger, but frequently tested it for fun.

It worked. Within minutes of being alerted, he could be gone.

He swapped hands with the dumbbell and mug, just as his mobile phone rang. He put down the mug and answered it, keeping up the reps with the weight.

It was Bronwen Buckland, Tommy's girlfriend, who lived in the small caravan with him.

Conrad could not help but grin slightly at the voice and his mind's eye vision of Bronwen. Tommy, Conrad thought, had done far too well with her. She was out of his class. She was a stereotypical raven-haired gypsy beauty who often wore blousy tops and flowing skirts, though more regularly tight-fitting jeans and skimpy shirts that accentuated every curve, of which she had plenty. Conrad lusted after her, and one day, assisted by Viagra, he would pin her down and she would say nothing about it. A pleasure to come.

'Bronwen, my darling,' he cooed.

'Conrad, they're here – they're back.'

The wind direction changed again and smoke from the fires drifted back across Hawkshead Farm.

Henry stepped out of the side door and peered up into the sky, seeing low cloud coming in from the moorland. He frowned and selfishly hoped there would be another change in wind direction.

A small SOCO tent had now been erected over the body of the guy Henry had mown down, which was a good thing. He wanted to keep away from it, avoid any contact so as not to be accused of contaminating evidence. He knew how the guy had died. He'd witnessed it in close-up and didn't need to know anything else.

He walked around the tent and entered the four-car garage for a short browse around the remaining cars which had survived unscathed. He could not fail to admire them. They were every sports car enthusiast's wet dream and so very, very expensive.

'They are nice – even I can see that.' Daniels had followed him.

'Yep.'

'This garage looks like quite a new build, even though it sort of matches the brick and stonework of the main house and the barn behind,' Daniels observed.

Henry hadn't realized that. 'You're right.'

'In fact . . .' Daniels stepped back out of the garage and pointed up to the front of it. Henry followed her and looked up. She was pointing at an inlaid stone with '2016' carved into it and set in the brickwork.

'The point at which they became wealthy?' Henry suggested.

'Who knows?'

He continued the tour of the garage with Daniels, then stepped out and walked towards the barn behind it, trying to rearrange his thoughts – and suddenly wondering if he was up to this. He'd been retired a few years and time had definitely blunted his edge.

Daniels looked at him with a puzzled expression.

'Just wondering if I've undercharged for this.'

'You're cheap at the price,' she complimented him. 'In one fell swoop, you will have earned more than half my annual salary in four weeks. Not bad going. Not that I'm bitter or anything.'

He blew out his cheeks and attempted to get his detective superintendent hat on once more. It felt a bit cockeyed.

'Right – basic stuff. First question: since we did that job over in Yorkshire, have you worked on a murder investigation?'

'Not as such.' She gulped. 'Not at all. Been to a couple of murder scenes as on-call detective.'

'OK, not a problem, but I'm feeling just a bit wobbly about this. I know Rik said you were to be my chaperone, Diane, but what I really want is a right-hand . . . woman. People have changed, procedures have altered, policies, too – so you're my conduit back into the force.'

'I get that.' To Daniels it seemed as if they'd already covered this, but Henry needed to get it right in his own mind, so she humoured him. He was obviously nervous about the whole thing.

'You will be my dumping ground for temper tantrums and general irascibility.'

'That goes without saying.'

'But that goes for me too. It's a two-way street.'

She nodded.

'I would guess there are a few DCIs out there who might just feel they've had their nose put out of joint, to say the least, because I've been given this job, and maybe rightly so. So you need to know that if I ask you to do something and some of the – pardon this – *twats* you might come into contact with are downright rude and awkward, you will be acting with the full authorization of Rik

Dean, and if you get any shit whatsoever, refer them to him.' He took a breath. 'I have a feeling we'll be treading on some big toes here, but we have been given a job to do, and you know what I say to any of those twats?'

Daniels guessed. 'Fuck you?'

'Correct.'

Henry's phone rang. Rik Dean.

'Henry, how's it going up there?'

'OK. The scientific people are here now, as is the pathologist, although I actually haven't found him yet . . . I'm glad you rang. This is what I want to happen if you want to retain my services.'

'About that . . .'

Henry guffawed. He knew a grand a day for twenty days was really too good to be true.

'I've spoken to the chief and she's not happy, so it's three weeks – fifteen days – at a grand a day, subject to acceptable progress and reviews, then with an option for another five days. So you'd better bust your ass!'

'That new Land Rover's getting further and further away.'

'But you're still up for it?'

'There are dead people here, so yes. Always my motivation.'

'Good man.'

'Now let me tell you my conditions. I do not want to travel every day to a major incident room at some police station or other, so we run this side of the investigation from The Tawny Owl.'

'What? From licensed premises?' Dean was aghast. 'The chief won't allow that.'

'We can use the conference facilities in the annexe, make a couple of bedrooms into offices, bring in computer links – we've even got broadband in Kendleton now, you know, so IT shouldn't be a problem. Get a HOLMES operator out here,' Henry said, referring to the Home Office Large Major Enquiry System which was the standard computer system for murder enquiries. 'I'll put them up for free if necessary, and if there is any need to provide overnight accommodation for anyone' – he glanced at Daniels – 'it can be arranged.'

'You've really thought this through, haven't you?'

'Nope, all off the top of my head. It should be possible in this day and age, shouldn't it? And it makes some sort of sense. From what little I already know about the Yorks, a lot of our enquiries will probably be over the border in Yorkshire and beyond anyway, so we're extra close here.'

Rik Dean heaved a heavy, defeated sigh. 'I'll sort it.'

As he was talking, Henry had meandered into the garage, walking back and forth around the cars and generally looking around at nothing.

Henry then told Dean the authority he wanted Daniels to have, which was met by another heavy sigh and then agreement.

'The chief will flay me alive,' he moaned.

'Lie back and think of England,' Henry suggested, then ended the call. As he stood behind the line of the three cars, he rotated slowly and looked at the rear wall of the garage with narrowed, puzzled eyes.

Daniels, who had followed him, saw the look. 'What?'

Henry reached out and tapped the wall with a knuckle.

'Not sure, maybe nothing.'

Henry was no DIY enthusiast but he knew he was looking at a stud wall with a plasterboard sheathing held in place by socket-head screws with square tops. He tapped the wall again, this time with his ear up against it too. It made a hollow sound.

Henry had first searched a house for stolen property when he was a nineteen-year-old patrol constable. He had later attended a course where he was taught how to apply a bit of logic to searching anything from a person to a vehicle to a factory to a forest, and one early lesson he learned about searching buildings was to tap every wall: hollow walls needed to be investigated because sneaky miscreants often hid things in them.

It wasn't great detective work. It wasn't luck. It was just bog-standard coppering coupled with experience.

He moved outside the garage and walked around it, carefully scrutinizing everything.

Daniels watched him, knowing where he was coming from. She was an experienced searcher too and had once found two missing – abducted – kids in a wall space behind a wardrobe in the suspect's bedroom.

As she followed Henry, he was reeling off what he wanted for this investigation as well as surveying the garage structure.

'Fast-track action menu,' he said. 'You taking notes?'

She wasn't, but said she was, happily confident in her memory.

'Intelligence, scene forensics,' he rhymed off. 'Scene assessment, which we've started, victim enquiries, motives . . . media, because once they get hold of this, we'll be swamped by them.' He paused. 'Post-mortems, other critical actions . . . identify suspects . . . I could go on.'

He was now standing at the back corner of the garage, tilting his head as he looked along the rear and side walls, trying to weigh up measurements in his mind, comparing what he had seen inside to what he was seeing outside.

And what he was seeing, if he was right, was a very big space between the inner and outer walls. The proportions did not seem right.

Daniels sidled up to him. 'I know what you're thinking.'

Conrad Costain sat at the dining table in his static caravan as Tommy Costain and Brendan O'Hara heaved the holdalls crammed with money out of the back of the vehicle that had picked them up in Hornby earlier.

Their route to the travellers' site in Blackpool had been circuitous and discreet and without problems, but both Tommy and O'Hara were relieved to have landed back in what was essentially a fortress with escape routes. Not only did Conrad have his own personal way off the site, but tunnels had been dug under two other caravans in case cops or other unsavoury characters came calling.

Eventually, all the money was deposited.

Tommy sat opposite Conrad, the money between them. O'Hara lounged by the door next to Stan. Bronwen was outside, looking in.

The driver who'd brought the boys back from Hornby had left with instructions to take the car far away and destroy it.

Conrad leaned back, looked at the money, looked at Tommy and half smiled.

Tommy said, 'We did it, Gramps.'

Henry rummaged through a tool chest in one corner of the garage and found a set of Allen keys, then looked along the wall, seeing it was constructed from half a dozen plasterboard panels, each held in place by four screws, one in each corner.

He inserted an Allen key into the bottom right-hand corner of the panel closest to him, unfastened it, and did the same with the screw in the left corner. Next, he reached up and, keeping his left hand splayed out across the centre of the panel, he removed the two remaining screws.

As the panel fell naturally backwards, Henry allowed gravity to help him remove it and placed it to one side.

Beyond, a cavity was revealed, about a metre deep, all the way to the breeze block that lined the inside of the back wall.

It was empty.

Henry put his head into the space and attempted to look along the length of the wall, but each section was a sealed area and he could only see as far as the dividing panel. Each piece of plasterboard was essentially the lid on a large upright box, so each would have to be removed.

'What do you think?' he asked over his shoulder to Daniels who had been watching his DIY skills in action. 'All of them off?'

'Can't do any harm.'

'I've got at least ten names I can call myself,' Tommy Costain argued.

'But only one set of fingerprints, as you found out this weekend,' Conrad countered him. 'They have you on file, so if you get arrested again for something else, you won't be going anywhere and they'll nail two murders on you – one being a cop. We'll never be able to break you out again and you'll be so far down the hole you won't see the light of day, Tommy.'

'Then I'll just have to keep moving, keep a low profile, trust the community to cover for me – which they will! I still want to be involved, Gramps.'

'You will be. This' – Conrad swept a hand over the money – 'is just the start.'

Tommy punched the air, then turned to O'Hara, still lounging sullenly at the door.

'You got a face like someone slapped it real hard.'

'Unfinished business,' he said. 'Unfinished business for Cillian and me.'

Daniels took the Allen key out of Henry's fingers and began to remove the second panel just as Professor Baines, the Home Office pathologist, made his appearance. He'd been out of sight under the crime scene tent.

'Henry Christie, as I live and breathe,' Baines exclaimed. 'You're supposed to be retired, living in a pub and rogering the landlady. Your life should be bliss, so what in God's name are you doing here, sniffing around a brutal crime scene?'

'Morning to you, too, Professor.' Henry smiled at the man who always reminded him of a stick insect with FA Cup ears. They had known each other for more than thirty years and during this time Henry and Baines had developed a great professional/personal relationship and spent many occasions – usually after gruesome post-mortems – discussing violent, sudden deaths over a pint in a pub. Over the years Baines had become fascinated by Henry's rollercoaster love life which had captivated him as much as gunshot wounds and dental pathology, and as Henry looked at him, he saw Baines take a sly, knowing look at Daniels, then back at Henry with a double-lift of his sprouting eyebrows as he jumped to the wrong conclusion. Henry shook his head and said, 'Why I'm here is a long story and I'll tell you in a minute.'

'But they've brought you back into the field?' Baines persisted.

'Kind of.' Henry grinned. 'What can you tell me about the guy in the tent?'

'Injuries consistent with having been run over by a very heavy vehicle. A post-mortem will confirm it, obviously, but I'd say massive brain trauma, crushing and severe internal injuries.'

Henry nodded. 'I take it you've had a look at the bodies in the house?' Henry had walked up to Baines and turned away from Daniels who, being tall, could easily reach the screw heads at the top of the second panel.

'I have,' Baines confirmed. 'As well as the dismemberment, I'd guess that both individuals had been tortured prior to death. There are cigarette burns on the faces and arms, and from what I can see without moving them, they look like they've been beaten too.'

Henry took this in. Behind him, Daniels undid the last screw holding the second panel in place and then, keeping it steady, she let it fall back naturally from its upright position.

'Nothing of interest in here, boss,' she told Henry.

He turned and nodded, looking at the empty cavity.

'Boss?' Professor Baines mouthed.

'If the cap fits,' Henry said.

'Shall I carry on?' Daniels asked.

'Might as well.'

She rested the panel against the first one and began work on the third panel along.

Henry asked Baines, 'When can you do the post-mortems?'

'Well,' he said with a tut, 'the bodies are certainly stacking up. The police sergeant is my priority, then I'll have to do the young lad from the infirmary, then the two in the house here, then the lad in the tent. Altogether probably four days' non-stop work, so it will be the day after tomorrow.'

'Can you get someone else in to help?'

'It's a possibility, but these PMs need a top-class pathologist and, not to blow my own trumpet, I'm the top of the tree.'

'Well, you know what you're doing,' Henry agreed.

Daniels had managed to unscrew the third panel and was carefully removing it.

'Woah!' she said. 'Would you look at that?'

Conrad Costain supervised the counting of the money. Much of it was already in vacuum-packed blocks with the amounts written on the labels and he had no qualms about accepting the figures.

Bronwen had helped with the counting of all the loose notes which were tied up with elastic bands, and when she'd finished and added up all the figures, she declared, 'Two million, four hundred and ninety-two thousand pounds, six hundred thousand euros, and a quarter of a million dollars – plus some spare.'

Tommy had watched the process with a smile on his face. He would have helped, but arithmetic wasn't his strongest point.

'How much spare?' Conrad asked.

'Just over six hundred pounds.'

'OK, divide that up across the site. It's not much but it's a pint or two.'

Bronwen nodded.

Conrad said, 'I thought there would have been more . . .' He shrugged. 'Still, beggars and all that . . .'

The counting and calculating had all been done on Conrad's dining table. O'Hara hadn't even watched, sitting out front on the path, hunched over with his elbows on his knees, fingers interlocked, rocking back and forth with a very bleak, dangerous expression on his face.

Conrad came out and sat down next to him and leaned in close.

'You knew Cillian better than me – will they be able to identify him?'

O'Hara thought about this and said, 'Eventually, yes.'

'In that case, we should not claim his body back, because if we do, the police will then draw a line from him to us, which we should avoid,' Conrad said.

'Fuck that! He was my friend. We did stuff together.'

'I know, I know,' Conrad said calmly. 'That doesn't mean to say we don't get his body back, does it?'

The two exchanged a knowing look.

'The other thing we need to deal with – you need to deal with for yourself and for me – is the man who killed Cillian: Henry Christie, you tell me.'

O'Hara continued to look at Conrad.

'That is a name I never thought I would hear again. Although I don't know him personally, he is a man who needs to be in our sights. First because he can identify you and second because our proud family, the Costains, have a long, sordid history with that man.'

'How is that?'

'He used to be a cop and our family was always in his sights. It was his intention to bring us down and destroy us . . . he even succeeded in getting one of us killed.'

'Troy! I remember. I was only a kid . . .'

'He got away with it. He used him and then got him into a situation in which he died. Our honest, legal attempts to nail Christie failed, but he's always been on my back-burner – and now he's at the front of the barbecue.'

O'Hara's nostrils were dilating with increasing excitement as the old man spoke.

'So now, Brendan O'Hara, what I want you to do is this: bring back the body of Cillian Roche so we can bury him privately. Then bring me the body of Henry Christie so we can put him on a fire and listen to him scream as he burns. Failing that, just bring me his head and we will have one great game of football with it.'

* * *

Henry helped Daniels to lift and slide the panel off before looking into the wall cavity she had created.

Which was crammed with clear plastic vacuum packs of money all neatly arranged like another inner wall.

Henry carefully removed one of the money bricks, gently so the rest would not fall out – rather like playing millionaire's Jenga. The label indicated it contained £10,000 in Bank of England twenty-pound notes. Based on that, he stepped back and did a quick count.

'Thirty-five high by ten across in this section. What's that?' he asked Daniels expectantly. Her face contorted as she attempted to do the multiplication in her head and with her fingers.

'Three hundred and fifty blocks times ten thousand,' Baines cut in, saving the detectives a bit of grief. 'That's three and a half million – rough estimate.'

Both detectives were stunned.

'Three and a half million quid!' Daniels said.

Henry looked at the remaining panels. Three more to go.

The next cavity was similarly packed with money bricks.

'So we're up to seven million,' Henry said, 'plus whatever disappeared from the kitchen, which I reckon was a bit less than what is in one of these cavities.'

Two more panels remained.

Daniels went down on her haunches and began to loosen one of the bottom screws with the Allen key.

Henry's mobile phone rang. 'I'll just get this.'

He stepped out of the garage. Rik Dean was on the other end of the line.

'Chief's a bit reticent about setting up at The Tawny Owl, more from a logistical point of view than anything.'

'She can be as reticent as she wants,' Henry said. 'I've just discovered another seven million quid and I'm running it from the pub, tell her.'

'You've just discovered what?'

Henry's answer was interrupted by a shout from Daniels. Henry wasn't quite sure what she actually said, but it was something along the lines of 'Oh, fuck me! What the actual fuck? Jeez! Fuck, fuck, fuck.'

THIRTEEN

Still clutching his phone, Henry swerved back into the garage on hearing Daniels' profanities to find her and the professor staggering under the weight of the plasterboard panel she had been in the process of removing. As she removed the last screw, she'd had the palm of her free hand supporting the centre of the panel, just as with the others, so it didn't topple out. She had expected to lower this one away from the wall and stack it.

However, the crushing weight as it fell forwards took her completely by surprise.

As did the two trussed-up, cellophane-encased bodies that had been leaning against it, their combined weight being the reason why the panel fell out.

Baines had stepped across to assist. Henry was only moments behind as she struggled to keep the panel from injuring her.

Henry grabbed one side. Baines grabbed the opposite and between them they took the weight, allowing Daniels to duck out, reposition herself and take hold of the top of the panel which they lowered to the garage floor as the two bodies rolled away in opposite directions, coming to a stop, faces up.

Henry stepped back.

They were the naked bodies of two males individually wrapped in chicken wire, then cellophane, their heads encased in plastic bags, then wound with duct tape before being propped upright in the cavity.

Both looked to have catastrophic head wounds.

'I'll be honest,' Daniels gasped shakily, 'I wasn't expecting that.'

She shared a look with Henry who said, 'Nor me. You OK?'

She let out a very long breath and nodded. 'The house that just keeps on giving.'

Henry looked into the cavity and saw eight automatic pistols and two machine pistols, plus maybe a dozen boxes of nine-millimetre ammunition on the floor space, then he lowered himself on to his haunches – his knees cracking hollowly – and looked at the two bodies more closely.

'Two males,' Baines said over his shoulder. 'Late teens, early twenties, one white, the other black – both with terrible head wounds.' He bent down next to Henry, contorted his head to get a better view. 'They've each been shot by a large-calibre gun placed to their temples – I can see gunshot residue even from here – and the exit wounds are quite awful.'

'How long dead?' Henry asked.

'Hard to say until they're unwrapped and on slabs . . . but quite recent.'

Henry said to Daniels, 'Observations?'

'I think we've discovered a clearing house of sorts,' she speculated. 'Money counted and prepared for laundering; bodies prepared for disposal and maybe storage of weapons and ammunition.'

Henry could not disagree.

There had been a time when Henry Christie, because he was a career detective (other than those dark times when he'd been suspended or sidelined to run such departments as Special Projects or, as happened once, dumped back into uniform), could have reeled off verbatim most of the contents of the Murder Investigation Manual. Not because it was the be-all and end-all of investigating murders, but because it helped to keep minds focused and on track, and sometimes it was useful to have boxes to tick; and not least because he'd had some input into writing the 2006 version of the manual having found himself ditched for a fortnight of brain-dumping, workshops, blue-sky thinking and focus groups at Bramshill House, then the headquarters of Higher Police Training, set in the beautiful Hampshire countryside. It had been a turgid two weeks, offset by some serious drinking and flirting with an equally bored female detective from South Wales.

Henry knew there was always a temptation to run full tilt at crime scenes, especially ones like Hawkshead Farm, champing at the bit because you knew that somewhere out there were violent, dangerous offenders to be tracked down, doors to be kicked in, killers to be hauled out, but he knew those moments would have to wait. Even though he also knew that the 'Golden Hour', that critical period of time in any police investigation when time is of the essence, had long since passed.

Yes, he knew he had to get things rolling, get detectives out on the streets, get intelligence analysts digging into computer databases, and some of those things he did get underway.

But it had to be a case of first things first to keep a tight hold on the reins.

He had to keep things simmering until the scene had been properly taken care of, because, as he was fond of saying, 'You only get one chance at a crime scene,' and he had to implement a detailed, planned, professional approach, systematic and disciplined.

And it was hard – because he had forgotten a lot, and therefore he was running on adrenaline and hope for a while.

Throughout the day at Hawkshead Farm he kept in constant touch with Rik Dean, who was now based at Lancaster Police Station and had set up a Major Incident Room, as Lancashire Constabulary had suddenly been gifted one of the most complex multiple murder investigations they had ever faced.

The murders at Hawkshead Farm – of the Yorks and the two, as yet, unidentified males found in the wall cavity – the murder at the infirmary, followed by the brutal breakout and the murder of the custody sergeant, and then by the attempted murder of Henry and the disappearance of the large amount of cash . . . to Henry they all seemed to be connected to the grubby street murder committed by Tommy Costain in the early hours of Sunday morning.

It was all going to take a lot of unravelling, but when it started to run, Henry had a feeling it would be like pulling a loose thread on an old cardigan.

But the thing was, until that point was reached, the basics had to be done.

Which is why he stayed at the farm, directing operations with Daniels on one shoulder, Professor Baines on the other.

The very last thing done at the end of a long day was the removal of the bodies to the public mortuary at Royal Lancaster Infirmary, which meant, of course, five extra corpses, in addition to any bodies already there and any that might arrive from the hospital wards.

It was going to be cramped.

Henry knew the mortuary wasn't particularly large, so he had contacted the infirmary to open up the emergency morgue on site in a separate building in the grounds. It was a place used more than people knew – opened for serious multiple fatal accidents on the motorway, or once following a flu epidemic a couple of years earlier that knocked down a lot of older people like skittles. By the time the bodies from the farm were packed and ready to be moved, the emergency mortuary had been opened, the chiller fridges switched on ready, and there was plenty of room to store them.

In order to maintain the chain of evidence, Henry followed the grim convoy of undertakers' vehicles – one carrying the lad he had mown down, another with the two cavity-wall bodies on board and another with the jigsawed bodies of John and Isobel York.

The money and weapons found in the wall had been taken by armed police escort to headquarters. The guns would be stored in the safes in the firearms range, and the money was going to be transferred to a security firm for depositing in a bank vault in Preston – all the while followed by cops with guns so the drivers didn't get greedy fingers.

Just before getting into Daniels' Peugeot, Henry walked the scene once more to keep it clear in his mind and had a quick chat with the members of an Operational Support Unit serial – one sergeant, six PCs – who'd been tasked to keep the place locked down and secure overnight and prevent access to anyone, especially the media, who had been gathering at the gate, demanding answers and photographs. Henry had referred them to Rik Dean who would hold a press conference the next day in front of the cameras.

Finally, the morgue convoy set off, Daniels' car at the rear, following one of the most macabre processions ever.

It was a slow journey during which Henry became increasingly exhausted, fighting to keep his eyes open. It would have been very easy to nod off.

'I'll nip home for another change of clothes,' Daniels said. 'Once these bodies are locked away.'

'OK,' Henry said.

It seemed a very long time since they had been to Daniels' flat to pick up her first change of clothing.

The transfer of bodies into the mortuary went without a hitch using the combined efforts of the undertakers, cops and mortuary staff, after which Daniels drove down to St George's Quay, pulling into her allotted parking bay and groaning at the sight of a car she recognized parked on the quay itself.

'Shit.'

'What's the matter?'

She shook her head as though she was trying to rid her brain of weevils. 'That car.' She pointed to a silver Mazda.

'Ahh,' Henry said, understanding immediately, or so he thought. 'Want me to come up?'

'No, no, it's fine,' she said, then, 'Actually, yes, please. I think he might be a handful.'

'Do you want to brief me first or not?'

'Duh – bounced into a bad relationship with a married man who wants his cake,' Daniels said sadly. 'Slight problem – he's a uniformed inspector at Lancaster, Brian Uttley. And I just want it to go away. Don't want to hurt anyone like I got hurt.' She held up her left hand, the ring finger of which was devoid of jewellery. Henry had noticed this previously, but hadn't said anything, not his business. He remembered that when he'd worked with her in Yorkshire, she had been wearing an engagement ring.

'I recall the ring,' he said.

'Mmm.' It was a bitter 'Mmm', said with clasped lips. 'Short version – bad marriage, he cheated, twice, we split, acrimonious, but no kids, thank God. I rented places, got transferred up here, bought this flat. I'm virtually penniless, but things can only go up now, I guess. But, y'know, one lonely evening I bumped into Brian at a retirement do and the rest is history. Should never have got involved. So, look, Henry, I'm quite capable of chucking him out, but I'm just too knackered to get into a stupid tit-for-tat, and maybe your presence would be helpful.'

He followed her into the converted warehouse and up the lift to the top floor where they stepped out and she entered her apartment.

In which Brian Uttley lounged on the sofa, feet up on the coffee table and with what looked like a whisky in a glass in his hand.

Henry hovered in the hallway and Uttley did not clock him.

Daniels sighed heavily on seeing him and said, 'Brian, you

need to go. I haven't got time to argue about it, I'm busy and I need to get going – and I want my key back. This whole thing is one big mistake.'

'I don't think it is.' His expression turned baleful.

Daniels held out her hand. 'Key – and go.'

'But I love you.'

'You don't know the meaning of the word, Brian. I'm sorry, sorry we ever got involved, but you have a wife and family and I won't be second best in any relationship.'

He swigged back his drink and rocked forward.

'Please go. I'm tired. It's been a long day, so let's just end this.'

He moved quickly and accurately. In a tangle of limbs and a blur of speed, he was up on his feet and had Daniels pinned against the wall with his right hand squeezing her windpipe.

Before Henry could react, Uttley staggered back, clutching his balls before dropping with a sudden gasp on to one knee.

'You black bitch,' he growled through a shot of agony, then he saw Henry. 'Who's this old fuckwit? Your new shag?'

Daniels lurched sideways, rubbing her throat.

'I wish,' she snarled.

'I'm her minder, though she doesn't really need one.' Henry jerked up his thumb. 'Time to get going, Brian. And leave that key.'

'Sorry you had to see that,' Daniels said. 'Unsavoury.'

'Scratch the surface, find a racist.'

'I know! But I would have thought the "old fuckwit" reference would have wounded you more?'

'Not so much the "fuckwit"; it's the "old" bit,' Henry said. 'But at least you got your key off him, and if he's got any sense, he'll back off.'

The journey back to Kendleton had been more or less silent and a little brooding on Daniels' part. She had massaged her neck and used a karate-chop gesture to stop any conversation starting. She wanted to be alone with her thoughts for a while, and Henry got the message and closed his eyes. She only made the apology as she pulled on to The Tawny Owl car park.

'It would probably end his career – an affair with a black woman,' she smirked, seeming to get some of her humour back. 'Not the affair, but the black woman bit. And the fact he just pinned me to a wall.'

'Well, look, if it's any consolation . . .'

'Whoa!' She stopped him brusquely with a karate chop again. 'Not sure anything good will come at the end of that remark.'

They stared at each other, then broke into smiles.

'Let's eat,' Henry said.

Henry had pre-ordered food, and after they'd had a quick wash down and a change of clothing, they reconvened in the public dining room where they sat opposite each other and were served with a lamb shank each, beautiful meat that fell off the bone, melted in the mouth.

'That is to die for,' Daniels said, savouring the food, rolling her eyes with pleasure as she once more put her half-hearted vegetarianism to one side.

'Yeah, not bad. Local, too.'

'You've got a great place here, Henry,' she told him. Last time she had been here, picking him up to take him to Yorkshire to investigate the unsolved double murders, Henry's fiancée, Alison, had been alive and had been almost jealous that Henry was going away with another woman, albeit to investigate two murders.

'I'm sorry about Alison,' she said simply to him.

'Are we moving on to personal things now?'

'Only if you like.'

'Mm, OK . . . thank you for the sentiment,' he said. 'After Kate died, Alison was the best thing that ever happened to me.' He shrugged. 'Corny line, I know, but true. The best lady I could have ever met and she didn't deserve to die, certainly not in the way she did at the hands of a psychopathic ex.' He almost added, 'But I did get some payback,' but decided not to. 'So, you – engagement, shit marriage, divorce . . . affairs,' he concluded enigmatically.

'Life's rich pageant.' She grinned.

'So, are we up to date now?'

'You know you're a really nice man, Henry?'

He guffawed. 'In spite of my gambling, drinking, smoking, drug taking, whoring and addiction to pornography?' he joked.

'In spite of all of them.'

'You're making me blush.'

'It's true, though . . . Dunno, something about you.'

He shifted uncomfortably, grabbed his beer and took a large sip. 'Let me put you right, OK? I'm a bloke who is probably thirty years older than you . . .'

'Twenty-five,' she corrected him.

'Twenty-five . . . Yet I still harbour red-blooded feelings, so don't ever forget that.' He gave her his best, piercing lustful stare. 'But when I say red-blooded feelings, they need to be supported by a blue tablet, if you know what I mean? I have a supply because I can now get them free on prescription, although I have never yet tried one.'

Daniels grinned. 'Not even with Maude?'

Henry lifted his beer. 'Cheers.'

After the meal they went into the private accommodation and sat next to each other on the sofa. Although they were both struggling to stay awake, Daniels used Henry's laptop balanced on her thighs to log into Lancashire Constabulary's database where numerous messages awaited her.

The first she accessed was from Rik Dean which contained a link to a mugshot file in which Dean had culled more than thirty photographs of young men matching the e-fit pictures Henry had put together with the police artist. It was clever stuff, but Henry could not see any who looked like either of the two killers as he peered at the screen while Daniels tabbed through.

'How about searching for photos of youngsters just linked to the travelling community? Males between the age of seventeen and twenty-four, say, who've been arrested for violence or drug offences in the last two years? As a start.'

'Could do, but I think we'd be swamped.'

'In that case narrow it down to very violent offences and also look at travellers who have been arrested, bailed and then failed to turn up to court.'

She looked at him quizzically.

'Just thinking out loud,' he said.

She nodded, stifled a yawn and began tapping away on the laptop, entering some of the parameters Henry had suggested in a search on the National Crime Database, which included offenders at large and bail-jumpers. She pressed 'send' and leaned back. 'This could take some time.'

Henry sat back too, horribly aware of Daniels' presence in such close proximity.

To stop any inappropriate thoughts, he said, 'Three general things at play here: the Yorks and what they were up to, then their deaths and the Costains. Obviously, there is a link, but I think that their deaths were probably . . .' His words drifted off as he tried to marshal his train of thought.

Daniels offered, picking up on it, 'Probably planned, but at the same time opportunistic? Not part of the same thing?'

Henry sat forward eagerly. 'Yeah, yeah . . . if the Yorks are a clearing bank, say, for some big-time crims who use them to launder money and bury the dead, and the Costains lucked into that and decided, as the Costains might, to empty the vaults and also make a profound statement – i.e., scare people shitless with their violence – and do other stuff in Lancaster linked to a turf war, it strikes me that they are up to something we, the cops, aren't aware of yet. And the fact that Tommy was broken out of police cells means – and I know this sounds basic – that we have to ruthlessly track this man down, as well as the other two guys who were cheeky enough to vape in my pub – well, the remaining one.'

Henry looked excitedly at Daniels who, he saw, was struggling to keep her eyes open.

His mobile phone rang: Rik Dean.

The two spent about twenty minutes talking through the possible ways forward and, despite himself, Henry offered to have an early meet-up at Lancaster nick with a few other key detectives now on board to plan strategy. Henry was beginning to think the whole thing was too big to run from Th'Owl and he might have to concede defeat on that point, much to his chagrin. He had sort of envisaged a Poirot-like denouement in the lounge of the pub, surrounded by suspects and finally turning dramatically to unmask the murderer.

He hung up.

Daniels had continued her computer search but had listened to the conversation. 'Seven o'clock, eh?'

Henry nodded. 'Better earn my dosh.'

They both looked simultaneously at the wall clock: ten thirty.

'Night cap? In the bar? My shout?' Henry suggested. 'I should probably show my face and let Maude know where we're up to with the Yorks. She can cross them off the call-round list.'

'Sounds good.'

They went into the busy bar. Many of the locals clustered around Henry, wanting to have the lowdown on the murders, and were disappointed when Henry told them his lips were sealed.

Maude, it transpired, had gone home and left a note at the bar to say she would be back in the morning. The Post-it note on which Henry had scribbled the registration number of the Dodge Ram was also still behind the bar. He showed it to Daniels.

'See, told you,' he said triumphantly.

They took a whisky each outside on to the patio. Just the one was enough as both felt the day spent on their feet had taken its toll.

They walked back into the accommodation, said a quick good-night and went into their respective rooms.

Henry perched on the edge of his king-size bed and the energy drained out of him like a spirit leaving a body. He flipped off his trainers, chucked his clothes into a heap and slid naked under the quilt. He still slept on 'his' side of the bed, still missed Alison with a terrible anguish within him which he could only just now control.

He thought briefly about Daniels, knowing he liked her a lot, but only as a friend now. Anything else would have been inappropriate.

He fell asleep with images of mutilated dead bodies swimming around his cranium, but he knew he would not have nightmares over them. Those days had long gone.

In the bedroom further down the hallway, in her cropped pyjamas, Daniels lay awake for a while reviewing the day and also thinking about Henry, whom she liked probably too much. And then, as she began the drift into the vortex of sleepy images, she thought about being crushed by two dead bodies falling on top of her and knew the nightmares would come.

In fact, Daniels woke from a deep, dreamless sleep, without having had one nightmare.

She was not sure why she woke.

She could have said a noise, a creak, a footfall.

But that would not have been the truth. This was only the second night she had spent at The Tawny Owl but she had already learned that this section of the premises, the old part, did nothing but make creaking and groaning noises. She guessed it was like being on an old schooner. It had its own life and she understood that. The floorboards and timbers made groaning noises as they contracted and expanded with heat and cold. The old heating pipes sounded as if someone was playing them with a spoon. They were all noises to get used to, part of the fabric of the building, part of its charm.

Which made her realize that what had caused her to snap awake was a feeling. A shiver down her spine because there was some other kind of presence here.

She did not know if the place was supposed to be haunted.

Perhaps it was, but Henry had never mentioned ghosts.

Up to that point, Daniels had kept her eyes firmly closed – but now she opened them.

The room was in darkness, but under the door she could see light from the hallway outside.

She propped herself up.

A shadow flitted past: someone walking down the hall.

Daniels tapped the Fitbit she wore on her right wrist in lieu of a watch: two forty-nine.

It was maybe not surprising someone was up and about in a place like this. The bar would have stayed open until well after eleven; she wasn't sure if there were guests in any of the rooms above her. She half remembered Henry telling her he'd cancelled all bookings because of the moorland fires.

However, someone knocking around probably wasn't unusual.

Ginny slept in the room next door with her boyfriend. It was possible they were just going to bed.

Then she tightened up as the shadow came back under her door and stopped. And did not move.

Daniels swallowed, swung her legs out and sat up quietly.

The shadow was still there.

Her nostrils flared. She swallowed.

Someone was standing outside her door at almost three in the morning.

The handle started to turn very slowly.

Let it turn, she thought. The door was bolted from the inside.

She exhaled a slow, dithery breath.

The handle stopped turning. The shadow moved away.

Could it have been Henry? Creeping about in the night, wanting to try his luck? Surely not. For one thing, he didn't have to creep. She realized that he could have crooked his finger and she would have gone running to him, despite the age difference and what others may have thought.

But Henry would not be creeping about like the Midnight Rambler. Not his style.

She stood up and padded softly, barefoot, to the door and pressed her ear to it. Nothing, though she felt the chill of a draught on her toes, which was strange, as if an outer door had been opened. Slowly, she drew back the bolt which, unlike everything else in this place, was silent. She couldn't remember if her door creaked on its hinges so she twisted the handle and gently pulled it open a fraction of an inch.

She put an eye to the gap which gave her a view along the hallway towards the fire escape at the far end. The lounge door was opposite and the door to Henry's bedroom a little further down.

Outside Henry's door, with his left hand curled around the door handle, was a man in a black hoodie, jogging bottoms and trainers. He held a long-bladed knife in his right hand alongside his thigh.

Daniels saw all this in one microsecond as the man went into Henry's bedroom.

It was probably an age thing. Henry was exhausted, but his slumber was fitful and loo visits frequent, so he was not resting particularly well, even though he was desperate to sleep.

Following his latest loo call, he had returned to a very dishevelled bed and had managed to purge his mind of everything. It seemed to have worked. Sleep arrived.

Until the scream.

Loud, piercing.

His eyes shot open to see a knife blade slicing down towards his head.

The oldest instinct – survival – kicked in. He rolled to one side just as the knife would have imbedded itself in his eye socket. He moved with such momentum that he dropped off the side of the bed, hit the floor and kept rolling, but by doing so wrapped himself unintentionally in the folds of the quilt. He started to desperately kick himself free and scrambled to his feet to see two figures fighting in the half light.

Daniels had grabbed the intruder from behind as the point of the knife impaled Henry's pillow, cutting through the memory foam. The man had reacted with terrible violence, bucking, kicking, trying to spin and stab the blade into Daniels' chest. She fought back like a maniac, twisting and contorting to avoid the blows and hoping to fuck that Henry would wade back into the fray.

The hooded man threw her off and, as she teetered backwards, came at her with the knife raised, then descending. Daniels saw that he was wearing a mask shaped like a demon's head under the hood.

She screamed as Henry powered in, hurling himself across the bed and launching himself into the intruder, bringing him down to his knees and shouting into his ear. The knife dropped from the man's grip, but he managed to do a backswing with his right hand, catching Henry on his jaw with a lot of force, knocking him sideways. The backs of Henry's knees hit the bed and his legs gave way as the man, still fighting, kicked out at Daniels, then scooped up the knife, turned for the door and was gone.

Henry got to his feet, intending to give chase, but Daniels shouted, 'Get something on! I'll go after him.'

'Everything was locked up,' Ginny promised him sincerely. 'Alarms set, all the toilets checked. We do it every night without fail.'

Having been woken by the commotion, Ginny and her boyfriend, Fred, came to their bedroom door just in time to see Daniels sprinting down the hallway to the fire exit, chasing the dark shape ahead of her.

Henry, now decent, looked at the splintered door and surrounding frame of the fire exit, which should have set the alarm off when opened.

'I know you do. He must have fixed the alarm somehow,' he said, inspecting the jemmy marks in the wood. He glanced at

Daniels who looked ill. 'Are you all right?' Henry hadn't noticed, but her right hand was clamped across her left forearm and blood seeped through her fingers. 'Hell, Diane!' he said as she slowly removed her hand to reveal the slash wound across the muscle.

'He caught me with it.'

Henry took her injured arm and raised it tenderly.

'It doesn't look too bad,' she said, even though it was obviously hurting her.

'Bad enough.' Henry said. He looked at Ginny and her very ashen-faced boyfriend behind her. 'You think you can try and turn out Dr Lott?' He was referring to the local GP and Owl regular. 'If he gets arsey, tell him he owes me and his tab will be called in.'

'No, no, it's fine,' Daniels insisted. 'I'll clean it up and put plasters across to pull it together. I'll see the doctor in the morning.'

Henry was still carefully inspecting the wound, holding her arm gently. It wasn't a deep cut, just a slice, and it was obvious the blade had been phenomenally sharp. She had been lucky. It could have half sliced her arm off. He'd been lucky, too. His head could have been skewered to his expensive pillow.

Henry let go of Daniels' arm, then closed the fire door and did something that would have caused palpitations to a Health and Safety inspector: he bolted the door. 'Ginny, Fred, are you guys all right?' They nodded, but they were as pale as newly washed bedding. Henry shooed them back to their bedroom. He ushered Daniels into his bedroom and sat her down on the edge of the bed.

She saw the pillow. So did he.

'Blimey,' he said, imagining his head there. He went into his en suite and came back a couple of moments later with a small first-aid kit. He took out some antiseptic wipes and began dabbing Daniels' wound.

As he concentrated on the task, she watched him.

'You saved my life,' Henry said without looking up. 'By screaming.'

'You saved mine too – by naked diving.'

'Um, yeah, sorry about that.'

'I'm glad you didn't stop to pull some pants on,' Daniels said. 'Do you think you've been targeted because the suspects know you saw them and because you killed one of them?'

'That would be my first conclusion.'

He dabbed the wound delicately with some tissue, then carefully stretched two plasters across it to draw the edges together. 'I reckon that will do for the time being.' His face was level with hers, just inches separating them.

'Thank you,' she said.

They stayed that way for a moment longer until two things happened simultaneously to make them jump apart and stop the foolishness.

Daniels' Fitbit buzzed to tell her she had completed her steps for the day and the front doorbell rang.

'Jake Niven,' Henry said.

Although Henry knew he should have phoned 999, he also knew that to get any cops to Kendleton, despite the violent nature of the attack, would take forever. So he'd called Jake Niven on his mobile, knowing that he slept with it at his bedside, and he had responded as quickly as it had been humanly possible to do so, landing at The Tawny Owl about ten minutes after the call, even though he was half dressed and half asleep.

Henry had to admit he was relieved to see the local cop.

Intruders and assaults in the middle of the night were things much younger people could deal with, mentally and physically, and Henry had to admit he was feeling a bit jittery.

Niven did a search of the pub and grounds and found nothing, but promised he would do it again later when the sun rose properly; in the meantime, he would keep a watch on the premises.

Henry returned to his bedroom. He looked at his sliced-open pillow again, went into the en suite, knelt down by the toilet, pushed up the seat, dropped his head into the bowl and was sick.

As good as his word, Jake Niven settled into his Land Rover outside Th'Owl. Henry had told him it wasn't necessary, but he felt better with Jake on guard and, as a result, managed to get back to sleep for a couple of hours and awoke feeling relatively refreshed. He showered, dressed and then made his way to the kitchen where the morning chef was already getting the snacks prepared for the imminent arrival of that day's fire service shift.

Henry snaffled a couple of bacon sandwiches and two mugs of

coffee and took them out to Niven who was slumped uncomfortably in the front of the police car with his legs spread across the seats. At first Henry thought he was asleep, but Niven had spotted Henry approaching in the side mirror, sat up and opened the door.

'Sustenance and thanks,' Henry said, handing the food and drink over, gratefully accepted.

The air was still clear this morning but against the distant rising sun there was a haze. The work of the firefighters was going to continue.

Henry and Niven munched and drank contentedly for a while, feeling as though peace had returned to the village, which was slightly shattered when Niven said, 'Apparently, the fire dudes had a few heart-fluttering hours yesterday. The wind caught the flames up on Lune Fell' – he gestured with his mug – 'and next thing they know they're chasing flames towards the village. Only another change in wind direction saved everyone from being evacuated.'

That was always going to be an issue, Henry knew.

Niven went on, 'If we're not careful, or lucky, we might end up with forest fires like they have in California.'

'Malibu Beach.'

'Without the beach bit.' Niven grinned. 'Anyway, they've dug out a few temporary firebreaks on the other side of the woods, which should work; there's talk they need more digging, but let's hope it doesn't come to that.' Niven munched as he spoke. 'How are you feeling?'

'Surprisingly OK. Happy to be alive, as is Diane.'

'She did good. Do we need to get her arm looked at?'

'Dr Lott will sort it and I'll get the CSI to call in on the way up to the Yorks' place to photograph the wound and have a quick look around, though I doubt there will be much to find.'

'Do you reckon the guy who paid you the visit is one of the killers? The one you didn't run over?'

'Oddly, no,' Henry said. 'Different type of weapon, different mask, different clothing . . .'

'Someone else out to get you, then?'

Henry shrugged. 'Who knows?'

'Anyway,' Niven said, changing the subject, and gave Henry a meaningful stare. 'You two?' He raised his eyebrows in a nudge-nudge suggestive way. 'You and Ms Daniels? Yes or no? She is very attractive.'

Henry said a blunt, 'No.'

'Phew . . . thank goodness, because the thought was making me nauseous.'

Henry took a stroll around the grounds to see if he could spot any traces left by the intruder. Finally, he reached the fire door by which the offender had entered and then escaped without triggering the alarm. Henry found that worrying. The guy had used quietly applied brute force to open the door with a jemmy or screwdriver but hadn't set any alarm bells ringing. Henry re-inspected the door, now unlocked, then stepped inside so he was in the hallway of the owner's accommodation where the alarm panel was situated.

Daniels came out from her room and joined him, looking at the panel which controlled every external alarm point in that section of the premises.

'You can get cheap and fiendish things to override alarm systems now,' she told him. 'Shut 'em down, enter buildings, do what has to be done, leave, reset. He must have had some device like that.'

'Doesn't help that this system is out of the Ark,' Henry said glumly.

'You're right. It does need a serious upgrade. You've got to keep one step ahead of the opposition.'

'Thanks for that. What happened to the good old days when Billy Burglar just put expanding foam into the alarm boxes? I always thought that was pretty ingenious.'

'As you say, old days.'

Henry looked at her to see if she was taking the piss out of him. She was and she smirked at him. 'How's the arm?'

'Sore.'

'Our friendly neighbourhood drunken doctor said he'll come and see you before surgery, but be careful with him. There's every chance he might amputate it by mistake.'

'I'll watch out for the bone saw.'

They walked back into the pub to get some food for Daniels, then went to sit in the wide bay window of the dining room.

'Normally, we'd be full at this time of year. Walkers, holiday makers, people passing through,' Henry said, gazing at the empty tables. 'We'll weather it, though. I'm already getting a lot of enquiries for autumn, so filling up nicely, and there's a lot of local goodwill invested in the place – most of it from when Alison was here. We inherited quite a legacy,' he said wistfully. 'Just hope she thinks we're doing her proud.'

'I'd say she does.'

'Hey, did you know I'm a trained barista now?'

'Barrister?'

'No, coffee maker . . . bareeesta,' he said, accentuating the Italian.

'Your skills are astounding.'

As they sat there, Henry spotted Maude making her way across the village green for her day's stint as volunteer coordinator. He watched her progress, knowing that Daniels was eyeing him with a cheeky smirk.

Henry shook his head, rose and left Daniels to her breakfast. He went to meet Maude on the front steps, where he told her what he could about the previous night's incident in the pub. As he spoke, her face grew increasingly shocked until eventually she just had to throw her arms around him for a big hug.

Daniels saw Henry stiffen uncomfortably, and also saw Maude's face of bliss as she enjoyed the squeeze just a little too much.

Henry disengaged himself and Maude trotted into Th'Owl with a crooked smile of lust quivering on her lips.

Daniels chuckled to herself. *Poor Henry*, she thought.

Also watching was Jake Niven, still stationed in his Land Rover, who laughed uproariously at Henry's predicament and discomfort.

Henry looked over his shoulder at Daniels' face in the bay window, then looked at Niven and gave him a less than discreet middle finger just as his mobile phone rang, which he answered while still staring daggers at Niven.

From her position, Daniels saw Henry stiffen again as he spoke into the phone. As he was still conversing, he turned and hurried back into Th'Owl, gesticulating to Daniels who picked up that something was amiss.

Just as he finished the call, he stepped into the foyer where they met up.

'Problem?' Daniels asked.

He waggled his phone. 'Rik Dean. One of the bodies has been snatched from the mortuary.'

FOURTEEN

Rik Dean had established the Major Incident Room at Lancaster Police Station in what, years before, had been the gymnasium on the top floor. That had been closed down by budget cuts and space issues – but mainly budget cuts. Gyms were a luxury and the whole social and welfare side of being a cop was on the wane through lack of funds.

Dean, Henry Christie and Diane Daniels plus a DCI Henry did not know were bunched around a desk in one corner of the MIR. A laptop was being fed images from the security camera which covered the entrances to the emergency mortuary at the infirmary. The screen was split into two, half showing the front entrance, half the rear – the entrance where bodies were brought in or taken out by vehicle.

They watched – riveted – as two men wearing hoodies bent at the front door with their backs to the lens. It wasn't quite possible to see what they were actually doing, although it was obvious they were engaged in forcing the door open. After a few seconds of concentrated work, the door shot open and the men entered the mortuary, closing the door behind them.

Henry clocked the digital time imprint: 02:05.

Rik Dean fast-forwarded the streamed images to 02:15.

On the right-hand side of the laptop screen the shutter door at the back of the mortuary started to rise.

'Do they have security patrols at the hospital?' Henry asked contemptuously.

'They do, but they'd all been called to the A and E department which was kicking off with some drunken yobs,' Dean explained.

'Diversion?'

'Coincidence,' Dean countered.

'No such thing.'

'We're looking into it anyway.'

Their focus returned to the CCTV images as the shutter door rose and a dark-coloured Transit-type van, the number plate obscured by tape, reversed up, but not quite close enough or at the right angle for the camera to get a good shot of the driver.

'At least three of them,' Dean said.

The next thing was a body bag on a gurney being wheeled out to the back of the van by the two front-door intruders. The van doors were opened, the gurney pushed up to the opening, and between them, one on each side, the men heaved the body bag across the gap into the van, dragged the gurney away and slammed the doors.

Both ran down the nearside of the van and out of sight of the camera, and a moment later the van drove away, leaving the gurney abandoned at an angle across the threshold, the two men presumably having jumped into the van on the passenger side.

The image then flickered to a new one – the view of the infirmary exit through which the van left. The camera was pointing directly at the front of the van and showed three figures sitting side by side across the bench seat. The one on the passenger side leaned forward, looked up at the camera and gave it several energetic V-signs.

The front number plate was also obscured by tape.

Dean rewound slightly, then paused the image of the guy flashing the V-signs. The face was looking up at the camera from underneath the peak of a hoodie and did not appear to be wearing a mask or covering his face at all – until Dean zoomed in and enlarged the image which, though it became grainier, confirmed he was wearing a tight-fitting latex-type mask.

'Like the ones used at the infirmary killing and here at the police station,' Dean said.

'But not like the one worn by the guy who tried to stab me and slashed Diane's arm a few hours ago,' Henry pointed out soberingly. Now that really was a worry for him, because perhaps it did mean that someone else had him in their sights.

'Doesn't mean to say it wasn't one of this lot, though,' Dean pointed out.

Henry accepted that, then said, 'And the body of the young man I ran down has been stolen and we still don't know who he is.'

'We have his blood, DNA, fingerprints and a photograph of his face, albeit somewhat distorted. We'll nail him, I'm sure.'

Henry blew out his cheeks. 'Why have they done this?'

'Probably to keep him from being identified, and then, by association, identifying the other killer.'

'Even though we know who Tommy Costain is?' Henry said.

'Could be a family thing,' Daniels suggested.

'How do you mean?' Dean asked.

She collected her thoughts. 'Say the lad isn't in our system – admittedly, that's unlikely – but if he isn't and we can't ID him, then if he was claimed by relatives, that would mean we *would* identify him. And then we would start to scrutinize them, harass them probably, because he's been involved in very violent crimes and we want to know who committed them and bring the offenders to justice. Who knows what we would uncover and how far this could all go? The family would therefore prefer to get the body back so they can pay their respects without us looking at them, and their lifestyle is such that they can do this, then dispose of him in any way they want without us finding out.'

Henry watched her talk, working through her hypothesis, more than impressed.

'Yeah, we know Tommy Costain, but he can disappear into their community too, especially if some of it is an organized crime group, say. He can live a normal life on their terms and we might never find him – or we might get lucky. Who knows? But travellers who want to stay off grid are notoriously hard to lock up, and even if we do find Tommy, he'll say nothing, not a damn thing.'

Dean looked at Henry, looked at the DCI, looked at Daniels again and said, 'How do we take this forward then, bearing in mind none of what we've just discussed even touches on the Yorks, which in itself is mega.'

To Henry, Dean still seemed overawed by the enormity of the task, maybe one of the biggest multiple murder investigations Lancashire had ever tackled.

'At the risk of repeating myself,' Henry said, 'I think the best way to prise open this can of worms is through Tommy Costain and the Costain family. I think we should throw all initial resources at him: he killed a drug dealer, he was sprung from custody – yeah, he killed the custody sergeant, but I think that was just a sideline for him, an opportunity not to be missed. Another drug dealer was finished off at the infirmary by the guys who killed the Yorks, and then all three rolled back to Hawkshead Farm to pick up the money they'd forgotten, or whatever.

'Tommy is the key – and if we don't move fast on him, he'll be gone in the wind,' Henry concluded.

'What about this morning's incident – you being attacked?' Dean asked.

'I don't know about that. Maybe it was one of these guys, maybe not . . . but whatever, it's unfinished business because – ta da! – I'm still here. Let's just concentrate on Tommy Costain.'

Daniels picked up the M6 from the Lancaster north junction, turning south and easing up to a comfortable seventy-five miles per hour and sticking to it. Henry lounged beside her, making himself comfortable for the journey which would take about forty minutes.

This was a route he had travelled many times over the last few years, though not too often recently.

After his wife had died and he subsequently fell into the relationship with Alison, he did a lot of commuting between his home in Blackpool and The Tawny Owl, eventually selling the house and moving to Kendleton in the latter stages of his career. It made sense, even if the village was out on a limb, but he'd grown to dislike spending time in a lonely house with vivid memories, and though it was a long way to work and back, the effort of returning to Alison each night was worth the hassle.

He smiled at those memories as he settled himself in the seat. A sideways glance from Daniels caught his grin.

'What?' she said.

'Wish I'd had a quid for every time I'd travelled this highway.' He went on to explain the logistics to Daniels who listened with a pleasant smile on her face.

'Kate and Alison were very special ladies from the sounds of it.'

'They were. I was lucky and probably didn't deserve them. Kate stuck with me through thick and thin – I met her at the scene of a murder, y'know? Love at first sight and all that . . . I treated her appallingly, yet somehow we made it through and I'll always be grateful to her. And we have two lovely daughters.' He blinked. 'Then, just as everything got ironed out between us, cancer got her and took her away so effin' quickly,' he said bitterly. 'The blink of an eye.'

'I'm sorry.'

'Then Alison. Couldn't believe my luck and I decided from the outset not to be an arse with her . . .'

Daniels said nothing as they passed the church spire in the picturesque village of Scorton alongside the motorway.

Henry kept looking out of the window, consumed by his memories, until a few minutes later when they left the M6 and filtered on to the west-bound M55. Not long after, Henry caught his first glimpse in a while of the Blackpool Tower on the edge of the flat horizon to the west.

'It's just as I remember it,' Henry said, mock-fondly, but cringing inside.

They had reached Blackpool – a place Daniels had, of course, visited, but never worked in. Henry directed her from Marton Circle at the end of the motorway on to Preston New Road towards central Blackpool, but then told her to hang a left on to Shoreside estate. As she followed his directions, Henry noticed with a chuckle that Shoreside had been rebranded 'Beacon View'. He assumed that 'Beacon' referred to Beacon Fell near Longridge, some twenty-odd miles inland and certainly not within view of the estate, other than on a very long ladder.

A sign proudly declared, *Welcome to Beacon View – a community for the people, by the people*. It was peppered with lead shot and obscene graffiti.

Henry had done much of his policing in Blackpool and therefore on the council estates within its boundaries. There were a few standout ones but, on the whole, Shoreside, now Beacon View, was the one he visited most frequently.

It had always been a poor, underfunded, lawless estate, having been allowed to decline from the 1970s with no real hope of rescue. Money had been chucked at it occasionally, usually to build children's play areas, but each one had been systematically demolished by uncontrollable youths. Council houses had been abandoned, trashed, then knocked down. A row of shops had been brought down brick by brick, with the exception of the end shop – a grocer/newsagent that survived only because its proprietor handled stolen goods. Finally, he'd succumbed to a turf war and was driven off the estate and the shop destroyed.

The council hadn't bothered to try to build others.

And the main catalyst for this decline was a certain family who lived in a large house on the estate, which had previously been a pair of semis, bought and knocked together – initially, without planning permission – to form one big house, six bedrooms, four bathrooms, two lounges, two dining rooms and a garage either side.

When the man from the council planning department had turned up with his clipboard to declare that there had been no planning consent and the houses would have to be separated again, he was tarred and feathered and chained to a lamppost. The council never visited again, and the police failed to get a prosecution. Planning permission was granted retrospectively.

This family controlled the estate and made good, law-abiding citizens cower in submission. They ran drug dealing and the fencing of stolen goods (a business wrested from the grubby hands of that shopkeeper). They intimidated and beat up people who complained about them, made their lives a misery.

'The Costains,' Henry said. 'Let's just cruise around and get a feel for how the newly named Shoreside has helped change people's lives for the better. Or not.'

Daniels drove slowly around the estate, hardly believing what she was seeing – the deprivation, the despair.

'I've seen some rough holes in my time,' she said, shaking her head.

'Blackpool all over,' Henry said. 'Some ultra-wealthy pockets rubbing shoulders with some of the poorest areas in the UK. Not sure what the answer is.'

Groups of teenagers were gathered on some street corners, watching the car with deep suspicion as it crawled past.

'They know we're cops,' Daniels said. 'We might as well have a sign on.' She turned right into one avenue on which all the houses were boarded up. A couple of young lads eyed them venomously and middle-fingered the car. One put a mobile phone to his ear and made a call.

Henry twisted to look over his shoulder to keep the two in view through the rear window. The lads stepped into the middle of the road, one still on the phone. Henry turned back to face front.

'Don't like that,' he mumbled.

'Look-outs?'

'Probably. Next left here,' he instructed her.

This was the avenue on which the Costain household was located.

Henry had witnessed the house go through several phases – from being the original pair of semis to becoming one big detached. He'd entered it on numerous occasions for various reasons, and he and the Costains had developed a healthy disrespect for each other verging on hatred – but he'd never been intimidated by them. He'd been frightened occasionally, but that had never stopped him doing his job.

It was a long time since he'd had dealings with them and, of course, he was no longer a cop with the authority that carried, so he had no intention of going bowling in . . . not just yet, anyway.

As the car got closer to the house, his heartbeat rose a tad and a bitter taste came into his mouth: a drip of adrenaline.

'The one on the right,' he pointed.

'It's a bloody fortress,' she said.

Six-foot-high fencing surrounded the house – just normal, substantial wooden garden fencing slotted between concrete posts, enough to deter nosy people or cops. When Henry had last been here, there was no such fencing, just a grotty, litter-strewn front garden. Now the house hid behind the fence with just one entrance through a six-foot-high mesh gate up to the front door and gates either side servicing the garages. A scrambler-type motorcycle was propped up outside.

'Yep, security's tight.' Henry saw a couple of cameras fitted below the eaves.

As the Peugeot crawled past, the front gate opened and two white youths, maybe late teens, stepped out and watched it. They were hard-faced lads, tightly shorn hair, and looked as if they worked out. They held up their phones and took photos.

'Bloody hell, they're on edge,' Daniels said.

'So they should be – then again, they always are. When you get to the end, loop back around. Might have a word.'

'You crazy? They'll eat you for dinner.'

'Trust me, I don't taste nice, although,' he added with a brazen double meaning, 'that is a matter of opinion.'

Daniels rolled her eyes. 'Oh, please.' She swung the car around and drove back along the avenue, putting Henry on the nearside and closest to the house and youths who, in the short space of time it had taken her to turn, had doubled to four little gents.

'I might ask if I can speak to Tommy.'

'Won't that alert them? Oh, forget I said that. I guess he'll know we're after him and this might be one of the places we'd come to.' She pulled in.

'You might want to keep the engine ticking over,' Henry suggested.

'Just what the hell are you doing, Henry? This is not a game.'

'Poking a hornets' nest with a shitty stick, probably. Here goes.'

Henry climbed out and walked across to the gathering youths – a couple more had arrived – giving them an affable wave and a cheery grin.

The phone cameras continued to click away, something Henry had not really experienced before, and it made him uncomfortable and slightly unsettled as he wondered if his brutal death at the kicking feet of a gang of lads would be posted on social media and go viral.

There was one lad who wasn't taking photos, though, who seemed to be the leader. He stood with his hands on his hips, looking down his nose at Henry.

'Hi, folks,' Henry said, using inclusive terminology because one of them was female. He addressed the one he assumed was the leader, gave a jerk of the thumb to indicate Daniels in the car. 'I know you've already ID'd us as cops, so that's DC Daniels and I'm Henry Christie.'

In the past he might have flashed his warrant card to underline his authority, but now he hoped that having nothing more than a Nectar card would not prove to be an issue.

The lad shrugged. On the tilt of his face Henry caught a glimpse of the look of Troy Costain, Henry's informant who had met an unfortunate end. Surely this could not be his son, Henry wondered, but didn't have time to do the maths with the dates.

'You're on dangerous ground here, old fella,' the lad warned Henry.

'Why would that be?'

'Pokin' yer nose in where it ain't wanted. Could end up bein' smashed flat.'

Henry gave him a reassuring smile. 'I haven't come for any trouble.' He was feeling slightly wobbly, though, and the 'old fella' jibe had got to him again, even though he knew it shouldn't have done. 'OK, fine, I get that . . . Any chance of you telling me your name? Just so we both know who we're talking to.'

'Not a chance in hell.'

'OK, fine,' he said again. 'I'll just say a couple of things, then I'll be off. First, don't forget who I am: Henry Christie. I have a long history with the family who live here and I've no doubt that some of the older members will have heard of me. Second, I need to speak to Tommy Costain. Urgently. He needs to contact me. Urgently. Have you got that?'

The lad's face remained largely impassive, although Henry did see a slight reaction to Tommy Costain's name.

Henry treated him to his best lopsided grin, then spun back to the car. It seemed quite a long walk with his back to the group and he fully expected to be hit by a house brick on the back of his head.

Nothing happened. He got into the car and Daniels drove away.

'I'm not sure I've ever held my breath for so long,' she said.

Henry kept his eye on the wing mirror. The leader was in the middle of the road making a phone call.

'I think it might be wise to get off the estate, ASAP, Diane.'

Following Henry's reverse directions, she took the route off the estate they had come in on, but as they turned one corner – oh, so close to leaving the estate – Daniels slammed on the brakes and the car lurched and stopped. Ahead of her, spread out across the avenue and blocking their exit, was a group of about a dozen youths, male and female, plus a couple of pitbull-type dogs on thick chains. The youths' faces were covered with scarves and in their hands they bounced chunks of house brick or stone; one had an iron bar like a jemmy.

'Shit,' Daniels uttered.

'Not a Sunday school procession,' Henry said.

Daniels crunched the car into reverse as the first brick sailed through the air, hit the bonnet and skimmed up over the windscreen, scratching but not cracking it, and skittered across the roof like a bouncing bomb.

In her rush, Daniels let out the clutch too quickly and stalled the car with a backwards kangaroo hop.

Three more projectiles the size of drinking mugs arced over and hit the car in quick succession – *bang*, *bang*, *bang*. The gang began to move forward menacingly.

Daniels kept her cool.

Henry gripped the handle above the passenger door.

She managed to restart the car and find that elusive reverse gear just as the youths split and spread down each side of the car, three of them staying at the front grille.

Henry's window shattered as the lad holding the jemmy bar swung it. Henry ducked sideways and managed to avoid the trajectory of the bar but was showered in thousands of shards of glass.

He cringed as the youth lined up again, this time with the intention of smashing him across the head.

On Daniels' side, one of the pitbulls reared up to her window, scratching, snarling and spitting what looked like snot and saliva, leaving a trail on the glass. She rammed her foot down, released the clutch and the car shot back, catching the arm of the youth brandishing the bar and knocking it out of his hand.

He screamed, swore and twisted away, clutching his forearm.

Daniels kept going, swerving backwards, but the youths stayed with her, baying like a pack of wolves on a buffalo. She deliberately dinked left and right, making them leap out of the way, even though they continued to throw rocks.

For Henry, this seemed to go on forever, but finally Daniels broke free from the mob and reversed at speed into a wide junction, pulling down hard on the steering wheel, bringing the vehicle around with a sickening lurch on its ancient suspension. Henry clung on.

She got into first gear as the youths swarmed on her again, but before they could properly regroup, she was accelerating away, feeling and hearing the thud and clunk of another half-dozen bricks and rocks on the roof, back window and boot.

She did not stop even when she reached the main road, but veered left towards Blackpool, not caring that she made someone brake and sound their horn angrily, or that she caused a speed camera to flash . . . she just stared ahead, wide-eyed.

Henry discharged a very long breath of relief, then looked at her, seeing the sinews in her neck and wrists quivering as tight as a straining steel hawsers, her nostrils dilating like mad and her lips a tight line.

As though he was unaffected by what had just happened, Henry laid his right hand on her forearm.

The gesture did the trick.

The tension flooded out of her and her whole body relaxed. Her shoulders drooped and she breathed steadily in and out.

'I know this car has sentimental value,' Henry said. 'But it probably is time to trade it in.'

She gave a nervy laugh. 'Fuck me, Henry! Y'know, not literally, but fuck me!'

'Damn,' he said, glad to feel the tension leaving him also.

'Weren't you scared?' she asked.

'Hey!' He gestured at his body with a sweep of his hand. 'Under this cool exterior lies a guy who is completely terrified. Go left at the next set of lights, then first right. I need a brew.'

'It'll all be on CCTV, won't it?' Daniels asked. 'Places like that must have loads of security cameras up . . . or am I being naive?'

'In my experience, if one goes up, it gets pulled down and smashed to pieces. There are no working cameras on that estate. We'd need a drone to keep an eye on it; even then, they'd probably shoot it down with a ground-to-air missile.'

Henry had directed Daniels to the Kentucky Fried Chicken on Preston New Road, a location he had visited on numerous occasions in his past for a coffee or a fast-food meal on the go. The fact it was open twenty-four hours was also a boon and three a.m. coffees for him there were not unknown.

'I can't believe they get away with it.'

'Lawless Britain,' Henry commented. 'Too many people in positions of power don't give a hoot about poor people; they're so out of touch it's unreal, wrapped up in their affluent cocoons . . . but don't get me going. I'm not good with politics, but nor do I like lawbreakers, whatever their motivation.'

'And people like us cops and the NHS pick up the pieces,' Daniels said despondently.

'Correct . . . anyway, back to our current position.' Henry brought them both back on track.

'Are they like that every time the cops call? Or have they something to hide?'

'Yes and yes. Unless we – you lot, I should say – go in mob-handed, I'm not sure we'll get anywhere with the Costains.'

They were both drinking coffee and eating fried chicken.

Daniels was still a little shaky.

'You did good there,' Henry told her, 'notwithstanding stalling the car . . . we could have done without that.'

'Slight malfunction. What do you think they would have done if they'd caught us?'

'Not worth thinking about.' He shrugged, although the phrase 'hanged, drawn and quartered' did spring to mind.

'Let me make this perfectly clear – you had no right to go on to Shoreside estate—'

'Beacon View,' Henry corrected Dean.

'Beacon View, then, and kick shins. You could have completely screwed up any operation I might have been planning.'

Dean was fuming at Henry, giving him the dressing-down he would never have been able to do in the old days because Henry always outranked him. 'You literally are a loose cannon . . . you could've cocked up stuff we had on the boil.'

They were in a very shiny office at the new police station at Blackpool. The old, crumbling cop shop in the centre of the resort had been closed down, and this new one built near the motorway junction at Marton Circle on the very outskirts of town. It had yet to be officially opened but was already in use. Henry noticed it had a great view of a Tesco superstore and he was already glad he never had to work from there. The old one was a decrepit monstrosity, but was slap-bang in the middle of things, had a great view of the Blackpool Tower and was a refuge for vulnerable people.

'So you were going to raid the place?' Henry asked.

'Well . . . not in as many words,' Dean flustered.

Daniels watched the exchange.

'So you weren't going to raid it?' Henry persisted.

'Well, we hadn't got as far as making any decisions,' he said defensively, 'but Tommy could be on his toes now you've alerted him.'

Henry couldn't help but grin. And shake his head. 'There's every chance he's on his toes anyway. Look, Rik, trust me; we won't have done any damage other than send a message that we know Tommy is among them, and the message will have gone up the chain of command that we're snapping at his heels and we won't back off. He'll be jittery, as much as he might not care about cops and the law, because they don't like us poking around into their affairs.'

'So what do you suggest?'

'Put the Support Unit on to the estate and later today descend on the house with arrest and search warrants and give it a good shaking. Guarantee you'll find something, even if it isn't Tommy.'

It was strange for Henry to step back into a world he thought he'd left far behind. As he and Daniels cruised aimlessly around South Shore in her car (with a clear plastic sheet taped over the smashed passenger-door window), his memories were vivid: of pubs visited and landlords hassled; of numerous houses and flats raided (occasionally with warrants) and occupants arrested; of car and bike chases and foot pursuits.

South Shore had kept him very busy indeed.

He was fond of saying that all human life could be found in Blackpool on the 300-metre-wide strip which ran from South Shore to North Promenade, because it often was.

'How does it feel to be sidelined so quickly – which is an occupational hazard of working with me, by the way?' Henry asked Daniels.

He was referring to Rik Dean's final outburst during which he told Henry and Daniels to get out of his sight until he worked out what to do with them, as clearly Henry could not be trusted.

She turned to him. 'Look at my face. Look at my colour.'

His brow furrowed.

'I've been sidelined all my life, Henry, whether through my sex or my colour. So, how does it feel? Shite.'

'Uh, fair point.'

She smiled genuinely. 'You're one of the few people I've met in this job who has treated me as a human being, an equal. And now you're not in the job anymore . . . But that doesn't help here, does it? Rik is steaming at you.'

'Ah, he'll get over it. He's a good cop. He'll work it out. There's just a whole lot going on at the moment and it must be hard for him to get his head round it . . . I'm sure he'll be on the radio soon, all contrite.'

'So, in the meantime, what are we doing?'

'I'm not sure,' Henry admitted. 'This area used to be my favourite hunting ground. I knew every bent – and straight – landlord and landlady. I knew the pushers, the dealers, the burglars, the fences; I knew every damn street. I've been beaten up in a few, too.'

'OK, that's the reminiscing part done. You were a good cop. I get it.'

'At least you understand that. Now the thing is, way back then the Costains were the premier dealers in South Shore and I imagine they still are. And they were always expanding, pushing their boundaries across the county. Last I knew they were headed by a guy called Runcie Costain. I'll bet what happened in Lancaster over the weekend was as a result of them either moving in or cleaning up. I wonder if Runcie's still the head man – that was years back and I don't really know what's gone on since.'

'So,' Daniels persisted, 'what are we doing here?'

'Just thought it might be prudent to have a chat with some people if they're still about. First port of call is to a club premises in Withnell Street – left here and it's on the left.'

Daniels stopped outside a club with 'For Lease' signs tacked on to it and boards over the doors and windows.

'Mm, maybe not. Runcie once owned this, as did some other lowlifes over the years, but it looks like it's gone the way of a lot of licensed clubs these days. Down the pan.' Henry used his phone camera to photograph the sign just in case he needed to contact the letting agent at some time.

'Where now?'

The PR cut in. 'DC Daniels receiving?'

She glanced at Henry, who said, 'Told you so,' because it was Rik Dean calling.

She answered and Dean said, ‘Can you and Henry make your way back to Blackpool nick? Some interesting things you need to see.’

‘Roger.’ Daniels tossed the PR over her shoulder on to the back seat.

‘Told you he’d forgive me.’

They were on Lytham Road heading north towards Blackpool centre on a road that runs parallel to the promenade. Out to his left Henry could see the framework of the ‘Big One’, the huge rollercoaster ride on the Pleasure Beach. Lytham Road rose over the railway line, then dipped as they reached the junction with Waterloo Road, which sliced across Lytham Road in an east-to-west direction, a small roundabout controlling the point where the roads intersected.

‘Spin around the roundabout and go back,’ Henry said quickly, just feet before the roundabout. Daniels had expected to be going straight on but she braked, flicked down her indicator and looped the car round in a tight circle as per his instruction.

Then she said, ‘What?’

‘Next left: Hampton Road,’ Henry said. They were almost at that junction and Daniels had to brake sharply again and turn into what was a short, dead-end road. ‘Now stop.’

She did.

On the junction was a large pub called The Flower Bowl, its exterior festooned with a multitude of colourful hanging baskets and tubs packed with flowers.

‘What?’ she said again, becoming irritated.

‘This is one of those pubs that has gone through many hands and facelifts,’ Henry explained, pointing at The Flower Bowl. It looked lovely. ‘Mostly run by landlords and ladies who didn’t mind drug dealing on the premises so long as they got their cut of the action.’

‘It looks really nice.’

‘Looks are only skin-deep.’

As he said this, he pointed further down the road at a motorbike parked up on the left-hand side. It was a scrambler-type . . . and Daniels let out an impressed, ‘Bloody hell, well spotted, Henry.’ This was the bike that had been propped up outside the Costain house on Beacon View – and now it was here.

'The Costains used to deal through this place. Maybe they still do,' Henry said.

Daniels was about to ask what Henry had in mind when the side door of the pub opened and a young man in light motorcycle leathers stepped out, tucking something down the front of his jacket, zipping it up, then fitting the scrambler-style crash helmet on as he trotted to the bike.

It was the youth Henry had been confronted by in front of the Costain house not long before.

'Don't know about you, but I want to have words with this lad without all his mates behind him. I guarantee he'll be a pussy cat.'

'Got you.'

The lad righted the bike off its stands and straddled it.

Daniels put her car into gear.

The lad started the bike with the ignition key, glanced in his mirrors, spun his head and saw the Peugeot crawling towards him. He recognized it instantly and reacted without hesitation.

Being a dead end, he had nowhere to go but back from where he came. With the ease of practice, he dropped his right leg, applied power to the engine and spun the bike, pivoting on his heel so that the rear wheel skidded one-eighty, and within a second he was face-to-face with the approaching car, like two cowboys about to duel in Dodge City.

The lad revved the engine, making it scream. Then he unzipped his leather jacket and slid his hand inside.

Giving Henry a bad feeling. Which was confirmed when the hand came out holding a heavy-looking automatic pistol.

'He's got a gun,' Henry and Daniels shouted in unison.

The weapon came up and was pointed at the two officers in the car, both instinctively cowering. Henry ducked left, Daniels right.

The lad fired. Two shots. The windscreen spider-webbed away from both holes but somehow did not crumble.

The bullets passed within inches of their heads and exited through the rear window which did shatter and crumble.

The lad slid the gun back into his jacket, put the bike into gear, applied power and slithered away past the two shocked cops, the whole incident over in a matter of seconds.

Daniels was enraged. 'Screw that for a lark,' she said through gritted teeth. Keeping the motorcyclist in view in her mirrors as he raced off, she executed a tight J-turn in the narrow road and set off in pursuit. Henry hung on, stunned by her ferocity, but liking it.

She did not stop at the junction, but veered left on to the main road – once more causing other cars to brake for her and sound their horns.

The bike was heading south along Lytham Road in the direction of Blackpool Airport, weaving in and out of traffic.

'Henry, you need to grab the radio and call this in,' Daniels told him.

He looked over his shoulder and could see Daniels' PR on the back seat, wedged in the corner directly behind her, about as far away from him as it could be and certainly not within arm's reach.

'I'm going to have to climb,' he warned her.

'Then climb!'

Daniels went for a dangerous overtake, then cut back in, narrowly avoiding a head-on smash, keeping the biker in her sights. He was still speeding south, obviously enjoying the chase.

Henry thumbed his seatbelt release and began to clamber through the gap.

Daniels swerved again and jammed the heel of her hand on the horn.

Henry tried to grab his headrest to swing himself up and over, but the bulk of his torso sagged against Daniels who gasped at his weight and pushed him off.

'Sorry. Not as pliable as I used to be,' he said.

He clambered through the gap and almost did a forward roll into the back seat, his legs kicking up into the air as Daniels braked and swerved again, then put her foot down, the momentum splaying him across the seat where he managed to sit upright and seize the radio.

The bike had reached Squires Gate Lane and turned left away from the seafront with the airport on the right. He gunned the machine so that by the time Daniels was on the dual carriageway he was just a speck in the distance.

Henry put the radio to his lips – then had a moment's hesitation.

In the past he would have just shouted his own name and rank over the airwaves. Now he had no rank and his name meant nothing. He had a fleeting feeling of helplessness.

He pressed the transmit button and said, 'Henry Christie calling on DC Daniels' PR to Blackpool comms – urgent.'

He saw Daniels' face screw up in the rear-view mirror.

'Caller repeat, please,' a comms operator said.

'Look, I'm with DC Daniels and we're in pursuit of a male youth on a scrambler bike who has just fired a gun at us. He is armed and dangerous. This is for real. DC Daniels is driving her own car and we're on Squires Gate Lane, heading inland, just passing the airport. The bike is well ahead of us, travelling in the same direction.'

It felt very wordy and long-winded to Henry who would have normally just snapped orders and instructions.

For a few moments there was an agonizing silence, then the operator said, 'Roger that . . . Please be aware that you are not authorized to get into a pursuit situation.'

'Got that,' Henry said.

'Alpha Romeo Seven receiving?' the operator called up.

'Yeah, received that,' came the reply from the Armed Response Vehicle covering the area. 'We are near Tesco at Marton – will make. The motorbike could be coming towards us. Any further details?'

'Yes, confirmed, still Squires Gate Lane,' Henry cut in and gave details of the bike, including the registration number and a description of the rider, plus a warning about the handgun and that he had fired at cops already.

'Detective Superintendent Dean to the ARV,' Rik Dean's voice came on air. 'Authorization to arm given.'

'Received, sir,' the ARV replied.

While Armed Response Units were allowed to self-authorize, depending on the circumstances, it was always good to have backing from further up the chain of command.

Up ahead from Daniels and Henry, the motorcyclist shot through a set of lights on red at the junction with Common Edge Road, going straight through on to Progression Way, still heading inland.

Henry leaned forwards in the gap between the seats.

'Unless the ARV is moving like stink, that guy is gone.'

Daniels did not say anything, just kept her foot down and concentrated on weaving her way through the traffic, but when she reached the set of lights the bike had just jumped, there were two solid rows of cars ahead of them, the lights were back on red, lines of cars were crossing from left to right, and in an unmarked car without lights or horns there was no chance of getting through.

And the bike was gone.

Henry realized it could have disappeared anywhere now: left to Blackpool, straight towards the motorway or on to the country roads that crisscrossed the flat lands of Peel and Balham.

His despondency was clear as Daniels gave up and slowed to join the traffic.

'Hell's teeth,' he said, looking around at the damage to the car. The two bullet holes in the front window, the rear window gone, the passenger-door window repaired with the plastic sheet, and so much bodywork damage. 'Never mind, he'll come again.'

'Romeo Seven to comms,' the ARV called up, using the abbreviated form of the call sign.

'Go ahead, Alpha Romeo Seven.'

'Romeo Seven – got him!'

FIFTEEN

Henry had to stop himself from saying, 'Cheer up, it might never happen,' while Daniels took a long, slow, careful circuit of her car on the police station car park. Her face flitted from sadness to grief, to some kind of perverted amusement, then back.

'I inherited it from my dad,' she said, something Henry knew all too well. She had kept it mainly for sentimental reasons, although it had proved to be a reliable workhorse for her. She inhaled, then exhaled a long pissed-off sigh.

She re-stretched the piece of polythene she had used to cover the broken side window and thumbed the sticky tape back into place.

The damage caused to the bodywork from the mini-riot was extensive and would probably make the car an insurance write-off, too costly to repair, given its value.

'Looks like the scrap yard . . . bloomin' heck, Henry – and I've got to get home tonight, and you too! It's not fit to drive.'

'Get a screen repair guy in, then claim it off insurance.'

'Mm, maybe.' Daniels shrugged helplessly. 'Let's go and see how our prisoner is doing.'

They walked around the front of the new police station to gain access and made their way to the custody suite where they found Rik Dean in a head-to-head conflab with another detective, breaking apart when they saw Henry and Daniels.

'Hey guys, you did good,' Dean congratulated them.

'In spite of my earlier meddling?' Henry reminded him.

'Swings and roundabouts,' Dean said. 'Come and look.'

He led them into an office just behind the custody reception desk, where TV monitors were keeping an eye on each cell in the complex. Most cells, as per Blackpool's sausage-machine reputation, were full.

Dean pressed a button on a control panel and the image from inside just one cell appeared.

'Matey boy,' Dean said. 'Claustrophobic.'

The camera lens, fitted high and flush in one corner of the cell, showed the occupant, whose name was Jamie Costain, the lad who'd taken pot-shots at Henry and Daniels. In the subsequent pursuit he had lost control of his scrambler bike as the ARV flashed across his bows, and came off the machine which wedged itself under the front wheels of the ARV. He tried to run, but the two armed officers were out of their vehicle in a flash, guns drawn and ready, more than happy to shoot the lad. He had seen this, heard their warnings and stopped, hands held high. Under clear instructions, he had removed the gun from under his jacket, kicked it away, gone down on to his hands and knees, then his belly, with his arms splayed out, then hands finally clasped behind his head.

The police had found a kilo bag of cocaine on the bike and ten rounds of ammunition in his pocket.

He wasn't going anywhere fast.

And now he was in a cell, wearing a baggy forensic suit two

sizes too big for him, but he wasn't sitting up or just lying on the bench; he was in one corner of the cell, kneeling with his face pressed up to the wall, his hands behind his head.

'Well spotted.' Dean beamed. 'If nothing else, this lad will be going a long way down that tunnel for a long, long time.'

'So I am forgiven?' Henry said.

'For the time being,' Dean said reluctantly.

'What's the plan, boss?' Daniels asked.

'Hit the house on Beacon View – hard – and see if we can flush out Tommy Costain.'

Henry narrowed his eyes. 'Has anyone been informed this lad has been arrested?'

'Not so far,' Dean said.

'Does anyone *know* he's been arrested?'

'Word travels, I suppose, but as far as I know, not yet.'

'Anybody interviewed him yet?'

Dean said no.

Henry said, 'Let me speak to him.'

'Uh, don't think so.'

'What's the point of paying me a grand a day, then? Let me speak to him now before you do anything else. Ten minutes under the radar – that's all I ask.'

'What can you do that any bog-standard operational detective can't do? You've been out of it for years – you lose your touch.'

Henry interlaced his fingers, flipped his palm outwards and extended his arms, cracking his knuckles.

'I might be able to tap into his inner psyche.'

Henry was accompanied along the shiny, new male corridor by a gaoler who opened the first cell. Henry noticed the complex was already beginning to reek of the bitter smell of men in custody: a combination of sweat, urine, alcohol, shit, general body odour and a dash of fear. Even new paint could not suppress it.

The gaoler stepped back from the door but hovered behind Henry.

The lad did not move. His face was crammed into the corner of the cell as though glued there.

Henry walked in and sat on the bench behind him.

'Jamie, my name is Henry Christie,' he said softly. 'I'm the one you spoke to outside the house in Beacon View and the one you fired shots at. I have a very good reason to be furious with you right now. However, I'm the one who can help you here, but only if you are prepared to help me too. And to show you I mean business, I'm going to take you out of this cell to an interview room to have a nice chat with you. How does that sound?'

With his face still pressed into the wall and his voice muffled, he replied, 'Sounds good.'

'This is unofficial, Jamie. It's not going to be recorded on tape or video and there will be no entry on the custody record.'

The prisoner frowned.

Henry continued, 'That way, when anyone looks at the custody record in the future – and they will – all they will see is that you were in your cell, climbing the walls, OK?'

'Not following.'

'And because the CCTV system is so new in this place, it just stops working from time to time, so there will be no video recording of you being taken from and then put back in your cell.'

'And?'

'That means this is a secret conversation between you and me. I will deny it ever happened, and so will you, and no one will be any the wiser. No one will be able to say it happened or didn't happen. Get my drift?'

'I still don't get you, and why would I want to talk to you anyway?'

Henry said, 'This, Jamie, is to protect you because, thing is, if any of your family, friends or partners in crime even suspected you'd talked to the police, what do you think might happen? To you, that is?' Henry's voice was smooth yet dangerous. He was loving it.

'They'd kill me.'

'Exactly. So they don't need to know, do they? However, there is a catch to all this.' Henry smiled. 'If you don't help me now, first off, it *will* leak that you have been chatting to me and, second, you *will* go back in that cramped, confined, tiny cell. You will be incarcerated for as many lengthy periods of time as possible and you will find yourself on a three-day lie-down – you know what that is?'

Jamie nodded. 'Three days here in the cells for further questioning,' he said bleakly.

'Correct – an extra seventy-two hours in the traps, after which, when you are charged and put before the magistrates, I will ensure that you are put on remand, probably to Strangeways – Manchester Prison as they call it these days. A very nasty, overpopulated place, and I will have no power over how you are looked after there, but it will be very bleak. So, think about this: three more days here, in a cell, shit food, no visitors because of the seriousness of your crime, no phone calls, and then weeks, maybe months, while you wait to go to trial, bail refused. I can make the wheels of justice move very slowly.'

'You can't do that!'

'And after the trial,' Henry ploughed on remorselessly, 'I suspect you will be sent down for two life sentences for attempting to shoot dead two cops, plus ten years for other firearms and drug offences, and I'll bet that bike you were on doesn't have insurance, you probably don't have a licence, it'll probably be stolen, so you'll get fines on top of that prison sentence. And yes, I'm taking as many bites of the cherry as I can! So, you see,' Henry said to Jamie's mesmerized face and held out the palm of his right hand, 'your life, for what it's worth, is in my hand.'

With a snap, he closed that hand into a bunched fist.

Jamie jumped.

'Do we understand each other?' Henry wanted to know.

Jamie nodded.

'OK, the thing is you took pot-shots at me and my colleague. You were then stopped by armed officers and found in possession of a gun, ammo and a ton of drugs – all the things Crown Court judges despise, yeah?'

Jamie nodded – and swallowed this time.

'Now, just like this' – Henry clicked his finger and thumb – 'I can make various bits of that scenario disappear.'

'How do you mean?'

'Well, although it pains me, I can completely delete the gun side of it – because you missed me.'

Jamie watched him. His mind was being blown sentence by sentence.

'The gun can disappear, and with it two counts of attempted

murder. So, in the blink of an eye, your sentence has been reduced from life to ten years. That, if you're a good lad, means five years in reality. But if I additionally put a good word into the judge's ear hole and say how helpful and remorseful you've been, that could easily reduce from ten years to six, which means you'd be out in three, just in time for your twenty-first birthday. How does that sound? Not only that, I could ensure you got bail from here rather than a remand in custody.'

'Why would you do that?'

'Because I've got bigger fish to fry than a minnow like you.'

'Oh, God.' Jamie deflated, as though his lungs had been punctured. 'You're after Tommy!'

'And his murderous henchmen.'

'Brendan O'Hara . . . no, no, no . . . I can't do that. I'd end up sliced to pieces like those two people up at the farm.'

'You know about that?'

Jamie nodded.

Henry fidgeted slightly on the chair. He knew he'd put a wedge into the crack. 'Tell me.'

'Uh, I don't know much, just shit I'd overheard.'

'Which was?'

'Those people at the farm. They launder money for big gangs down south – London an' that.'

'Is that all they do?'

'Far as I know . . . what d'you mean?'

'Nothing,' Henry said. *They do much more than that*, he thought. 'Go on.'

'Well, I know Tommy and Papa Conrad wanted to get in on the big stuff down south, wanted to start running county lines for 'em up here, but the people down in London didn't want to know us gypsies. That got Tommy and Papa Conrad mad as wasps. They'd found out about that couple and what they did, so they decided to show that lot down south, teach 'em a lesson – so they brought in Roche and O'Hara.'

'Who are they?'

Jamie shrugged. 'Killers, I suppose. Don't really know 'em, but they done a few things for Papa Conrad. They're not from round here. Peterborough, I think. They do driveways, too.'

'Remind me not to hire them . . . So you heard all this?'

'Bit at a time . . . and then Tommy blabbed some more stuff over the weekend.'

Henry waited. He now recalled why he loved being a detective.

'We went up to Lancaster – business that Tommy wanted to sort face-to-face, like. It were all kickin' off up there, everybody at each other's throats, and Tom decided he wanted to put an end to it. Someone had ripped him off, too, an' he were going to make a statement.'

'A written statement?'

Jamie chuckled. 'Hardly. A killing one, more like.'

'What part did you play?' Henry asked, mindful that this response could skew what he was trying to achieve here.

'I, uh, followed a guy for Tom, then held his bird and kept nicks for Tommy while he dealt with the guy up a back alley.'

'Dealt with him?'

'Kicked him to death – but two cops were literally just walking past and they nabbed Tom. I legged it. Tommy didn't drop me in or anything,' Jamie said ingenuously, not realizing he was dropping himself into some other mire by admitting this.

'Such a good guy, that Tommy,' Henry said, unable to hide the sarcasm. 'However . . . back to the names you mentioned – Roche, O'Hara, Conrad?'

'Yeah, Roche an' O'Hara . . . I know they've done jobs for Papa Conrad. They love it. They were already coming in to do the couple and they got a few extra jobs, like at the hospital and then getting Tommy out.'

'So who's this Papa Conrad?'

'You don't know Conrad?' Jamie asked incredulously. 'Mind, I suppose he's under the radar pretty much. He's the Costains' head man – like, uh, the Godfather. We just call him Papa.'

'The head man?' Henry had to admit that, as much as he knew a lot about the Costains, he'd never come across Conrad. 'OK, let's start with Tommy, shall we? We're going to raid the house on Beacon View. Will he be there?'

Jamie shook his head. His mouth visibly clamped up.

'What and who will we find there?'

'Nowt interesting. A gun, some ammo, coke, weed . . . the attic's a cannabis farm.'

'But no Tommy?'

Jamie shook his head again.

'Where is he, then?'

'I can't tell you.' He began to look petrified.

'Can't or won't?'

'Won't. Look, I know you've promised to keep all this a secret, but if rumour does get out that I actually told you where he . . . where he might be, I'd be dead f'sure, and I wouldn't see twenty-one. So, y'know, if it comes to hey-lads-hey and I end up looking Tommy in the eye, I want to be able to tell him, "No, Tom, I didn't say a word to the cops." That bit has to be true. Understand?'

Henry said, 'Write it down, then.'

Jamie's mouth went crooked and his face twitched with shame. 'Thing is, Mr Christie, I can look Tommy in the eye and say, "No, I didn't tell 'em anything," and I can also say I didn't write it down either. That bit he'll know is true.'

'How's that?'

'Can't write. Can't read, either . . . well, just bits, but I really can't write even me own name. I put a cross on the custody record.'

'So, essentially, you are no use to me whatsoever and we're back to square one: life imprisonment twice over.'

'No, no, no, no,' Jamie gabbled in a panic.

It was an A–Z road atlas of Lancashire that Henry had snaffled from the comms room bookshelf, tatty, well used over the years, but now mostly obsolete with the advent of GPS technology. Henry liked the feel of the ring binding because he was still a map man, and although his Audi was fitted with a satnav, he always checked new routes by map first. He liked the perspective they gave. He knew he was getting too old for the world.

He laid the book down between himself and Jamie Costain.

'Turn to the street map of Blackpool South,' Costain said. Fortunately, the lad did have some knowledge of printed maps.

Henry did: pages 108 and 109.

The interlinked maps showed Squires Gate Lane horizontally dissecting the pages, going from west to east inland from the Irish Sea.

Alongside that road was Blackpool Airport, showing a crisscross of runways.

North of Squires Gate Lane was the cluster of streets forming

South Shore; then the whole southern section of the map was Lytham St Annes.

Inland, the streets petered out and the land became open, flat farmland known as the Mosses.

Henry swivelled the book around for Jamie to look at. His eyes roved the two pages.

Then he looked at Henry meaningfully, lifted his right forefinger and placed it down on West Moss Lane in Higher Ballam.

'So I've said nowt, written nowt, yeah?'

Henry nodded agreement.

Jamie raised his hand and offered it across for Henry to shake. 'So we have a deal?'

Henry noted the exact point where Jamie's fingertip had rested, then spun the map back around to himself and closed the book before he looked contemptuously at Jamie again and the hand hanging in what seemed like no man's land.

Henry did not shake it. Jamie withdrew it.

'I'm a man of my word, Jamie,' Henry assured him. 'If what you have just indicated leads to the location and capture of Tommy Costain, then the allegations of attempted murder will be dropped . . .'

Jamie looked relieved.

Henry's next word was 'However' and that struck terror into the young man's breast. 'However, I'm not sure that even I can stop you being charged with actual murder.'

'What d'you mean, *actual* murder?'

'In case you didn't know, keeping lookout for someone who is kicking another person to death makes you just as guilty as the person doing the kicking. You've committed murder, Jamie: cold-blooded, brutal, nasty murder. You're just too stupid to realize it.'

Jamie wilted in his chair. His young, unshaved chin began to wobble; his mouth quavered and blobs of tears formed on his lower eyelids, then spilled out down his cheek as he transformed into what he really was under the tough guy exterior: a stupid, vulnerable, immature kid who had just destroyed any possibility of having a half-decent life.

And though Henry wasn't too proud of this, the feeling of why he liked being a detective so much was strong within him, particularly one who investigated murder. The dead could not fight for themselves. People like him did that.

SIXTEEN

Although it had been some years since Henry had first set foot in the Costain house on the Beacon View estate (previously Shoreside), it seemed that no one from the police had been in it in recent years, which gave him food for thought and a hint at what the current state of policing was – timid.

He kept that little gem to himself as he sketched the layout of the knocked-together semis from memory on a piece of paper. He had tried to get Jamie Costain to do this, but now that he faced the possibility of a murder charge, Jamie had withdrawn all labour.

What Henry was doing wasn't ideal, but it would have to suffice under the circumstances and would serve as a map for the officers leading the intended raid on the house.

Somewhere he definitely had not been before was the spot on the map indicated by Jamie Costain's fingertip.

It had not taken much to identify what he was pointing to: the location of a permanent travellers' site (which seemed a bit of an oxymoron to Henry), known officially and without inspiration as the West Moss Lane site. It was supposedly managed by the council, although there was only one brief mention of it on the council website, dated some ten years ago. Recent police records showed only one visit to it as a result of a complaint about a year ago concerning a noisy car.

Henry, Dean, Daniels, two other detectives and the uniformed ops chief inspector were in conference about strategy, but none of them knew anything about the actual layout of the site near to Ballam, which was a big problem.

'Who went to the job about the noisy car?' Henry asked.

The chief inspector looked at his iPad. 'PC Bromilow . . . he's on duty in the town centre today.'

'Get him in here,' Dean said. 'We need to know what we're going into.'

'Good idea,' Henry said. 'I'll be honest. I knew this site existed when I was based in Blackpool, but I don't ever remember any problems on it, or any links to the Costains . . . and this Conrad Costain intrigues me.'

'Not having problems now starts to look a bit suss,' Dean said.

'Too quiet to be true,' Henry said.

'Although that stereotypes travellers,' Daniels warned them lightly. 'They're not all tarred with the same brush. Most want quiet lives. The people we're dealing with are an organized crime group who may be travellers, but they are using the greater travelling community to hide their criminal enterprise.'

'I know, I get it,' Dean snapped. 'So.' He eyed Henry. 'Depending on what PC Bromilow says, this is pretty much your show, Henry, in terms of the planning and execution.'

Henry could have said a cynical 'Cheers' but didn't. He was buzzing inside, wanted to get on with it. He looked at the assembled cops. 'My suggestion is to hit the house on Beacon View first. Kick the doors in, flood the place with' – he was going to revert to type and say 'hairy-arsed cops', but stopped himself when he saw Daniels out of the corner of his eye – 'officers. Maybe give the occupants just enough time to relay the raid to anyone concerned, such as Tommy Costain or this Conrad guy, which will give them the impression we are barking up the wrong tree and might just lull them into a false sense of security.

'I mean, it won't be a surprise to them at Beacon View because Diane and I have already laid the groundwork, as it were, so they already think we believe Tommy might be hiding there.'

'And hopefully,' Daniels continued for him, 'Tommy will think he's safe and sound while, unbeknownst to him, we'll have a team ready to go crashing through the gates of the site, warrants at the ready and maybe catch Tommy and this O'Hara guy, who we don't really know much about.'

'One issue is keeping it quiet about matey in the cells,' Dean said, referring to Jamie Costain. The police were now at the very limits of not allowing him a phone call or access to a solicitor and, legally, were struggling to keep his detention quiet. Dean knew that once these rights were allowed, Tommy would certainly be alerted and on his toes, if he wasn't already.

'Why not . . .' Henry began and gave Dean a certain look that made him wince a little and dread what was coming. 'Why not release him on police bail pending further enquiries for our job?' He indicated himself and Daniels. 'And then, as he's walking out of the door, arrest him on suspicion of the murder over the weekend in Lancaster, where he kept nicks for Tommy? Stick him back in a cell, contact Lancaster and get them to come down and pick him up – when they have someone available to do so' – Henry winked – 'then, when he reaches Lancaster, nick him and deny him his rights all over again?'

Daniels regarded him with shock, seemed about to protest, but then relented and said, 'It's a plan.'

Dean was obviously crumbling inside at the prospect. 'It's very iffy.'

'Needs must, Rik. Think about the bigger picture. Ultimately, we can afford to lose Jamie out of this because he isn't a major player, but we can't afford to lose Tommy. We just have to keep a lid on Jamie for another, what, fourteen hours? Feed him with KFC and McDonalds, stick him in a holding cage, keep him content and then tomorrow morning give him all the phone calls and solicitors and rights he wants, and if he sues us, so be it. Sorry, sues you, because it's your decision, not mine. I'm a civvy.'

Dean did not like it one little bit. It was written all over his stressed-out face.

'Either that or we take him out in the boot of a car for a very, very, very long ride,' Henry suggested.

Dean's head dropped into his hands as he thought about his career crashing and burning.

Henry just shrugged and said, 'If we crack this whole thing in about twenty-four hours, you can have my outstanding fee to pay for legal costs. But it won't come to that.'

'How do you know that?' Dean asked.

'Because Jamie will not moan, not least because ultimately he's getting a bloody good deal and we can play down his part in the murder.'

Dean swore as he visualized a queue of 'no win, no fee' vulture lawyers lining up to doorstep him.

Henry briefed Dean on his quickly hatched plans.

Two staggered raids.

The first would take place at five thirty the next morning when an inspector leading a Support Unit team, backed up by firearms officers, a dog patrol and other uniformed cops and a couple of detectives, would swoop on the house on Beacon View, back-and-front it, open doors with sledgehammers or door-openers if necessary, swarm in, brandish a warrant and begin the search for murderers on the run, namely Tommy Costain and Brendan O'Hara (whose details still remained vague). Hopefully, they would find all sorts of goodies in the house as they dragged folk out of and upturned their beds and other furniture, and then finally entered the attic to discover a cannabis farm.

Henry suspected that almost from the first bang on the door, the whole of the Costain clan who were part of the organized crime gang, wherever they may be, would somehow be alerted, which was part of the plan, really. Henry guessed they would probably have a ring-round system.

The next raid would take place at five forty-five when a number of officers would emerge from hiding in the fields neighbouring the West Moss Lane site, then move in and surround it in order to nab anyone thinking of scaling the walls.

Henry had considered making a polite entry to the site, knocking on the gates and asking to be allowed in, but he thought that would give Tommy and O'Hara too much time to secrete themselves.

He had therefore decided on the hard, fast, brutal approach instead.

The afternoon was spent planning the raids but keeping the actual target addresses a secret because Henry – unpopularly – suggested that would be the wise course: if the Costains were anywhere near as organized as they seemed, then it wasn't beyond the realms of possibility that they might have someone inside the police feeding them information.

By four thirty, after several read-throughs, obtaining the necessary warrants from a friendly magistrate and running the whole thing past the eyes of the chief constable, the two linked operational orders were completed. Henry became quite tongue-tied when Rik Dean suggested that the operations be called 'Kate' and 'Alison'.

He wasn't expecting it, and although neither woman would have felt honoured to have police operations named after them if they'd been alive, he was quite touched.

When the session was over, Henry sidled up to Rik Dean and thanked him.

'It's nowt, really, is it?'

'You'd be surprised,' Henry told him and patted his shoulder but stopped short of a man-hug.

'What are you doing now?' Dean asked him. 'You can come to ours. Lisa would love to see you. It would be a bought-in pizza probably, but y'know?'

'I'd love to, but I need to show my face at The Tawny Owl; otherwise, Ginny will think I've done a runner. I haven't really explained what I'm up to, so I need to do that.'

'How are you going to get back up there? Aren't you in DC Daniels' half-wrecked car?'

Henry checked her and said, 'Hopefully, the magic windscreen repair chap will have been, so it won't be too breezy.'

'OK. I need to get on with getting resources. Gonna take a lot of personnel, this. A lot of phoning to do. So – see you back here at four thirty, latest.'

Daniels did a quick hit and run for another change of clothing from her flat in Lancaster, and despite getting snarled up in horrendous tea-time traffic in the city, they were back in Kendleton by six o'clock.

Henry caught up with Maude and a chief fire officer.

Concern was continuing to grow about the direction of the fires as another change of wind direction blew the flames relentlessly towards the woods around the village. Even dumping tons of water from a helicopter failed to achieve anything of significance. There was more talk about digging firebreaks, which would require a considerable number of people.

Henry listened to all this, wondering when it would stop.

The fire officer thanked him for all the support provided by Th'Owl and the people of the village, then headed back to the moors. Henry had a few more minutes with Maude who had been grafting hard all day and looked shattered. He told her to lock up and go home.

After showering, Henry and Daniels met up for a bar snack and spent some time with Ginny, who was more than happy for Henry to continue on his 'little police project' as he called it.

After that – and no alcohol – Henry and Daniels went to their separate beds and crashed out. They slept soundly for six hours and were on their way back to Blackpool by three thirty a.m., refreshed and eager to go kicking down doors.

There were some situations as a cop that always excited Henry, got his heart pumping, adrenaline flowing.

Being en route to a potentially dangerous job in a police car was at the top of his list. Weaving through traffic, seeing the reflection of the blue light on other vehicles and shop windows, and hearing the two-tones from within the car was a great sensation and one he had missed when he became a detective. Detectives rarely rushed to anything.

Entering a pub which was kicking off inside – with backup on the way – was a good one, too – though, again, that was mainly a uniform memory.

The anticipation generated at a briefing was another of his favourites, knowing that in a short space of time doors would be battered off hinges, bodies would be hauled out of beds, bad people might get caught and contraband recovered.

That old feeling hit him at the morning's briefing at the new police station as he lounged at the back of the conference room, looking across the heads of the packed assembly of officers in uniform and plain clothes, listening to Rik Dean (who he knew had been up most of the night pulling it all together) talking from behind a lectern on the slightly raised platform at the front. He delivered what Henry thought was a pretty good briefing.

Once done, the officers filtered out, murmuring excitedly between themselves, glad to be doing something positive, and headed out to their vehicles to board them and move out into pre-raid positions.

Dean came up to Henry. 'How was that?'

'Yeah, nice.'

Dean nodded with satisfaction and went out, leaving Henry with Daniels.

Both were dressed in dark-coloured trainers, jeans and zip-up jackets, wearing stab vests and high-vis tabards bearing the word POLICE.

'How are you feeling?' she asked him.

'Lucky.'

At five thirty Operation Kate was underway.

The police moved in on the Costain house on Beacon View.

A convoy of vehicles had assembled on the main road a quarter of a mile from the estate entrance, and once a quick communications and radio check had been done, plus a check to ensure that all images from the bodycams of the first designated officers through the doors were streaming, Rik Dean gave the go.

Henry and Daniels were not going to be playing any part in this raid. They were in an unmarked police car in the narrow Peel Road just a few yards short of the junction with Ballam Road, and a couple of minutes away from the travellers' site on West Moss Lane.

The car was equipped with a dashboard computer linked to the audio-visual streaming that would soon show the progress of the first raid, and they could either watch all the images on a split screen or pick just one to follow.

The first officers through the front door would be highly trained Support Unit cops specializing in building entry, who, in a matter of seconds, would break their way in, then step aside as others entered, including the authorized firearms officers and the dog patrol.

Officers deployed to the rear of the property would prevent runaways and also smash the soil pipes coming down from the two main bathrooms and put a fine mesh sieve under each to catch any drugs that might be flushed away.

Henry and Daniels watched the images with anticipation as the personnel carriers began their short journey on to the estate. It was exciting, if slightly blurred, viewing.

About ninety seconds after being set in motion, the officers had reached the house, were swarming into position and the front door was being hammered open with clear and unambiguous shouted warnings accompanying the entry.

* * *

Tommy Costain lay alongside the naked, warm Bronwen, snoring loudly as he had been doing for the last three hours, keeping her awake and making her increasingly irritable until, finally, despite repeatedly digging him to shift and change position, which had no effect, she'd had enough.

Wearily, she sat up on the edge of the bed, rubbed her gritty eyes, then stood up, pulling a dressing gown around her.

She looked at Tommy and swore, then walked to the door of the tiny caravan, picking up Tommy's phone on the way, plus his cigarettes and lighter, and opened it, noticing his pistol on the worktop next to the sink and wishing he would be more subtle with the thing. She tapped a cigarette out of the packet and lit up, inhaling the smoke deeply into her lungs, then exhaling it with pleasure into the early-morning atmosphere as she stood on the top step and looked at the approach of dawn.

The site was deadly quiet, nothing moving, not even the dogs which were usually a pain.

She took another drag, exhaled. Then she frowned slightly, tilted her head and listened, sure that somewhere in the distance – way, way off – she could hear the hum of a helicopter. More than likely it would be the police one.

Another drag, then she glanced at Tommy's phone and began to tab through, looking at the social media shite.

It might have been her imagination, but she thought the sound of the helicopter was getting closer.

She read something about *Love Island*.

Then the phone, which was on silent, showed an incoming call from Billy Thursday, one of Tommy's running mates who lived at the house on Beacon View. Bronwen thought that extremely odd. A phone call at five thirty-four.

She swiped the screen. 'Tommy's phone,' she answered.

'Cops are here, all over the place,' Billy's voice said urgently. Bronwen could hear a lot of rustling, quick footsteps, a banging noise and shouting. Billy said, 'Shit!' and the phone went dead.

Bronwen tossed the cigarette away and rushed to Tommy to try to rouse him, tell him the news. Even as she shook him roughly, she knew this would be hard work. Tommy had drunk a skinful of booze last night and had gone to bed very drunk. Waking him would be a nightmare.

She was sure the sound of the helicopter was even closer.

She shook Tommy even more fervently, having a very bad feeling about this.

'Target One – locked down and secure,' the voice of the on-ground commander of the house raid came calmly over the radio. 'Two males in custody – but neither, repeat neither, is Suspect One or Suspect Two,' he added, meaning that they weren't Tommy Costain or Brendan O'Hara. 'All mobile phone devices have been seized, but I cannot confirm if any calls have been made or not . . . Also a cannabis farm discovered in the loft – perhaps two hundred plants. I repeat: no sign of Suspects One or Two.'

Henry heard Rik Dean acknowledge this.

There was a pause.

Henry and Daniels blew out their cheeks nervously. Daniels gripped the steering wheel firmly, tensing her fingers around it.

Suddenly, Daniels lurched sideways and planted a kiss on Henry's cheek. 'Good luck, pal.'

'Inappropriate,' he quipped.

'So sue me.'

Rik Dean's voice came over the airwaves: 'Operation Alison – go, go, go!'

It was always dangerous entering any area without a detailed map of the layout, but Dean had managed to get a police drone to fly over the site the previous evening and take a series of photographs from above, and he had a detective do a quick drive-by to take photos of the front gates.

The photos from the drone showed twenty static caravans, all, with one exception, splayed in a circle around the site; the exception was one van parked in the back corner, parallel to the back wall. There were two permanent single-storey toilet blocks and a fenced-off area with two industrial-size wheelie bins. A small caravan stood just to the right of the gates.

The photograph from the drive-by showed double gates made of sheet metal with barbed wire strung across the tops and fastened by a thick chain threaded through the gates, probably padlocked inside. The whole of the perimeter wall seemed to be made of corrugated metal panels, probably ten feet high and six feet long, slotted in between concrete posts.

The drone photo showed half a dozen vehicles on site, all pickups, plus a panel van of some sort just to the left of the gates.

Dean had not wanted to alert anyone to the police interest in the site, so all other information was pulled from public records on the council website which said the site had been licensed for twenty years, did not specify how many people lived there and reported that the main point of contact for the travellers was a man called Conrad Costain, but there were no further details of him.

The numbers on site were an issue for the police. If there were four people per van, that would make about eighty on site, and if they all decided to be difficult, there could be major public order problems.

Because of that, fifty uniformed cops were going to wade in, backed up by ARVs, two dogs, detectives and a Police Support Unit search team. That did not include officers hidden in the fields around the site.

It was going to be fun, especially since the first knock on the door was by bulldozer.

The opening salvo of the raid went well.

Driven by an experienced traffic cop with all the right credentials, the hired bulldozer turned into West Moss Lane from North Houses Lane and trundled towards the site entrance.

Fifty metres short, a radio call went out to the police helicopter, which was hovering on station at Blackpool Airport. It rose swiftly into the sky, travelling due east, and at exactly the same moment that it came to hang above the site – turning on its bank of hugely powerful night-sun searchlights, instantly bathing the camp below in a bright light – the bulldozer smashed its way through the front gates, lifting them easily off their hinges, like a parent lifting up a baby gate.

Two police personnel carriers came in its wake, fanning left and right, discharging twenty Support Unit cops who deployed through the site like well-drilled ants to their pre-designated targets – caravans – while behind them a full firearms team drove in, crammed into a Transit van; these officers poured out and formed a widening circle.

Thirty-plus officers were in the camp within thirty seconds.

Which is when the door of the small caravan just to the right of the smashed-down gates opened and a figure appeared, seemingly brandishing a handgun.

Two armed officers responded instantly.

They fired.

Eight shots.

Each one was on target and the figure went down, thrown back into the back by the impact of the nine-millimetre slugs to the chest, and was dead before hitting the floor.

SEVENTEEN

It was the hail of gunfire that woke Tommy Costain. His eyes opened to see Bronwen stagger back from the caravan door and slither down the floor-to-ceiling cupboard, blood spouting from her multiple entry and exit wounds, while, in reflex, she seemed to toss the gun in his direction. It skittered across the laminated floor.

Light flooded the caravan from the helicopter hovering above. There were shouts, bangs and other noises, and Tommy knew the police had found him and somehow killed Bronwen in the process.

He threw off the sheet and scampered across the caravan on all fours, picking up the gun, then sliding back against the sink, having to look at Bronwen's bullet-riddled body as he shouted obscenities at the police and threatened to shoot anyone stupid or brave enough to come for him.

The siege then lasted for four hours.

'She came to the door, gun in hand, looked like she was going to shoot. The officers were well within their rights to open fire.'

Henry was speaking for the first time to Conrad Costain, who had been discovered in his caravan, half in, half out of his pyjamas, desperately trying to get dressed. The old man's inner seething rage was plain for him to see. As was the rage of the Doberman sitting next to him, which kept a beady eye on Henry and a constant snarl on its quivering upper lip, showing

Henry his very nasty-looking teeth. The old man glared at Henry and then at Daniels, who he looked at with disdain. She held his gaze steadily, almost willing him to say something about her colour and sex. In the end, Conrad turned his head back to Henry and stroked the dog's head.

'She would never have used a weapon,' Conrad said. 'She was probably just handing it over. She had nothing to do with anything that Tommy may have been caught up with – which, I swear, I know nothing about.'

'I've seen footage from a body camera on one of the officers,' Henry told him. 'She appeared at the door holding the gun as if she might fire it, not holding it by the barrel to hand it over.'

'She made a mistake.'

'A bad mistake and died for it. It was a very fast-moving situation and a split-second decision had to be made.'

'And you and your officers will pay dearly for it,' Conrad promised.

'That may be so, Mr Costain, but we have a dangerous situation still running, and until that is resolved and Tommy Costain gives up his weapon and surrenders to the police, there is nothing to discuss – other than the possibility of you helping us.'

'Why would I do that? I don't even know why you want him – he's just a lad staying here, that's all.'

Henry had to stop himself from laughing, knowing that Conrad was well aware of what Tommy had done. However, to keep him on board he just said, 'Tommy is wanted for some serious offences, including murder, Conrad. That's all you need to know and now he's barricaded himself in the caravan, and if he doesn't come out with his hands held high, he will end up dead unnecessarily. We will have no choice other than to storm in, and it will not end nicely. And you, I believe, are the man in charge of this site, so he will listen to you. Is that correct?'

Conrad regarded Henry with hate-filled eyes, but also with some consideration for his words. 'Yes, he will.'

The Doberman's lips curled even further back to give Henry an even better view of his teeth.

'What's he called?' Henry asked, indicating the dog.

'Satan,' Conrad replied. 'But you can call him Stan.'

*   *   *

Following the shooting of Bronwen, it had taken the police over an hour to take any real control of the situation as site residents poured out of their homes, angry, wanting trouble, itching to fight, making it doubly difficult to keep a lid on things when it was imperative to establish a secure perimeter around the caravan where Tommy was holed up.

Six-foot-high screens were brought on to the site and erected in a semi-circle about thirty feet away from the caravan, which meant that it was possible to evacuate people and also keep them out of sight of the caravan. The bulk of the bulldozer also proved a useful barrier for the police to hide behind, with little chance of any bullets penetrating the thick steel plates it was made from, ricochets being more likely.

The sheer number of police officers under Rik Dean's control and his determination to use physical power should it be required ensured that the residents eventually went noisily but peacefully from the site to be bussed to a local village hall where they were told to wait as patiently as possible.

It was far from ideal and not part of the plan. Planning is all well and good, but it only lasts as far as contact with the opposition and then things usually go to rat shit.

The only person not to leave the site was Conrad. Henry had been keen to speak to him about the Costains, but first get him on board with ending the siege.

'I'm an old man and I don't need this,' Conrad moaned.

'You and me both,' Henry agreed. To be fair, he was much younger than Conrad and was hugely enjoying the situation, although he did regret the death of the woman, which looked like a terrible tragedy. But that was one of the problems when a gun is picked up, even with the best of intentions. A gun in someone's hand usually gave a firearms officer little or no choice in the matter. It would be a very long, drawn-out legal matter, Henry knew, but he was sure the police would be exonerated.

They were in Conrad's caravan, which turned out to be the one on the drone photograph situated at the back of the site next to the perimeter wall. It was luxurious, spick and span, with an array of highly polished horse brasses on the walls and other arty pieces that betrayed Conrad's gypsy heritage.

Up to that point Conrad had been in his pyjamas.

'I need to get dressed,' he told Henry, who nodded. They'd been talking while sitting around the dining table and Conrad slid off the seat and made his way to the large bedroom at the far end of the caravan, leaving Henry and Daniels alone with Stan for company. Annoyingly for Henry, the big dog edged up to Daniels and looked at her with big 'love me' eyes. She stroked him and he lapped it up, though when Henry spoke again, a deep, warning growl came from somewhere deep in its chest.

'What he doesn't know is that he's going to get his collar felt as soon as we resolve the situation with Tommy,' Henry whispered. 'You'll be doing that. I don't have that power any longer.'

Daniels nodded. 'Good. I already don't like him. His dog is lovely, though. Aren't you?' She rubbed Stan's head.

Henry stood up and looked around the caravan. 'It's well looked after, must be worth a ton of money.'

'Which comes from where?'

'Good question.' Henry rubbed his face, his eyes still taking in the interior of the van. He stopped suddenly and went visibly still.

'What have you seen?' Daniels asked. Her eyes followed Henry's gaze, but all she saw was a coat stand with a few coats slung on it.

Henry was about to respond, but his words were interrupted as Conrad appeared from the bedroom, fully dressed now, pulling on a windcheater. 'What do you want me to do?'

'OK,' Henry said to Conrad, 'one person has already died and it is vital this siege ends peacefully without further bloodshed. Do you understand that?'

Conrad nodded. 'Of course.'

Even though Henry did not fully trust Conrad, he knew this was one option that needed to be explored, so he explained, 'We have a hostage negotiator on the scene now who is an expert at dealing with situations like this. I'm going to take you to meet her, OK? She will brief you and guide you about establishing a dialogue with Tommy and, all being well, we can end this peacefully. I really do assume that is what you want to happen. Oh, and please take your dog with you.'

* * *

Rik Dean was in control of the standoff with Tommy and the past hour had seen little contact with him. Tommy had closed the caravan door with his feet without exposing himself, and until Conrad, with the dog now on a lead, was ushered along by Henry, Dean was seriously considering going in for Tommy as all approaches to him had so far dwindled and failed. There was only so much time to be allowed for these kinds of situations.

Henry stood back behind the bulldozer and watched as the hostage negotiator took Conrad to one side and began to talk urgently to him.

After about ten minutes, Conrad was positioned in a safe spot and given a loudspeaker.

'Tommy . . . this is Papa Conrad . . . your grandfather,' he began.

'I knew it,' Henry said to Daniels.

'Henry – what did you see in the caravan?' she asked.

'Uh, not certain, but—'

'Mr Christie?' Henry and Daniels turned to the ops chief inspector, Pollack, who had just approached them. He was in charge of securing and searching the site. 'You need to see this.'

Pollack beckoned Henry and Daniels to follow him. He led them across the site towards the walled-off rubbish disposal area where two wheelie bins stood side by side, but just before getting to it, he veered to one side and went to the back doors of the panel van that Henry recalled seeing from the drone photograph, parked to the left side of the gates. A very pasty-faced, poorly-looking, young uniformed PC was standing at the van. Henry thought he looked quite peaky, more so when he seemed on the verge of vomiting but managed to swallow it back.

Pollack opened the van doors – at which moment Henry and Daniels both realized where they had seen this vehicle before.

'We found this in here,' the CI said, standing away and letting the pair look in.

It was a body bag.

'It's empty,' the officer added.

'Right,' Henry said.

'Follow me.'

Pollack jerked his head and they traipsed behind him and around the van to the wheelie bins. He stood next to a green-coloured, industrial-size one and said, 'I think this is for biodegradable waste.' He grinned at his little joke. No one else did.

He raised the flat lid and the stench hit them immediately.

Behind them they heard the constable retch again.

Henry and Daniels covered their noses with the cupped palms of their hands and looked in, both knowing what they would see.

Lying on top of four waste-filled bin bags was the terribly injured body of the young man Henry had mown down at the Yorks' farm, whose cadaver had subsequently been stolen in a gruesome raid at the emergency mortuary behind Royal Lancaster Infirmary, the body having been whisked away in the van Henry and Daniels had just looked into.

Daniels twisted away, revolted by the stench, a combination of a decomposing human being and, as Pollack had cheerfully quipped, biodegradable waste. Henry looked for another moment before nodding to the CI to shut the lid.

Daniels wasn't sick, but the smell had done nothing for her.

'Poor lad,' Henry said. 'Poor, poor lad. No dignity.'

'They took him just so we wouldn't identify him,' Daniels said vehemently as she wiped her mouth with the back of her hand.

'I guess they might have got round to incinerating him,' Henry speculated. 'Just keeping him in the bin so he stayed fresh . . . another reason why Papa Conrad's coming with us.'

Henry nodded at Pollack and went back with Daniels to where the siege was still playing out.

They caught the last few words of Conrad over the loudspeaker.

'Come on, Tommy . . . you know what to do . . . you know you have to come out with your hands up . . . do it, boy. Do it for Bronwen, do it for me, do it for yourself . . .'

Henry had to admit that he sounded pretty persuasive.

For a few moments there was complete silence and then the caravan door opened a crack and the handgun was flung out on to the concreted area at the foot of the doorsteps.

'I'm coming out,' Tommy called from within. 'I'm not armed . . . I'm not even fucking dressed.'

The door opened further to reveal Tommy standing on the edge clad in only a pair of boxer shorts. He raised his hands to head height, then came down the steps. Henry could see the young woman's body propped up behind him, not having been moved for the last few hours.

Suddenly, Henry recalled something. He grabbed Daniels' arm. 'Come on . . . something's nagging at me.'

He manoeuvred her away from the cluster of cops and hurried in the direction of Conrad's caravan, which they entered, Henry just steps ahead of Daniels. He stopped and looked around, swivelling on his heels.

'Something,' he said quietly.

'What?'

He made a cutting gesture with the edge of his hand, trying to concentrate. And then it was there – right in front of him.

'Brendan O'Hara,' he said, quietly again.

'What do you mean?'

Henry walked across to the coat stand, the type often found in hallways of houses, but today found in Conrad Costain's caravan. There were six S-shaped hooks at the top, with an umbrella stand at the bottom. Four coats hung from it, and there was an umbrella and a walking stick propped in the lower section.

Henry took the coats off one at a time and laid them on the dining table.

One was a tweed sports jacket. Another was a long raincoat. Next was a hoodie, but the last one was a donkey jacket. Henry lifted it off the hook and held it aloft with his forefinger. It was a heavy, soiled, work jacket.

'Keep your voice down,' he warned Daniels. 'This belongs to Brendan O'Hara.'

'How the hell d'you know that?' she hissed.

'I didn't know who he was at the time, but I do now.'

'Like I said . . .' Daniels insisted.

'They came to The Tawny Owl for a drink; I asked them to vape outside. Remember?'

Daniels nodded eagerly.

'One was wearing this jacket. That would be O'Hara, the red-haired one.'

'How the hell do you know it's the same jacket?'

Henry spread the jacket on the table and pointed to the left side. 'Because of this.' It was a faded business logo. The words were cracked and all but unreadable, but Henry smoothed them out and was convinced, as he had been before, they said something about 'ground works'.

'Shit,' Daniels mouthed.

'O'Hara's here too,' Henry said, and his eyes started to rove. Clearly, he wasn't in the living room, dining room or kitchen area of the caravan as they were all open-plan, which left the bathroom/ toilet and the two bedrooms.

There was no one in the loo and a quick search of the bedrooms, under and over the beds and looking into the wardrobes, showed he was not there either.

Henry stepped outside and scrutinized the caravan, slowly walking around it. Daniels stayed with him, knowing exactly what he was doing: working out the dimensions, as he had done with the garage at Hawkshead Farm. He could see the caravan had no wheels, or they had been removed, and the whole structure sat on a rectangular brick apron about two feet high, which served to keep the whole thing off the ground. He walked the whole perimeter, kicking the bricks, checking to see if there was some way to gain access under the van, but could find nothing other than a couple of fixed air vents which were impossible to see through because of the angle of the slats.

'Solid,' he said, looking into Daniels' eyes.

'How do they do any repairs, then?' she said, returning the look. 'If they can't get underneath.'

He grinned wickedly. 'Because there's another way, maybe?'

She blinked. And in that blink of her eyes, Henry fleetingly realized what a very bad man he was, because he realized that he liked her eyes very much. He stuffed that thought firmly away and went back inside the van to the living area, which was plushly carpeted.

He went to the corner by one of the settees underneath the front window and used his finger and thumb to pull the thick carpet slowly backwards to reveal the flooring underneath, made of a composite of plywood and Styrofoam in which was a hinged trapdoor flush with the surface, with a ring-pull to open it.

Daniels stood to one side as Henry hooked his finger into the ring and slowly opened the trapdoor, as if opening a cellar door.

There was a quick movement, the sudden appearance of a white face in the dark looking up at him, but then Henry threw himself aside, grabbing Daniels as he did, because the next thing he saw was the single barrel of a sawn-off shotgun pointing up. He dived away before the flash and bang of the weapon as it was fired upwards, punching a hole through the roof of the caravan.

He and Daniels rolled into an untidy heap. Henry disentangled himself and scuttled back to the opening, holding his breath and then looking into the abyss to see the shotgun lying on the ground and a pair of feet disappearing into the opening of a tunnel which Henry quickly worked out went underneath the wall of the site, out in the direction of the surrounding fields.

'Escape plan,' he muttered. He sat up with his feet dangling, then dropped into the cavity underneath the caravan which he discovered, as he fell unsteadily, was almost five feet deep.

'Henry, what are you doing?' Daniels shouted.

'Going after him.'

He went down on to his knees and peered into the tunnel which had a string of lights with low-wattage LED bulbs affixed to its roof for as far as he could see – and he could also see the figure of Brendan O'Hara slithering along the tunnel, pushing himself on his back using his heels to propel himself.

Henry glanced around, then back up through the trapdoor to see Daniels' face peering down and said, 'There's an awful lot of money down here,' pointing to stacks of vacuum-packed cash, all in neat piles in the cavity which stretched the full length of the caravan, exactly like a cellar.

His attention turned to the tunnel, which looked to have been excavated professionally, with wooden supports and planks across the top and bottom. It measured perhaps three feet across and two feet high . . . and O'Hara was getting further and further away. He shouted up to Daniels, 'Get some of those cops outside the site into the back field. This has to come up somewhere . . . I'm going after him.'

He did not hear Daniels shout, 'Henry, no!' but plunged in on his stomach and began to crawl forward, using his forearms to drag him along and feet to push him, like a royal marine on an assault course, with his head angled upwards so he could see ahead where O'Hara was way in front.

He had managed to travel about thirty feet into the tunnel, with

O'Hara maybe forty feet ahead of him, but realized that his prey had stopped moving and was kicking at the roof of the tunnel.

Henry had a premonition then and, with a terrible sensation in his guts, began to scrabble backwards because he knew what was going to happen.

He heard O'Hara laugh.

Then, like a mini avalanche, the tunnel roof started to collapse. Henry knew he could not move quickly enough to escape. He raised his face and saw the supporting timbers begin to crumble and the whole thing cave in and come remorselessly towards him as the ground above burst through. All he could do was wait to be consumed and buried by tons of earth and planks of wood, knowing this was the place in which he would meet his death.

Daniels had dropped into the 'cellar' and looked into the tunnel to see Henry crawling along, and then there was a terrible creaking and rushing noise and she saw the roof come down and cover him. A rush of dirty, gritty air shot into her eyes and throat and almost choked her.

Coughing, she tried desperately to waft away the smog caused by the collapse.

'Henry!' she screamed and scrambled into the tunnel as the collapse had not affected the first fifteen feet of it. She went in blindly because the fall had ripped down the meagre lighting system and plunged it into darkness. As she went along it, she heard the timbers creak ominously. 'Oh God, oh God,' she intoned and then had to spit out a mouthful of grit while she slithered forward, using her toes to propel herself and reaching ahead with her hands, shovelling soil aside and behind her, desperately hoping to feel Henry's feet.

He was still alive, although his lungs were clogged up with dirt. By resting his head on his arms he had managed to form a small air pocket and although the weight of the soil on top of him was enormous, crushing, the supporting roof timbers had collapsed over his back in an inverted V-shape which helped to protect him.

Wriggling slightly, he was sure none of his bones were broken.

That said, he realized he had little time to get out of this and the thought produced a terrible, rising dread inside him as his breath began to get short and his heart rate doubled. He knew then that if the collapse didn't kill him, it was possible that his heart and lungs would explode of their own volition, maybe even before his little air supply ran out.

He moved his legs and almost jumped when he felt someone's hands wrapping around his ankles and heard the words, 'Henry? Henry?' faint through the mass of compacted earth encasing him.

So he wriggled his feet again to let Daniels know he was still in the land of the living, though probably not for much longer unless she got a shift on.

The realization she was there had an immediate calming effect on him because he knew she would not give up on him. With that thought, his heart began to beat a little less fast, his breathing slowed down a touch and he tried to stifle the panic: he knew he could trust her with his life. He also hoped she was good with a shovel.

EIGHTEEN

Daniels was too tired even to drive on to the upper car park at Lancaster Police Station, so she ran her car on to the kerb and stopped on Marton Street, ignoring the double-yellows, pretty sure that there wouldn't be too many traffic wardens knocking around at eleven thirty at night.

She climbed out and peered in through the locked front door of the station, seeing that the security screen on the front desk had yet to be replaced and the notice pinned to the door telling the public the police station was closed until further notice, but if the matter was urgent to pick up and use the emergency phone on the wall by the door.

She walked across the car park and let herself in through the police-only access door and made her way up to the deserted CID office where she slumped down at her desk, beyond exhausted but just feeling the need to check there was nothing outstanding she could deal with quickly before going home, showering and hitting her bed to sleep for as many hours as she needed. She was supposed to be back on duty at five the next afternoon, but she wasn't even bothered if she slept past that.

There was nothing pressing in the paperwork.

She leaned back, tilted her head and swore, feeling weak and pathetic, reliving a series of images of her day since entering the travellers' site in Blackpool at dawn.

The dead girl: completely innocent, taken down by eight bullets because she'd been naïve enough to come to the door with someone else's gun in her hand and appear to point it at armed cops.

The appalling sight of Cillian Roche's battered, already putrefying body in the wheelie bin, put there to await disposal by whatever means, just so the police would be unable to make any connection to Tommy Costain, Brendan O'Hara and Conrad Costain.

And the faces of those three men as they were arrested.

Tommy: on the ground being handcuffed.

Conrad Costain: protesting his innocence and saying he was too old to be locked up, as he too was cuffed and hauled away.

Brendan O'Hara: greeted by two armed cops, weapons drawn, waiting for him to emerge at the far end of the tunnel in which he had hoped to murder the man lawfully pursuing him by triggering a mechanism designed to destroy the tunnel in just such circumstances. It had been greatly satisfying to watch him get bundled roughly into the back of a police van, protesting his innocence.

Then she recalled the dirty face of Henry Christie when, through her almost superhuman efforts, she had clawed and dug wildly and moved what seemed tons and tons of earth, first uncovering his feet and legs, and then, along with his own huge exertions, pulling and dragging him free of the landfall, until the moment when both of them were back at the tunnel entrance, coughing, spluttering. And then at last everything calmed down and they sat there leaning against a wall of stacked money, maybe £10 million, and Henry slid his arm around her shoulder and they hugged each other with clear tears of relief streaming through the grime on their faces until Henry cupped her dirty face in the palm of his hand, looked her in the eye and said, 'Thank you . . . you seem to be making a habit of saving my life.'

They had hugged again, but did not kiss, and climbed weakly

from the cellar under the caravan in time to witness the three detainees being put into separate vehicles and driven away to three different police stations.

Paramedics from an ambulance that had been called to the site checked them both over and, remarkably, they seemed fine, even though Henry could not stop coughing up 'shite', as he so colourfully insisted on calling it, much to Daniels' revulsion.

Henry really wasn't all right, but he insisted on keeping going for the day after both of them managed to get a shower at the police station and buy a change of clothing from the nearby Tesco store. Even though there wasn't a view of the Blackpool Tower from the new nick, Henry admitted it was handy to have a superstore within walking distance.

Neither Henry nor Daniels were involved in processing and interviewing the prisoners – this was being dealt with by dedicated detectives who had been on standby as part of the operation – but they watched all the audio-visual feeds from the three police stations as the interviews progressed and were able to offer comments and advice along the way.

Even by the end of the day, there was still very much more to do – this was just the start of a long investigation which, when the Yorks were mixed into the equation, meant that Lancashire detectives would be travelling far and wide – and finally Henry and Daniels withdrew and she took him all the way back to Th'Owl. She gently refused the offer of a nightcap and another night at the pub. She wanted to get home and become a jelly-like blob in the privacy of her own flat.

But she still just wanted to call in to check her desk first.

'DC Daniels receiving?'

She flopped forward in her desk chair and fumbled for her PR in her bag. 'Yes, go ahead.'

'Location, please,' the comms operator asked.

'CID office, Lancaster.'

'Brilliant – I'm on the line to a female who is at the front counter, says she needs to speak to you urgently.'

'Me? Can't anyone else deal with this?'

'Asked for you by name,' the operator said.

'She still on the line?'

'Affirmative.'

'Tell her I'll be down in two minutes.' Through gritted teeth, she added, 'Unbelievable.'

'I'm sorry I ran – but I got a bit jittery and lost my bottle . . . well . . . sorry.'

'That's OK,' Daniels said. 'I understand.' She was in an interview room off the front foyer of the police station talking to the woman who had come forward as a witness to the explosion, but who had disappeared when Daniels rushed out to the emergency at the infirmary. With everything that had happened, Daniels felt the explosion that had killed a mother and a child was in the dim, distant past. She wasn't even sure how that investigation was progressing.

She looked at the thin woman with the badly dyed red hair who had begun to tell her about her friend who had been killed.

Daniels was struggling because her brain was currently in a fuzz, but she said, 'We were talking about Andrea Greatrix, weren't we?'

The woman nodded.

'But you didn't tell me your name.'

'It's Madeline Talon and I want to tell you what was going on in Andrea's life, what she told me, what I overheard. If I can, I want to save a kid's life and someone else's life too.'

'What's the name of the kid?'

'Jenny Howard. That's Andrea's daughter . . . she's about ten. Howard is the surname of her father.'

'And she is the child that wasn't at the house when it exploded?'

'Correct. That's because her father had literally stolen her.'

'OK, and what's the name of the other person whose life you want to try to save?'

'I think' – her face screwed up as she tried to remember – 'he's a detective – least he was back then . . . I've got it, I've got it . . . Christie, Harry Christie maybe . . . yep, that was deffo his name, and I know for a fact that if he isn't dead by now, he will be soon.'

The knife was a kitchen knife with an eight-inch blade of German stainless steel, perfect for cutting, slicing and chopping – hard, sharp and durable.

The person holding it stood in shadow on Kendleton village

green looking towards The Tawny Owl where the knife had been used, almost to fatal effect two nights before, but luck, reactions and an intervention had meant the intended target managed to survive.

Blood dripped from the tip of the knife.

It was after midnight when Henry finally managed to usher the last of his excited customers out of the pub, all having been eager to hear his story. Although he had been as exhausted as Daniels, he had been willing to regale them with an account of his brush with death.

With a whisky in hand, Henry stood outside and watched the last couple stagger away towards the village.

Silence descended. He was alone. He sniffed the atmosphere, then did one of the things that he despised other men doing. He pressed one finger against a nostril and blew hard down the other in order to dislodge even more dirt from up his nose. It seemed never-ending. He did the same with the opposite nostril and hoped no one had seen him.

At least it cleared his nasal passages for the moment, until it accumulated again.

He sniffed the atmosphere once more and this time could smell the aroma of the smoke from the moorland fires.

His mobile phone rang: Diane Daniels.

'Henry?' she said urgently. 'You need to listen to me – does the name Robert Howard mean anything to you?'

'Off the top of my head, nope. Why? What's the problem?'

'I'm still in work and I'm looking through the archive database of old murders, and in 2009 you arrested a man called Robert Howard, who was a PC based up here in Lancaster, for murdering his wife, a detective sergeant called Jo Howard.'

'Oh yes, I recall it well. And now I think about it – Andrea Greatrix, you mentioned her. The woman who died in the explosion. She was the woman Robert was seeing. He had an affair with her and Jo found out about it, which is why it all went very wrong. Andrea was pregnant by him. So?'

'That attack on you in your bedroom, the guy with the knife?'

'I remember that like it was only yesterday.'

'Don't be facetious, Henry . . . this is serious. I have reason to believe it was Robert Howard.'

'I thought he was in prison?'

'He got out two weeks ago.'

A movement to Henry's right caught his eye. He spun as a figure stepped out from the shadows. Henry saw the glint of a knife blade.

The figure moved towards him, into the light, pointing the knife in his direction.

Henry lowered the mobile phone from his ear, seeing the blood on the blade, blood on the clothing.

The girl, maybe ten years old, was dishevelled, dirty, a pretty face but with terror streaked across it, nothing on her feet, bleeding toes. She opened her fingers and dropped the knife with a clatter on the flags.

'I think I've killed my dad,' she said simply, almost zombie-like. 'Only he wasn't my dad. I didn't know him. I didn't know him at all. He said he was my dad, but he killed my mum and he kidnapped me and I . . . I knew he wanted to kill you, too. But I was frightened and I took the knife and I stabbed him in the chest and in his neck because I was afraid. He's in a van over there.' She pointed weakly across the green, then sank slowly to her knees, looking pleadingly at Henry, tears cascading down her filthy face.

'Please help me. My name is Jenny.'

NINETEEN

There was no space on the car park of The Tawny Owl, so Daniels drew in a little further down the road in her Peugeot. All the car windows had been repaired, but the bodywork was still a mess and she was planning to scrap it and buy a more up-to-date run-around, as much as it pained her to do so.

She walked back to the pub, threading her way through a gathering of about twenty people, men and women, milling around on the car park, all dressed in work overalls, wellington boots, with disposable face masks and work gloves, reminding her of an episode of *Doctor Who* she once watched where the population was under threat from a killer virus. At least she thought it was *Doctor Who*. It could have been *Star Trek*.

A fire tender was parked in the road, behind which was a huge tractor with a four-wheeled flatbed trailer attached to it, and behind that was a tracked JCB excavator with a man sitting in the cab.

Propped against a wall was a line of spades and pickaxes.

Dressed in the same garb as the people assembled outside, Henry came out with Maude in tow, also dressed similarly.

She smiled at Maude who smiled back insincerely with a disapproving look and edged haughtily past, leaving Daniels with Henry.

'What's going on here?'

'Community action,' Henry said proudly. 'The fires don't seem to want to stop; they're creeping towards the village again and the fire service think a firebreak might save us from disaster, so we've hired a man and his excavator, got permission from the landowners and we're off to go dig-dig-digging.'

Daniels smiled warmly at him. 'You're feeling OK, then?'

'Yeah . . . yeah, all good here.' He patted his chest.

'And Maude?' she teased.

'She's lovely, but not my cup of tea, even with all that dosh in the bank. We're good friends.' He kept smiling. 'What's happening in cop world?' he asked. In spite of Rik Dean's pleas for him to stay on and help out, Henry had decided to withdraw his services, claim a couple of grand but forgo the remainder. He knew his life wasn't as a cop anymore. He had a business to run, in a place he loved, and was as sure as he could be that he would not be drawn into coppering again.

'Tommy, Conrad and O'Hara all charged with numerous offences ranging from murder to . . . multiple murders, I suppose. They're not going anywhere, and Papa's going to end his days in the slammer if I get my way. I think he was the most evil of the lot, actually – but I did like his dog. Oh, and I also arrested a lad called John Dishforth for the initial assault on the lad who got killed in the infirmary. And the York side of things – not much progress on that, but it's a big one.'

'What about Jamie Costain?'

'On bail for murder . . . and guess what? His dad *was* Troy Costain, apparently.'

'So he caught the claustrophobia gene?'

'Seems so.'

'Well, all excellent news.'

'Have you got a minute just to chat?' she asked.

They went into the dining room and sat at a table. 'I've spent the last two days talking to that traumatized child,' she began. 'As you already know, Robert Howard was having an affair with Andrea Greatrix ten years ago, which was the catalyst for him murdering Jo Howard when she found out about it. Unfortunately for him, you rocked up and scuppered all his plans to cover it all up. The additional problem for him was that Andrea was pregnant with that little lass, Jenny. Robert was released ten years into his life sentence on licence – as per the idiocy of the criminal justice system – determined to claim his daughter. Andrea wasn't having any of it, with the end result that he killed her and her younger daughter by another man, then made off with Jenny. He kept her in the back of a van, tied up, gagged, promising it was all going to be all right. But he bore one last killing grudge – to murder you for destroying his life.'

Henry laughed harshly. 'Pretty sure he did that when he had an affair, got another woman pregnant and then killed his wife who wasn't too happy about it. His life was going down the pan long before I stepped in and noticed the McDonald's wrappers. But what do I know?' he shrugged.

'Hmm?' Daniels did not understand that reference.

'Nothing – go on.'

'Anyway, that's where I'm up to . . . and, you know, once again, I don't think I'm cut out for this murder lark. Spending time with that little girl has made me realize what I am good at – and that's protecting kids and other vulnerable people.' She shrugged. 'It's what I do best, and maybe hunting down murderers is just pie in the sky.'

'Well, for what it's worth, I think you're a brilliant, fearless detective and you'll be fantastic at whatever you choose to do – and that includes being on FMIT. Trust me, I know a good detective when I see one.'

She sat back, frowning. 'Henry, I haven't asked you yet, but I will now the dust has settled a bit.'

He shifted uncomfortably.

'What the hell – *what the hell* – made you go after O'Hara in that tunnel?'

'I keep asking myself the same question. The hunt, I suppose. The challenge. The anger. But I have to say that just a few feet into the bloody hole I started doubting it, even before the thing collapsed. I always think I'm thirty years younger than I am, if you know what I mean?' He gave Daniels a wistful look. 'Anyway, I'm glad the little girl is in your capable hands, Diane, but if you'll excuse me, I have people waiting and a firebreak to dig.'

They hugged each other and she followed him out to the front of the pub where, clearly, everyone *was* waiting for him. The tractor fired up; the excavator fired up. Everyone began to clamber on to the flatbed while Henry swung up into the tractor cab, plonked himself on the smaller passenger seat alongside the driver and gave a cowboy-style 'let's get moving' swish of his hand. The convoy, led by the fire tender, set off towards the moors.

Daniels watched it all drive past, noticing Maude observing her carefully, thinking she was going to give her one of those two-fingered 'I've got you in my sights' eyeball gestures, but then they had all gone and she walked back to her car.